Two-time RITA® Award nominee and Golden Quill award winner **Jennifer Morey** writes single-title contemporary romance and page-turning romantic suspense. She has a geology degree and has managed export programs in compliance with the International Traffic in Arms Regulations (ITAR) for the aerospace industry. She lives at the foot of the Rocky Mountains in Denver, Colorado, and loves to hear from readers through her website, jennifermorey.com, or Facebook.

Also by Jennifer Morey

A Wanted Man
Justice Hunter
Cold Case Recruit
Taming Deputy Harlow
Runaway Heiress
Hometown Detective
Mission: Colton Justice
A Baby for Agent Colton
Front Page Affair
Armed and Famous

Discover more at millsandboon.co.uk

COLTON'S
FUGITIVE FAMILY

JENNIFER MOREY

MILLS & BOON

First Published in Great Britain 2018
by Mills & Boon, an imprint of HarperCollins*Publishers*
1 London Bridge Street, London, SE1 9GF

Colton's Fugitive Family © 2018 Harlequin Books S.A.

Special thanks and acknowledgement are given to Jennifer Morey for her contribution to the *Coltons of Red Ridge* series.

ISBN: 978-0-263-26609-2

1218

To Harley. May his fight for life prevail.

Chapter 1

White Christmas lights twinkled in the otherwise dimly lit log cabin; a fire crackled; *It's a Wonderful Life* played on a DVD. Demetria "Demi" Colton hung the last ornament she'd picked up in town. Stepping back, she admired the end result. She folded her arms and smiled, feeling a welcome upturn of the corners of her lips.

Perfect.

Teal, magenta, blue and lime-green round ornaments mixed with other fun, animated character ornaments and sparkly sprigs of blue-colored berries. She'd wondered if the end result would be too gaudy but the tree looked beautiful. She'd put it in the corner of the living room, flanked by windows. Only she and Wolf would enjoy viewing the lights from outside— hopefully. She didn't want company.

She had worried she wouldn't be able to have a tree this year, but she'd come up with a disguise so she could go into the little town not far from here. She'd changed the color of her hair from red to black and cut it into a pixie almost a year ago, when she'd first gone on the run. A brown wig, black-rimmed glasses and hippie-themed clothes were diametrically different from how she had dressed before. Working as an independent bounty hunter she had worn practical clothes—clean, neat and tidy—but she also liked to dress up and go out. She did not turn away from a Little Black Dress when the occasion fit.

Thinking she heard something outside, Demi moved to the front window and parted the heavy drapes that reached the floor. She saw nothing other than darkness beyond the porch lights. On one side of the cabin the front entry jutted out farther than the living area inside, one thing she really liked about the place. There was room to remove winter clothes, put shoes under the white bench and hang jackets on hooks above. She'd bought a no-slip multicolored rug to put over the wood floor.

The weather forecast had called for snow tonight and tomorrow. She loved snowstorms, one positive about being forced into hiding with a five-month-old baby, and this storm had prompted her to stock up on essentials since it was predicted that over a foot would fall. The single-lane driveway that wound its way a quarter of a mile from the highway would be impassable for days, shaded by a dense, dark forest.

Snowflakes drifted down right now, nothing too

ominous, but a light layer of white already covered the ground. She'd be safe tonight, a rarity.

Letting the drape fall back into place, she turned toward the living room of the small cabin and shut off the lamp beside the sofa. She left the light on over the stove all night. With the Christmas lights, it was just bright enough to see. The cabin wasn't big, with a kitchen, dining area and living room, and two bedrooms down a short hallway. One bathroom.

She had constructed a secret room where Wolf slept, and a baby monitor on the kitchen counter kept her apprised of his well-being. She'd created a hidden entrance in her bedroom closet. She'd divided the second bedroom into two. Call her paranoid, but given her fugitive situation, her first priority was Wolf's safety. And she had an escape plan if anything went wrong. She slept easier at night knowing her son was locked in a secure place. She shouldn't have to do any of that. She shouldn't even be in this preposterous situation.

Anger flared. Innocent of the alleged murder of her ex-fiancé, framed unjustly, she had no way of finding evidence to clear her name. That infuriated her. It would infuriate anyone in this situation, but her temper demanded some extra control. She screamed into pillows on occasion, banged on the mattress. Sometimes she just did a few laps around the cabin to vent steam. The real killer better not get too close. The least she'd like to do was give him a bloody nose.

"We aren't succumbing to anger anymore," she said aloud. She didn't feel like going to bed yet, too restless and in one of those moods where, bored and caged, she didn't know what to do with herself.

She tried to take in her home, to let it soothe her nerves as it often did. The living room took up the front, with the kitchen to the rear left and the smaller dining room to the right, the hallway between. She'd found a used furniture store in town and used the cash she'd taken from her account to survive on the run. That had been another sore point. She should not have had to tap into her savings, most of which had come from an inheritance from her mother, who had ended up marrying someone with money after she divorced Demi's father. She had died in a car accident a few years ago.

A tall dark-wood bistro table with white trim and very few scratches stood in the dining room. She hadn't hung anything on the log walls. The blue patterned sofa was against the wall near the entry, and two high-backed chairs flanked a wood-burning fireplace near the dining room. A cream and tan area rug warmed the room.

The kitchen had come with stainless steel appliances and beautiful gray granite countertops with white cabinets and pendant lighting above the snack bar. She sat at one of the two blue-cushioned stools each night for dinner, after she fed her adorable baby.

If she had to spend a lot of time isolated and on the run, she needed a calming environment, and this cabin had provided that, thanks to a good friend. Being alone had its challenges, however.

"I just need to be around people more." Maybe she'd started to go a little crazy being cooped up in this place for so many months.

If she could socialize again, then she could stop

talking to herself. She had Wolf, but a five-month-old couldn't talk back yet.

Thankfully, her inventive disguise allowed her to go to the nearby small town for supplies and visits to the library where she kept tabs on the Groom Killer investigation. She'd used the computer there to read news reports and dig into the background of the bogus witness who claimed to have seen her fleeing the scene of her ex-fiancé's murder back in January. She'd believed he would lead her to whoever framed her. And why. And she'd been right.

Hearing that sound again—a sort of thump—Demi returned to the window, but when she pushed back the drape a bit, the Christmas lights were reflected on the glass. She saw nothing, but heard a muffled scraping on the other window.

Heart leaping into faster beats, she hurried to the fireplace mantel where she kept a wooden box containing a pistol. She had mounted a rifle on the wall in the hallway and kept another pistol in her bedroom, on the top shelf of her closet.

When she heard a piece of glass part from the window and the sound of a gathering winter storm grew louder, she realized that whoever had carved a hole in the glass, A, had specialized equipment, and B, was a professional. Although she didn't see him, she listened as he unlocked the window and slid it open.

Flipping off the safety, she racked the slide and moved out from behind the Christmas tree.

"Come one more inch into this cabin, I'll shoot and keep shooting," she said.

The man had already climbed inside and when he

heard her, he rolled or fell onto his behind, brushing the branches of the tree and jingling ornaments. The drapes slid off him to reveal a familiar face.

Lucas Gage looked up at her with his sexy dark eyes. His chestnut hair was mostly hidden by a black beanie, but the scars on his left cheek and above his right eye were a clear identifier. A bounty hunter, like her, he'd been her nemesis for years. He must be feeling mighty triumphant right now. He'd found her.

Instead of gloating, however, he let out a long breath and said, "You're okay."

He hadn't expected her to be? And was that relief she saw and heard? Surely he hadn't *worried* about her.

"Get your hands where I can see them," she ordered.

He held up his hands, amusement spreading over his face. That always annoyed her. He was always so cocksure of himself and seemed to enjoy riling her. It didn't help that he was a good bounty hunter—a legitimate Red Ridge Police Department bounty hunter with a K-9. Whenever she felt spurts of envy or insecurity, she reminded herself that she didn't have to play by any PD rules.

"Thanks to you, I'm going to have to find another place to stay," she said a bit harshly.

"You don't have to run anymore."

What was he saying? Was that some kind of ploy to get her to trust him? If so, it was weak. How would she get away? How would she snatch up Wolf and get out of here?

She gestured toward the window. "You have a backpack or something out there? Handcuffs?" She'd tie him up and leave. By the time he got free, she'd be long gone.

"I didn't come here to take you in, Demi. You don't have to tie me up and run."

As if she'd believe him. A man like him would say anything with a gun pointed at his head.

"I came here to tell you the Red Ridge PD is almost a hundred percent sure you're innocent."

"Almost?" That was rich. Did he really expect her to melt in relief and blithely go with him?

He let out a long exhale, no longer so amused. "It's Devlin Harrington who's been killing all the grooms. Police just need the missing gun and hopefully prints or other evidence that will link him."

The police had no evidence against Devlin and he still thought she'd be safe returning to Red Ridge? "I know it's Devlin." She'd known for quite some time.

Devlin had behaved strangely toward her after she rejected his invitation to dinner one night. A few months later, she found herself accused of murder. While that hadn't made the connection for her, recalling that Hayley Patton had rejected him as well made her begin to wonder if that meant something. Sure enough, it did.

"I also know he's obsessed with Hayley Patton and a witness claimed to see me kill the last groom victim," she continued. "A low-level drug dealer with a rap sheet said he saw me fleeing Bo's murder scene. Really? That's a credible witness? Another witness was killed. Can no one see a pattern here?"

"The police do." Lucas moved slowly and began to

rise, keeping his hands up and looking at her warily, testing her.

"Stay on the floor." She took a step back. She'd never get away from him if he got the upper hand.

Lucas stood all the way up, his hands shoulder height. "I'm not going to take you in, Demi."

"How can you expect me to trust you?"

"You don't have to. Just believe me when I say you'll be safe in Red Ridge."

She wavered a few seconds before she skittered back to caution. She could *not* trust him.

"How did you know Devlin was obsessed with Hayley?" he asked. "One of the witnesses confessed to being paid, and that story was in the news, but what about Hayley?"

"I remembered how he used to watch Hayley. His girlfriend, Gemma Colton, brought him to a rare family gathering that her branch of the family deigned to attend. It was as though he forgot all about her when Hayley showed up. He had a creepy way of just staring at her. Then he'd make derogatory comments about Hayley, strange comments, like her dress was too short or she had on too much makeup. It was as though he thought she should be more modest. One or two comments like that and I wouldn't have noticed, but he always criticized the way she looked and he did in a weird way, as though he was offended. I also found a social media webpage of his. He assumed a different name but I recognized him in a couple of photos he had posted. He posted a lot about his *girlfriend* and never mentioned her name, but he had many, many photos of Hayley and made up stories about things they did together that clearly never happened."

"You need to give me the link. That's more evidence against him."

He was just trying to get her to lower her guard. He'd do anything to have another successful bounty to add to his rock-solid reputation.

They proceeded to have a stare down. Demi wasn't one to be uncomfortable, but Lucas's handsome face always threw her off. Not to mention his tall, muscular and fit body. She looked away first.

"The police won't arrest you, Demi. You can go home," Lucas said. Smooth talker.

Demi spotted the baby monitor on the kitchen counter and experienced a flash of panic. What if Wolf made a sound? Lucas might redouble his effort to haul her in if he found out she had his nephew in a hidden room.

"You say the police don't have the evidence they need to arrest Devlin. Well, they have evidence against *me*."

"They know the necklace was planted and the killer wrote your name in Bo's blood, making it look as though Bo wrote it as he was dying. They know the witness who claimed to see you running from the crime scene lied."

"How do they know that?"

"Everything came out because of a sexual harassment case last month. No one even realized it was connected until the pieces starting fitting together. Hunter Black—he's a cop with the PD—found out that an employee of Colton Energy lied about bigwig Layla Colton sexually harassing him. Her phone and email were hacked. Only one person would have a motive to ruin her and that's Devlin Harrington. He didn't want his father marrying her. Hunter found proof of the hacking and, in turn, other evidence was dug up—evidence that connected him to being the Groom Killer. Devlin is now on the run, like you."

Demi lowered her gun, stunned by this revelation. "What evidence?"

"A gun was found buried in his backyard. It's the same gun used to kill some of the victims, but there were no prints."

That further interested her. She resisted. This was Lucas Gage, Bo's brother and her longtime enemy and professional competitor. He could be playing her until he found Wolf—his nephew—and subdued her long enough to take her into custody. He had ample reason to want to get her, and get her good.

A gust of wind reminded her a storm was underway. If she didn't make a move now, she'd never get away. She walked into the kitchen and stopped at the counter with her back to Lucas. Blocking his sight of the monitor, she slid it between the coffee maker and the toaster oven. Then she turned to face him.

"That's very compelling, Lucas, but I'm not going anywhere with you."

When Lucas had first seen Demi from his vantage point on the floor, he hadn't recognized her. He'd thought he'd wound up at another dead end, breaking into a strange woman's cabin. Then the changes registered, the shorter hair she'd colored dark, the baggy hippie-like clothes. Her pretty green eyes were still the same, all full of fiery courage and defiance. She was the most fearless woman he'd ever met. The most competitive, too. She annoyed him as much as she intrigued him. He was sure she felt the same about him.

He still sat at the kitchen island and she stood on the other side, distrusting, still holding the gun. She might dress up as a hippie, but she looked casual but modern right now. The jeans flattered her shape, long legs and narrow hips. A soft blue thermal top was both practical on this cold night and attractive, molding to her form and reminding him that he'd always been attracted to those breasts.

He'd been so relieved when he realized he'd finally found her, relieved that she was the woman supposedly named Chelsey Carter whom he'd been tracking, and unable to deny that his relief stemmed from something much more emotional. She could handle herself and he felt bad for doubting her innocence, for going after her with more determination than he'd ever had for any other fugitive. Devlin Harrington had proved himself very dangerous, paying off fake witnesses and killing all those grooms. He'd do anything to preserve his evil way of life. More than he wanted to make amends for doubting her, Lucas wanted to protect Demi until the real Groom Killer was captured. One problem with that? Demi hadn't liked him *before* he started hunting for her.

"How did you find me?" Demi asked.

Her demeanor had changed. She'd softened. Had she begun to believe him? He studied her unreadable mouth and the slight angle of her face. Were her eyebrows raised a little more? The easing of tension would do that. But Lucas knew this woman more than she realized. She might have dropped some of her guard, but she most definitely did not believe him.

"Do you mind putting that gun away?"

She still held it aimed at him.

"If I was going to hurt you, or bring you back to Red Ridge against your will, I'd have already done it, Demi."

"You always were so sure of yourself."

He was a good bounty hunter. "I could say the same about you."

Her eyebrows twitched as though she hadn't expected him to say that, as though doubting his subtle compliment.

"How did you find me?" she asked again.

He moved away from the window and the Christmas tree, nearly certain she wouldn't shoot him. He took in her cabin. Simply furnished, but tastefully done, she'd made herself a home while she hid. At the kitchen island, he pulled a stool out and sat.

Demi stayed where she was with her gun still ready, waiting for an answer.

"I checked new and recent residents of surrounding towns and only one name came up as having no history until a few years ago—Chelsey Carter. The timing was off, of course, since you've only been on the run for a year. But I knew you could have found a way to fudge dates, so it was worth checking out. I wasn't sure if it was you," he said.

"That explains why you seemed surprised to see me," she said.

"How did you manage to get set up here? The false name. This cabin." He glanced around. "This is nice."

"I didn't have to fudge dates. I helped a fugitive escape a few years ago. She was innocent. This cabin belonged to her under a false name. She helped me the way I helped her."

"What fugitive?"

"Maddie Morrison. When she was on the run, she came here. One of her family members gave her enough money to buy this place and helped her clear her name. I assumed her fake identity, the one she set up for herself as Chelsey Carter. She took all the furniture with her when she left, so all I had to do was furnish and decorate."

"Didn't anyone in town get suspicious about another Chelsey Carter appearing every now and then?"

Demi smiled. "I went to town in disguise. I bought some hippie attire and a wig so I looked more like Chelsey. We have the same eye color. She's a little shorter than me, but not by much. Also, Chelsey didn't go into town very much, just to buy food. She never talked to anyone, either. No one noticed me, at least, not in a suspicious or curious way."

There was only one question left to ask.

Where was the baby?

Police had found a positive pregnancy test in her bathroom the day she'd fled. And just a few months ago, when she'd texted her brother from a burner phone to declare her innocence, Shane Colton had asked how the baby was, and Demi replied that he was fine.

Lucas looked around and saw no sign an infant lived here. He would have found her sooner if she'd had the baby under her own name. She must have gone to the hospital as Chelsey Carter. For months, until Demi had confirmed it herself via that text, her being pregnant, giving birth on the run, were rumors. He'd always hoped the rumors were true—and that the father of the baby was Bo, her ex-fiancé, his late brother. When he'd believed her guilty, he'd thought Bo getting her pregnant and then dumping her served as great motive to want to kill him. After he realized she hadn't killed his brother, he'd wanted the rumors to be true. A part of Bo would live on. Lucas's nephew.

"Where's the baby?" he asked.

"What baby?"

He watched her face closely. She'd answered deadpan. But he knew about her text to her brother Shane, who worked closely with the RRPD. Why was she lying?

"Is it Bo's?" he asked as though he didn't believe her.

"I don't know what you're talking about."

There it was, that ever-so-slight flinch of her eyes. She often did that when he made her falter.

"Come on, Demi, everyone knows you were pregnant when you fled. You were spotted—definitely pregnant—before you came here."

Could she have lied to her brother about the baby? Maybe she'd lost the baby. He swallowed.

"I did move a lot, from hotel to hotel and town to town. I adopted disguises."

She'd disguised herself as a pregnant woman? Disappointment filled him. So, there was no baby? No nephew? Bo would be gone forever, leaving no trace of the younger man with whom Lucas had been so close.

But what about the pregnancy test?

She put the pistol down on the counter and leaned her hip against the edge. She seemed entirely too relaxed. He began to suspect an act.

"I'm a little chilled." She rubbed her arms and left the kitchen. "I'm just going to get a sweater."

He watched her disappear down the hall. He leaned to the right but couldn't see all the way to the end. Standing, he walked to the threshold. A light was on in one room. Another door led to a bathroom and the one next to it must be for a second bedroom. Passing the bathroom, he peered into the first bedroom. It contained a twin bed and a dresser and not much more. It was a small room. At the end of the hall, he looked into the lit bedroom. A queen-sized bed with a colorful quilt, dresser and chair filled it. He looked back toward the entrance to the spare bedroom. The wall ended before the linen closet.

Where had Demi gone?

He entered her bedroom. There was no bathroom off this room. He opened the closet. Just clothes hanging and some folded on an upper shelf. Shoes lined the floor. He parted the clothes. No passage there. Hurrying to the hall, he opened the linen closet. Nothing unusual here.

In the spare bedroom he noticed there was no window on the left wall and the window straight ahead was right at the room's corner. He went there and looked outside. Snow fell much thicker now, but when he looked left, he saw the house extended farther than this room.

Going back to Demi's closet, he shoved the clothes

aside and searched the back wall. There had to be a hidden entrance in here. He felt the paneling until his fingers caught on a latch. Opening that, he found himself inside a nursery. The cradle was empty and the barred window was open. He shut it to keep out the cold.

He ran to the front of the cabin. Bursting through the front door, he saw Demi running for the Jeep through the heavy fall of snow. She held a bundle in front of her—the baby.

She had lied to him. She *did* have a baby.

"Demi! Wait!" he shouted.

Just then, gunfire erupted through the blowing wind and snow. Demi shrieked and had to duck in front of the Jeep. Lucas took out his gun and tried to determine the location of the gunman. It was difficult to see.

More bullets followed. Glass shattered and the Jeep sank as its front tire was blown out.

Lucas shot in the general direction of the gunfire. The gunman returned fire. Lucas pulled his head behind the pillar of the front porch where he'd taken cover, then leaned out and shot back several times.

Taking shelter again, he heard no more gunshots. He left the protection of the post and ran for the woods, seeing Demi with a crying baby still crouched in front of the Jeep.

Lucas slowed at the origin of the gunshots and saw footprints.

Chapter 2

Wolf's cries overpowered Demi's fear. Holding him against her in the baby carrier pack she'd put on, she tried to calm him and keep him quiet. How had Devlin found her? Had Lucas led him here?

The Jeep was useless with a flat tire. She'd have to change it, and how would she do that without being noticed or being killed? Had she been able to reach the Jeep before the gunfire exploded, Wolf wouldn't be in tears and she'd be gone. Now only her baby's safety mattered. She had to get back to the cabin.

If she could find Lucas's keys, she could still get away, but that would have to wait. Her conscience nettled her that she'd be leaving him here with a killer. No matter what he said, he intended to hand her over to authorities. What else could she do? She had to think of Wolf. If she was arrested, what would happen to him?

Seeing Lucas disappear into the woods, she ran to the cabin, going in the front. She took a moment to calm Wolf, rocking him and looking down into his teary green eyes. He had red hair and a cute face. Right now his cheeks were bulbous with his open and crying mouth.

"I'm sorry." She kissed his head. "I'm sorry." This was all Devlin's fault. Her son should not have to endure this. He should be sleeping in his crib, warm, safe and dry.

The baby began to quiet, looking up at her in a way that always melted her, with such trust and love. His sleepy eyes closed and opened. She'd put him to bed once she was sure he felt safe again.

Demi looked around the cabin. Lucas had left nothing behind. She went to the window he'd broken in through and looked outside. There was a backpack there.

She covered Wolf in the soft blanket and checked her surroundings on the porch, making sure the gunman had fled. Lucas had no doubt chased him through the woods. She hurried to the side of the cabin. Crouching at the backpack, holding Wolf securely against her, even though the baby carrier did that for her, she saw he'd fallen asleep. She dug through the contents of Lucas's bag. The main compartment held nothing but extra clothes and water bottles. The smaller pockets held other essentials like trail mix, a GPS and a small first aid kit. No mobile phone. No handcuffs. No keys.

Standing, she returned to the front, not seeing Lucas and not hearing any gunfire. He had his keys on him. She was trapped here. She closed and locked the door and put Wolf to bed. Seeing that Lucas had closed the window, she locked it and then the secret door before going back into the living room. It was cold in the cabin. She went to the window he'd compromised and closed and locked that. Getting duct tape from the kitchen junk drawer that served as her tool box, she taped up the hole in the glass. Before closing the drapes, she saw that two or three inches of fresh snow already covered the ground.

A knock on the front door told her Lucas had returned. He'd spent a while out there, tracking the shooter.

She went to the door and said, "Just go away, Lucas."

"I can't leave, Demi, especially now. Devlin got away."

He was that sure it was Devlin who'd shot at them? Devlin could afford to hire a gunman. He'd hired witnesses. Why not a hit man?

"Go away."

"Let me in."

"No."

"Demi…"

"No! Go away. You should have never come here." She kept her voice low enough not to disturb Wolf but loud enough for Lucas to hear her.

"You need me. Let me in."

"I don't need you," she snapped, her defenses flaring. What made him think she needed him?

"You have a baby. You need help. You can't defend him on your own. Surely you can see that. I can protect you both."

A few months ago, when she responded to Shane's text saying that the baby was okay, she'd immediately known she'd made a mistake. She could trust her brother, but he worked with cops. They'd know to look for a woman and infant. That had been a rare error on her part.

And Lucas did have a good point. When the shooter had fired at her, she'd gone wild with anxiety that Wolf would be harmed.

But this was Lucas offering his protection.

"How can I be sure you're going to help me?"

"You won't be. This storm is getting bad and you have a flat tire and broken windows in your Jeep. You need a vehicle. You can't stay here anymore, Demi. Once the storm clears, I'll get you out of here."

Did he speak with a silver tongue? Although she could not argue his points. Would she be better off finding another way to get herself and Wolf somewhere else?

"Let me in. We can talk about what to do in the morning. Devlin won't try to come back tonight. If he does, he'll be trapped in this storm."

With them? No, Devlin or his hit man would kill her and possibly Wolf. Then he could just take shelter in her cabin until the storm passed. The thought of Wolf hurt like that, or dead, made her sick.

Lucas could make it to town before the storm really got bad, but he'd return once the roads were passable again and she'd be hard-pressed to get away before he did. On the other hand, if she allowed him to stay, she could ride the storm out and wait for another opportunity to escape. She could take his keys while he slept. He'd be okay in the cabin until he found a way out. An outdoorsman like him could hike to the road or even town. By then she'd be long gone.

She unlocked the door, pulled it open and stepped back.

Lucas stood with snowflakes covering him, his gun held down at his side and his pack slung over his other shoulder. He looked manly and strong and sexier than she'd ever seen him.

"I knew you'd see reason." He grinned.

"This doesn't mean I trust you." She folded her arms.

He walked inside. "Oh, believe me, I know." He brushed the snow off himself and stomped his feet. He looked around. "Where is the baby?"

"In bed."

He looked at her. "Can I see him?" He put his pack down.

Indecision gnawed her. He must be wondering if the baby was Bo's child—if he had a nephew. What harm would it be to allow him a look?

She led him to her bedroom and the secret door, which she unlocked to allow him inside.

"This is a little overkill, isn't it?" he asked as he walked to the crib.

"You think it's overkill after being shot at tonight?" She came to stand at the foot of the crib. Wolf lay sleeping on his back, the blanket up to his chin.

Lucas turned on the light on the side table. Then he used his finger to pull the blanket farther down. He gazed at Wolf for endless seconds. Then his eyes lifted to catch hers. She saw the unvoiced question. Was the baby his nephew? Next she saw the pain of loss and a wish for some kind of link to his dead brother.

Empathy took her by surprise. She met his eyes for a while, flustered and reeling. This felt like a connection, but there could be none because this was her enemy.

To her amazement, Lucas averted his eyes first. "What's his name?"

"Wolf."

He returned to his silent and reverent study of the baby.

Demi looked down at Wolf, befuddled over what was transpiring. Could it be that Lucas had come here to help her? Or had seeing his nephew in the flesh confused him?

She folded her arms, feeling uncharacteristically vulnerable. Wolf was the most important thing in her life now. She'd had no way of predicting his importance before he was born. He'd been important as he'd grown inside her, but as soon as he came out into the world and gave that first cry, something had changed in her. When he'd been placed in her arms, she knew she'd never be the same. Every move he made, every twitch of his tiny arms, every shift of his head, was miraculous. When his newborn eyes met hers, she'd melted with love.

This man could take all of that from her.

When he looked up at her, she sensed he'd ask more questions.

"Let's let him sleep." Demi moved to the door and waited for Lucas to leave the room ahead of her.

He walked to the door and stopped, meeting her eyes as though guessing she didn't want to talk about Wolf's father.

"I'm going to board up the window, then I'll sleep on the sofa." He left the room.

Demi's heart slammed. He'd backed off. Maybe he'd recognized the mama bear in her. Maybe he had decided to table his desire to see and hold the child of his dead brother. Demi could not trust her intuition. With Lucas, she'd been wrong too many times to give in to the primal attraction that had plagued her from the first time she met him. Okay, so she was attracted to him. That didn't mean he was good for her.

Lucas lay on Demi's living room sofa, his head on his folded arms, fireplace flickering, staring up at the shadows flickering on the ceiling. He had so much on his mind he couldn't sleep. Demi's determination to get away, her protectiveness of Wolf and, most of all, her reticence in talking about Bo. Why did she feel that way? Did she feel threatened? He could see why she'd taken such precautions in fleeing and hiding, and even securing Wolf in his nearly impenetrable room. She must fear his being taken from her and, of course, harmed in some way. Did she also fear that Lucas would take the baby after he turned her in? As a relative, Lucas could get custody of the baby if she were in jail.

What could he do to convince her he had no intention of turning her in? Maybe all she needed was time—to trust him or for him to prove that Devlin had become the prime suspect in the Groom Killer case. He felt obligated to make amends for believing her guilty for so long. He also knew how stubborn she could be.

Hearing her moving in her bedroom, he saw a light turn on. He listened to her open the secret door. How many times did she do that during the night? Maybe she hadn't until now, when her location had been revealed and someone started shooting at her.

He heard her close and lock the door and then come into the hallway. She walked quietly, as though trying not to wake him.

"I'm not asleep." He pushed the blanket off and stood to see her frozen in the kitchen.

He had kept his jeans on but was bare other than that. He watched her take in his chest and arms and then lift her eyes. Blinking, she turned and took out a glass from the cabinet. Lucas liked how she stretched her body to reach the upper shelf. She wore a sleeveless nightgown that fell to her knees and inched up her thighs. She was barefoot, like him. The gas fireplace kept it warm in here. The cabin had forced air heating, as well, but on such a cold night with blowing snow, the cabin would feel draftier without the extra heat.

"Nights like tonight I wish I had a television," Demi said as she put the glass on the counter, the nightgown returning to her knees and her bare heels touching back down on the wood floor.

"I can't sleep, either."

Without acknowledging that, she opened the refrigerator and took out a milk container. He leaned against the island, the tree lights and fire the only sources of illumination after the refrigerator closed. He found it amazing that she'd managed to make such a welcoming home while on the run. Then again, as a bounty hunter, she knew how *not* to be found. Using a false name, plus her disguise, explained why it had taken so long for him to do so. She'd been on the run for a year. He should have known. He should not have underestimated her.

She glanced over at him as she finished pouring a

glass of milk, her eyes going down the front of him before turning to put the milk carton away.

"Where's Queenie?" she asked, in what must be a safe subject for her.

"She's with Elle." His dog was a beautiful Belgian Malinois, with a dark head faintly intermixed with chestnut brown that took over the rest of her body. She was one of the best ground and air trackers the Red Ridge Police Department's K-9 Unit had. His sister, Elle Gage, had a dog, too, and was a rookie cop at the RRPD.

"You didn't bring her?"

"I'll pick her up when we're back in Red Ridge."

"We?" She sipped her milk and sent him a barely contained scowl as she walked into the living room.

He decided not to argue just now. Wind gusted and pelted snow against the side of the cabin. He welcomed the time he'd be stuck here with her. Trailing her, he sat at the opposite end of the sofa, listening to the storm. Demi had left the gas fireplace burning on low before going to bed. Flames flickered and added light in the small space.

"You must have been working hard to find me," she said, putting her glass down on the side table. "You didn't always think I was innocent."

She said the last in a tone much more representative of her fiery spirit. She obviously did not believe he thought she was innocent, at least, not completely.

He put his feet up on the square ottoman and leaned back. "Oh, yeah. I tried very hard to find you when I thought you killed my brother."

"But now you've changed your mind."

She sounded like a smart-mouth. "With good reason."

"With no proof," she countered.

He again decided not to argue.

"Did everyone think I did it?" she asked.

"No, not everyone. Quite a few didn't think you would kill anyone. Shane and Brayden drove me nuts."

At the mention of her half brothers—Shane Colton, the ex-con turned private investigator and RRPD informant, and Brayden Colton, another RRPD K-9 officer—Demi's face lit up. They had defended her but she likely hadn't known that until now. He felt a little redemption inch its way into his regret.

"My brothers tried to exonerate me?" she asked.

"At first the evidence was difficult for them to ignore. After Tucker Frane was killed, Shane thought you were being framed."

"Tucker said he saw me shoot a man in the alley between Bea's Bridal and a French restaurant."

"That's why Shane began to suspect something was off."

She angled herself on the sofa, bending her knees and looping her arms around them, settling in. For what, Lucas would wait cautiously to find out.

"And Brayden?" she asked.

"Brayden would rip my head off if he had the chance."

She smiled big and sang a soft, "Yay."

"Aw, come on. It wasn't all that bad between you and me." The Coltons and the Gages of Red Ridge traditionally didn't get along well. Years of feuding had caused a rift, but Lucas had seen that change ever since Demi had been set up as the Groom Killer.

Her animation faded. "Yes it was. You always had to be the dominant top dog."

"You're freelance. I'm a bona fide Red Ridge PD K-9 cop."

The vixen poked out her pretty head. Stormy dyed eyebrows arrowed down. He hated how he loved that. Part of the reason they'd remained enemies for so long was he could never stop teasing her. He didn't think he'd be able to stop now.

"Bounty hunter," she shot back.

"Deputized bounty hunter." He winked.

"Ugh." She rolled her eyes. "Do you have to do that?"

He chuckled. "Only with you."

She eyed him. "You do it on purpose?"

He chuckled deeper. "I wouldn't say on purpose. I can't help it."

Her head tilted sideways a little. "You like yanking my chain."

"Let's just say I'm one of the few people who think your quick temper is adorable."

"Adorable."

He held back another chuckle. "Yes."

"Why do you think it's adorable? Adorable is not how I would describe myself."

He agreed. He would describe her as many things. Smart. Tenacious. tough. "It's adorable because you never realize I'm teasing you. You're innocent and then…not."

She said nothing. Someday maybe she'd relax enough to let the little things fall off her shoulders.

If she ever did, he would want to be the first man to date her that way.

"I also think you're defensive because of who your father is, Demi."

"What? You Gages hate all things Colton, no matter what side of the tracks we live on."

The snowstorm wasn't easing up anytime soon. They had plenty of time to debate.

"I know you're close with your brothers and sister, but what happened with your dad?"

"He's my dad."

"Yeah, but…"

"He's Rusty Colton, the low-down bar owner? Nothing compared to the other Coltons in town? Be careful."

"Hey, I didn't—"

"Didn't mean to what?"

Dealing with her temper had always been a chess game. He'd always had to plan his next move. But now, suddenly, this wasn't a game. Demi's temper had more depth than he'd ever realized. She could be touched off rather easily, but she never got abusive. Granted, she could tone down her intensity a notch or two, but she stood on solid ground. He'd actually always sensed that about her, and enjoyed how easily he could set her off.

"Why do you want to know about my dad? All you're here to do is take me in to be arrested. There might be a new prime suspect, but that doesn't mean I'm off the hook."

He gave up trying to convince her he wasn't here to take her in. Instead, he decided to be blunt. "We're going to be together in this storm for a while. Why not make the best of it? I'm curious, that's all. I've wanted to ask you about your dad for a long time."

Her controlled attack mode softened. She took a moment to answer. "My father doesn't care about anyone other than himself." She averted her eyes toward the Christmas tree. "The only good thing he ever did was produce me and my half brothers and my half sister, Quinn. He's my father and we spend time together, but it doesn't feel genuine to me."

He felt her conflict about being raised by a man like Rusty or fathered by him. Her mother had left him, or so Lucas had heard.

"You're not estranged?"

"No." Her slow response conveyed her confusion.

She had some kind of relationship with her father, albeit strained. "What about your mother?" He knew something about her history but not personal details.

"You probably already know all of us have different mothers. Mine died just a few years ago."

Lucas said nothing. Her line of Coltons wasn't the high end compared to those others in town. He hadn't paid much attention to that gossip, but Rusty's was the rough branch of the clan, their spawn not accepted by the wealthier Coltons. Bad reputation due to hard living.

"I'm sorry," he said.

He'd always thought Demi needed no approval from anyone. Her strength surpassed anything he'd heard about her father.

Standing, he strode to the window next to the tree, parting the drapes as though to survey for security, when in fact he needed the time to recover. Rusty tainted her reputation with those who didn't look deeper. Her brothers had proven themselves. Her sister, too. Did Demi feel she hadn't yet?

"I didn't know about your mother." He turned to look back at her.

She lowered her eyes, a telltale sign of the loss, the memory of her mother still painful.

"What was she like?"

Her eyes lifted. "Someone who should have never married Rusty."

"I'm guessing the mothers of all your siblings realize that."

She met his eyes and he turned from the window to keep up the contact.

"My father doesn't do much to change our reputations, but he is my father. There's nothing I can do to change that."

"If you could, would you want to?"

"No. What would be the point?"

He didn't respond.

She stretched her legs and rested her feet on the ottoman. "My mother was naïve, but not ignorant. She preferred to look at everyone in the best light. She saw good in everyone. Even Rusty."

He gave her time to go on.

"Rusty's bad qualities outweighed his good, but she only cared about the good. I suppose that's why she married him. I can forgive her because she was so full of love and because she finally took me and left. We had a good life without Rusty. We were close. I lived with her up until she died. I had just finished college." She rested her chin on her knee and drifted off in thought.

"I'm sorry. That must have been hard on you."

She shrugged, as though opting for bravery instead of acknowledging painful memories. "I had Brayden."

He knew she was closest to Brayden. "How did she die?"

"Car accident." She slid her feet off the ottoman and leaned on her elbows.

"I'm sorry."

She sat up and looked at him. "Stop saying that."

That he was sorry? He did feel sorry for her.

"You Coltons never cared much for any Gages. You're only putting up this fantastic front to lure me back to Red Ridge."

"You've always been interested in the family feud that's been raging for a century. I never paid it much attention. And I won't try to keep telling you I'm not here to take you in."

"The only reason I found the feud so interesting is there was plenty of feuding going on in my family. None of my father's other wives liked my mother. I barely saw my half brothers or half sister. I never understood what the feud was about. My family is about as broken as any can get. We were disliked because we have a low reputation. I guess I thought that funny… or silly."

She confirmed his notion that she needed no one's approval.

"How did you end up so close to Brayden, then?" he asked.

"I would run into him on occasion. We started talking and discovered we had a lot in common. We both love the woods and mountains. We liked the same kind of literature and food. And…" She stared at the fireplace with a soft smile forming. "We just…talk a lot. It's easy to be with him."

"Love of woods and mountains." No wonder Brayden had become a search-and-rescue specialist. He hadn't known until now why Demi had become a bounty hunter. He supposed it had something to do with that, but more so a desire to catch criminals, and for Demi, that included satisfying her outlaw spirit.

"I never thought you were a roughneck just because your dad is." Outlaw, yes, but she had soft spots he doubted even she realized she possessed.

"But you think I killed Bo."

"Did," he corrected her. "I know you're innocent."

She humphed.

Another gust pelted snow against the windows and outer walls. The storm showed no signs of letting up anytime soon. Lucas didn't mind. What he did mind was his reason for not minding. Being stranded alone with Demi filled him with excitement. Maybe more than redemption had drawn him here. Maybe Demi herself had. Her innocence might have had a bigger effect on him than he realized.

Chapter 3

Demi heard Wolf on the baby monitor. He'd started to cry. She got up and went to the secret door. Leaving that open, she flipped on the light. There was no overhead light in this room, just two brushed-brass lamps with bear-embroidered shades. She went to his crib to see what had awakened him. Judging from the smell, she didn't have to guess. Lifting him with a kiss to his pudgy cheek, she quieted him and then laid him on the changing table.

He didn't protest. In fact, she was pretty sure he enjoyed having his diaper changed. She bent to brush her nose with his.

"Don't you?" she cooed. "You like this."

He wiggled his arms and legs along with a baby sound of glee.

She smiled with a heart full of love. And proceeded to change him.

"You're going to be a clean freak when you get older, aren't you?"

He made the gleeful squeal again.

She cleaned him up and put on a fresh diaper. When she'd finished, she picked him up and held him, unable to resist. She was tired and needed more sleep, but these moments were just too precious to relinquish too soon.

"He's a good baby."

A jolt shot through her and she turned. Lucas stood in the doorway. How long had he been there?

"Sorry." He walked into the room. "I didn't mean to startle you."

"He likes eating and having his diapers changed. He doesn't even mind a bath." She looked down at his adorable face with his sweet green eyes looking up at her. He'd have her red hair, too. She was glad he'd gotten a lot of her features. She didn't want to look at him and every time be reminded of Bo.

When Lucas stopped before them, Wolf turned his head and fell into a long, curious inspection of the new face.

"Can I hold him?"

Demi couldn't explain why she was so overprotective of Wolf, other than having a madman frame her and police on her tail for murder. She saw no harm in letting him hold Wolf, not in the middle of a snowstorm. He wouldn't try to take Wolf and go.

She handed him over.

Wolf seemed glad to go there, immersed in rapt fascination with Lucas's face. She watched softness transform Lucas's expression like an instant connection had formed right then and there. Lucas put his finger near Wolf's hand and Wolf grasped it. Her baby had a strong grip.

"He's something else," Lucas said. "He has your eyes and hair."

"Yes."

"Is he Bo's son?"

After a few seconds she finally said, "Yes."

Lucas looked up at her and she felt the powerful meaning that brought to him. Bo might have veered off an honest path into murkiness and deceit, but they were still brothers.

"You were close to Bo?" she asked.

"When we were younger we were practically inseparable. Somewhere along the way he had drifted. I got busy with life and didn't notice until he started doing questionable things. Lying. Treating female coworkers with disrespect. He'd almost been fired from some early jobs for sexual harassment. That wasn't the brother I knew. I don't know why he changed."

She could see the sadness that brought him, but he also had many good memories. So did she. When she first met Bo, she must have seen the same traits Lucas had. Although Bo had darker hair and green eyes, he'd looked similar to his younger brother. He and Lucas were both handsome in a strong, clean-cut way. He'd also loved the outdoors, hiking and skiing, fishing—and dogs, of course.

She'd fallen for him right away and been certain he'd felt the same. She believed he had, anyway, and maybe hadn't stopped loving her even after she'd begun to withdraw. She'd caught him in various lies, as well.

Not major ones, just a series of little lies that made her wonder why he'd thought he needed them in the first place. But every time she questioned him he would fly into a rage. He'd frightened her once when he'd picked up an iron patio table and hurled it across the yard. That's when she began to think maybe he wasn't the one for her. When he left one night after another fight and came home drunk, she'd found another woman's number written on a business card. That had been it for her. They had broken the engagement.

"I don't know, either," she finally said. "He had a lot going for him, but he made a lot of bad choices."

Lucas watched Wolf fall asleep in his arms. "How did you get together?"

"I've always known him. I ran into him a few times. Then one day at the market he started talking to me. A few minutes later he asked me out. We had dinner, then went on a few hikes." She shrugged. "We just hit it off."

She wouldn't add that Bo had reminded her of a nonconfrontational Lucas.

"And then he showed you his new ways?" Lucas's eyes lifted.

"Yes, but he had some good points. He had his own business breeding dogs for the K-9 Unit and was so good with the mamas and pups. I can see how the two of you were so close before he lost his way."

A slight upward curve of his mouth told her he appreciated the comment.

"He could be charming. The only problem was, he was charming to other women."

"Yeah, and he got mixed up with the Larson twins."

Noel and milder-mannered Evan had caused Red

Ridge a lot of trouble, but the criminal twins were behind bars now. Bo could be a real rat, but he hadn't
deserved to be murdered.

"What happened between you and Bo?" Lucas
asked.

Unable to resist, Demi reached for Wolf. Lucas gave
him up and she held him, seeing him stir a little before
falling into sleep again.

"We started fighting a lot. He would lie about stupid things, things he didn't need to lie about. He had
a temper, too."

"He wasn't like that when we were younger."

"He wasn't like that until we got engaged. He asked
me to marry him, I said yes, and then I found out about
the harassment. It changed the way I felt about him.
After one fight, he left and spent his evening at The
Pour House and came home drunk." She eased Wolf
down into his crib and covered him. "The next morning I told him he had to change his ways or it was over."

"You broke up with him?"

"In essence. I gave him a chance to redeem himself.
I guess I still hung onto the man I dated, the man I'd
fallen in love with."

"You did love him?"

She wasn't sure why Lucas needed to know all of
this. Maybe talking about his older brother helped him
deal with the loss. "I loved a version of Bo."

"Did he try to change?"

"Oh, no. He was furious with me. He packed, took
back the ring and left. Not long after that, I found out
he was seeing Hayley Patton."

Lucas studied her, or maybe he wasn't really seeing

her, he was so deep in thought over how his brother had ended up so unreasonably callous.

"Did you know you were pregnant when you split up?"

She shook her head. "And I didn't see a point in telling him. To be honest, I don't think he would have cared."

"The previous version of Bo would have."

She supposed he was right, although at the time of the split she'd believed that when they first started dating, Bo had put on a front to win her over.

After a lengthy stare that began to heat up, Lucas scratched his head as though feeling awkward. "I'm going to be up for a while."

"Me, too. Should we make some coffee?"

"Sure." He led her out of the baby's room.

In the kitchen she went about preparing a pot of coffee, not hearing the snow blowing the way it had earlier. She kept thinking about how loving Lucas had been with Wolf. He seemed a natural with children. Before having Wolf, Demi would not have pictured herself as a maternal person. Now she knew that if she ever married, it would have to be to a man who would be a father to Wolf.

"Do you want kids?" she asked before she could stop herself. She didn't need to know that about him— Lucas—her rival and a Gage.

"No."

He answered so quickly that she stopped in the process of pouring water into the coffee maker to look at him.

"I haven't seen the family thing work out so well. It might be for some people, but not for me."

"So, not just kids, you're tossing the whole marriage thing into the trash along with that?"

"I wouldn't say trash. I chose not to."

That sounded rather harsh. Cut-and-dried. He'd live alone his entire life? What would make anyone come to such a drastic decision?

"Having a long-term girlfriend is the same as being married." She said that to test him more than anything.

"I don't think so."

He seemed so adamant. Demi couldn't help the disappointment that gripped her. She'd always been secretly attracted to him, but their volatile relationship had not left any room for soft sentiments.

She had to ask. "Why? I mean, why not get married?"

"My mother died when I was young. It tore my father's heart out and changed everything in our family."

She had known he'd lost his mother just as she had. "Your dad remarried but she died last year, too" she said.

He nodded grimly. "He still grieves for her and my mother, but I've seen him improve over the last few weeks. He told me he does much better on his own."

Alone. That sounded more like avoidance. "Better in the sense he doesn't have to worry about losing anyone?" Everyone was happier when they weren't alone. Humans weren't meant to live alone.

"I think that's why my brother turned into such a reprobate. He kept losing mothers. He may have felt abandoned, left to his own devices, especially after our mother died. My dad was no good for us during his mourning. He worked constantly and wasn't really there for any of us. It ripped our family apart."

Mourning that never stopped. His father must have drowned his sorrow in work and had been so consumed with it that he never had time with his kids. Maybe spending time with them had grown too painful. He'd had a family with two women he loved and both of them had been cruelly taken from him. His kids had been left to raise themselves.

Demi saw the coffee had finished brewing and poured two cups. "Sugar or cream?"

"Black."

She poured cream into her coffee along with a sugar substitute, her one nonnegotiable indulgence. Taking the cups, she went to the kitchen island and handed him his black coffee.

"What about your stepmother?" She took a careful sip of the steaming brew.

"By the time she came along, we were accustomed to taking care of ourselves. She was nice and everything, but she wasn't our mother and she never really tried to form any kind of bond with us. In all fairness, I don't think she could have, even if she tried. We all felt the loss of our mother. It wasn't just Dad who suffered."

Demi leaned her hip against the countertop. "After my mother died, I started thinking about having a family. Being alone didn't appeal to me. After I had Wolf, I realized I will never be alone. I will always have him. I can see why you wouldn't want to get married. My father didn't mourn the loss of any of his wives, but he wasn't part of my life. He didn't care about us. I would hate it if I ended up marrying a man like that. Even if he wasn't exactly like my dad, even if he had redeeming qualities, if he doesn't care about his kids, to me that is worse than if he died."

"Then we agree." He half grinned. "That sounds dangerous." He sipped some coffee and put his cup down behind him and to his side on the counter.

Dangerous because they had that in common— something important? She wasn't completely convinced. "In a way. I think there is too much importance placed on marriage, that too many people get married because that's what everybody else does. That leads to bad decisions. That said, you can't go through life expecting to lose the person you love if you marry them."

"Why not? Everybody dies. There is no free ticket out of that one."

"Well, no, obviously not," she said, "but look at how many people live their entire lives with the one they married. Just because your dad lost both wives doesn't mean you will." It seemed a weak reason to avoid marriage. Then again, she'd avoid it, too, if she wasn't sure the man would care deeply about his family.

"It's more than marriage. It's the whole idea of love."

So, he refused to love out of fear he'd lose it the way his father had? "You'll really go through your entire life never falling in love?" She felt another one of their notorious arguments coming on.

"Actually, I don't think about it," he said.

"You must, because you just told me you'll never fall in love or get married." He couldn't have come to such a conclusion without first pondering the notion.

"Are we going to fight again?" he asked.

Feeling her ire rise, she practiced control. With Lucas that did not come easy.

"You're just afraid," she said, trying to tone down the edge in her voice.

"No," he said. "I don't want to mourn over a woman, whether she leaves or dies, and I don't want the family drama that comes with it. Ever."

Like his father had. "Isn't that a little narrow-minded?"

"Aren't you narrow-minded when it comes to getting married? Trusting a man?"

He had her there. She couldn't call out his flaws when she had her own. "Marriage is also about trust, not just love. You either love the person you're with or you don't. Trust is a lot harder to gauge."

"I'm not with anyone," he said.

Come to think of it, she had never known him to be with a woman for any significant length of time. He dated often and he dated stereotypical beauties—fashion divas or sheltered, unadventurous women with not much going for them other than their looks. She bet he singled them out, knowing none of them would last.

Demi agreed that if you loved the person you were with and were sure you wanted to spend every waking moment with them for the rest of your life, then marriage didn't matter. But trust did. You trusted your partner with your money and your home. You loved the man.

"Neither am I."

"Then we've settled it. No love without trust because trust is too rare, and no marriage because marriage never works. Just companionship. That's what both of us want."

"Ooooh, something in common. How special."

He angled his head in response to her mocking. "You brought it up."

"What if you end up falling in love despite your best effort not to?" Her stomach did a flop when she realized she feared that as much as he did. What if she fell in love again?

"I won't."

Her ire rose again. How could he say that? She left her coffee on the counter and went to him.

"Then there's no danger in doing this." She put her hands on his chest and slid them upward as she leaned her body against his, looking up into his dark eyes with her best attempt at smoldering sexuality.

She saw the startled flinch in his eyes before he recovered.

"We've never tried this before," she said. "We were always so busy arguing and beating each other to bounties that I doubt it ever crossed either one of our minds."

"It crossed mine."

It was her turn to be startled. He'd considered romancing her? She'd daydreamed of it more than once. Those hot imaginings had always unsettled her.

"Well, I don't trust you and you will never fall in love, so…" She tilted her head as she rose up onto her toes. Looking into his eyes, she slowly moved her lips to his, barely touching. She felt his warm breath and smelled the faint remains of cologne.

Her heart beat fast and she had to take more breaths. She hadn't anticipated this—a real reaction to him as a man. She should have. Hadn't she just recalled all those daydreams she'd had of him? He'd admitted to having them, too.

His hands slid around her. They singed her with each inch they traveled from her waist to her back. Heat ignited and spread.

He pressed his mouth more firmly to hers and they fell into a moving kiss. As his lips caressed, hers answered. It felt so good she couldn't stop. She vaguely heard their harsher breathing.

His tongue probed for entry and she allowed it. From there a hungry feasting ensued.

His hands roamed down to her rear and she instinctively lifted her leg, needing more. He reached for the hem of her nightgown and, in doing so, his elbow moved back and bumped into his coffee cup. The cup tipped over and coffee spilled.

Demi stepped back and Lucas turned to right the cup. For a moment she could only stand there and watch coffee spread over the counter and drip over the edge.

What had just happened?

Snapping herself back into a semblance of control, she went to the paper towel holder and retrieved enough to mop up the mess.

"I'll get it." Lucas took the paper towels from her and began wiping up the spilled coffee.

His declaration that he'd never fall in love or get married gnawed at her. So did her lack of trust. This man would see to it she was arrested. She'd kissed him, and the chemistry taunted her. Attraction she expected but this…this was far beyond anything she'd ever imagined.

* * *

Lucas spent an awkward day with Demi. The snow-storm had gradually relented by midday and he was itching to get out of here. Another storm was forecast for later so they didn't have a long window of time. He also needed to get moving rather than be confined in this small space alone with her. Demi had always been bold, but he couldn't believe she'd pressed herself against him like that. Kissed him. Even more, he could not rationalize the punch it had packed. He'd thought of kissing her many times before but he had never anticipated such intense passion.

He wanted to stop it from cluttering up his mind. Unlike other women, she wouldn't leave him alone in his thoughts. She'd spent her morning with Wolf, feeding him and bathing him and dressing him. After she'd put him down for a nap, she'd come out into the living room and sat the sofa with a book, her glances wary and sometimes sultry.

"We should get going soon," he said.

Raising her eyes from the book, she sent him one of her distrusting looks.

"We can't stay here with Devlin out there. It's stopped snowing. He's going to be back." They should have left as soon as the snow let up this morning. Now the afternoon was growing late.

"Give me your keys, then."

He had kept them in his pocket to prevent her from leaving without him. "I'll drive you."

"Why should I go with you?" she asked.

"We can go to my cabin. I have a security system. Devlin won't be able to get at us there."

"Us."

"You and Wolf will be safe there."

"For how long? Until you convince me to go to town where I'll be arrested?"

"You won't be arrested."

"The evidence hasn't disappeared, Lucas. Police have enough to throw me behind bars until they're positive Devlin is their guy. But seeing me in jail is what you really want, isn't it?"

"No." Frustrated, he stood and paced to one side of the room and then went to the window next to the Christmas tree. It was still cloudy but there was no wind and no more snow fell. Drifts rolled across the landscape from the cabin to the trees. He saw no tracks and had gone outside to check for signs someone had prowled. There were none. They didn't have much time to waste.

He faced the room and Demi's cautious eyes. "You can stay at my cabin for as long as you like. I won't tell anyone you're there. My colleagues all know I went looking for you. I'll tell them I didn't find you. You can bring your disguises and we can search for the missing weapon used in Bo's murder. You can stay hidden until we find it and we have something concrete to clear your name."

Several seconds passed while she considered that. "Why would you do that? What reason do you have to help me? You think I'm guilty."

"I don't think you're guilty anymore."

"Still. Why help me? I'd be more inclined to believe you'd use my arrest as a convenient way to get rid of me professionally."

He scoffed. She sure had a low opinion of him. Well, her body certainly disagreed.

"I'm not that much of a shyster. Thanks."

She averted her eyes and he knew by her reaction that she saw his point.

"I owe you, anyway," he said, bringing her eyes back to him. "Not only for doubting your innocence, but for saving my life."

When she didn't seem to recall the incident to which he referred, he said, "Remember that bounty we both went after? The robbery suspect? He drew on me and you appeared behind him and stopped him from shooting me."

"I didn't save your life."

"He would have shot me." Lucas was sure of it. "I was so intent on getting him before you that I rushed too much. I went out into the open too soon. I didn't know where he had gone. I didn't see him go into that alley. You did, and you positioned yourself behind him."

Again, several seconds passed as she contemplated what he'd said. "That almost sounds like a compliment."

He hadn't said she was a good bounty hunter but he supposed he'd implied it. She *was* good. He had never admitted that, though. He had always been too driven to outmaneuver her.

"Please, Demi. Come with me to my cabin. It isn't safe here." She had to see that.

Her gaze went to the Christmas tree. "I don't like the idea of spending Christmas in hiding."

"I have a Christmas tree in my cabin."

Her eyes moved back to him.

"And exterior lights. You don't have those here." She only had the tree.

Still, she hesitated, but he felt her begin to sway.

"Aren't you tired of running?"

She let out a heavy sigh. "Of course I am. I miss my home and my friends."

"Then go pack. Let's get out of here while we still can."

At last she nodded. "All right." She stood and walked to the back of the cabin.

Lucas was immensely relieved and a little amazed that he'd actually gotten through to her. She'd agreed to go with him. She never would have done that before she'd been accused of murder. Their rivalry had been too strong. Add to that the fact that she was a Colton and he was a Gage and their feud only grew more intense.

Now, in the short amount of time he'd been alone with her, he began to sense a thaw between them. Certainly that kiss had melted a sizable chunk of animosity. He wasn't sure it was right to call it animosity, though. Maybe on the surface. Underneath, he had always thought their competition held more playfulness than that. He had teased her, after all. Now he had to face the fact that his attraction to her presented more of an issue than anything else.

What if you end up falling in love despite your best effort not to?

Her question haunted him. He suspected it would continue to haunt him after that kiss.

An explosion rumbled the walls of the cabin.

Lucas drew his pistol and rushed to the front door. He cracked the door open and cautiously peered outside. His truck was on fire. Someone had blown it up. Further, all the tires on the Jeep were slashed.

They had no way out of here. Except on foot.

Chapter 4

Throwing on a jacket, Lucas ran from the cabin. He heard a snowmobile. In the woods, he slowed to listen. The snowmobile noise grew fainter. He'd never catch the man.

Running back to the cabin, he saw Demi, armed with a rifle, standing outside the cabin.

"We're trapped here," she said, lowering the gun.

Inside, he closed and locked the door. "We'll hike to the inn a few miles down the highway."

"Hike?"

He knew she was thinking about Wolf. "We'll be all right. Dress warm."

She gaped at him a moment and then went to the rear of the cabin.

Lucas kept watch through the windows. Moments later, he heard the snowmobile return. Devlin emerged from the trees with an automatic weapon. He started shooting at the cabin. Lucas ducked out of sight with his back to the wall. Glass broke. Bullets hit ornaments on the Christmas tree.

He ran to the back of the cabin, grabbing his backpack on the way. Closing Demi's closet door behind him, he adjusted the hanging clothes to hide the back of the closet and then joined Demi in Wolf's secret room. He locked the door.

All the while, a hail of bullets struck the cabin and broke more glass and other items in the living room and kitchen.

Demi had finished dressing Wolf and had him in a baby packpack. He began to fret over the noise.

"Shh," Demi said softly, bouncing him. She had the rifle propped next to the door and he saw a pistol in a waist holster. She'd brought a backpack and winter clothes into Wolf's room. He commended her for her forethought.

The gunfire ceased.

Lucas exchanged a look with Demi. Where was Devlin?

Shortly thereafter, the sound of the door breaking down preceded more gunfire.

"I know you're in here!" Devlin shouted.

His booted feet thudded on the floor as he moved into the cabin. Lucas heard him come down the hall and stop at the door to the room next to this hidden area. Then his steps reached Demi's room. He shot his automatic weapon, tearing the room up for a few seconds before stopping. "Where are you?" he yelled.

Devlin began throwing things. A lamp. He tipped over the dresser with a roar.

"Where did you go?" He continued to rant. "How did I miss you running?"

His boots thudded into the hall. "Stupid. Stupid. Stupid! How could I be so stupid?"

More thrashing came from the living room. "I should have never drove away on the snowmobile. I should have attacked right away!" He roared again and then his footsteps faded as he left the cabin.

Lucas waited, listening to the snowmobile circle the cabin, then do a wider swath, and then the noise faded altogether.

"All right. Let's go."

Demi put Wolf's hood over his head and covered his head with a blanket. She herself had on a heavy winter jacket, a hat and gloves, and winter boots.

Lucas opened the window bars and the window. Demi had put a stepladder before the window. Lucas picked up the two backpacks and used the ladder to climb up and out. Dropping the packs, he took Wolf from Demi and she climbed out. He hung one backpack on his back and hooked the other over one shoulder while Demi put the baby pack back on. She followed him through the deep snow toward the front of the cabin. Flames devoured his truck. He'd loved that truck, his 2500 Laramie Crew Cab.

Once they reached the long, winding driveway, he slowed to allow Demi to catch up and walk beside him. He kept an extra-careful watch on their surroundings, listening for the snowmobile and searching for signs of anyone lurking in the trees. The snow wasn't as deep under the tree canopy.

"Why does Devlin want to kill me?" Demi asked as she hiked alongside him.

"Got me."

"The evidence is against me. He framed me."

He thought while he walked and kept vigil. "He must know police are after him. Even without solid evidence against him, he's now a suspect."

"Then why kill me? Why not just make a run for it?"

"He has. If you're asking why he'd like to kill you, you should ask why he wanted to kill all those grooms."

"His obsession with Hayley. He killed Bo so he wouldn't have her, and he probably killed all the others because he couldn't marry the woman he loved so therefore no one else could."

Lucas thought some more as he walked, glad to have something to focus on other than kissing Demi. "You were supposed to go to jail after he framed you. Instead, you went on the run. You got away. Now he's a suspect. His plan is failing and he likely blames you. You should be in jail, according to him."

"I guess we'll never know for sure. I can't climb inside the mind of an unstable person. Whatever his reason is, it won't make any sense to someone rational."

"Probably not."

They reached the highway. They'd be more out in the open now. If Devlin were to come after them again, he'd have to drive a car and not the snowmobile. Lucas made a mental note to check the local snowmobile rentals to prove Devlin rented one.

"How far is the inn?" Demi asked.

"I saw it on my way here. Maybe five miles."

"That's not bad."

Five miles was a cinch for him. He loved the out-doors and always made plans on his weekends off to do something active. He was, however, concerned over the lowering gray clouds. It would start to snow again soon.

"Do you walk a lot?"

"Yes. I love hiking in the woods. It's been great stay-ing at the cabin. I took Wolf every day."

"I love being in the woods, too. Camping. Fishing. Mountain biking and hiking."

"I haven't camped in a long time. I'm not big on fishing. I have a nice mountain bike, though."

He walked beside her, wondering how he'd missed the many interests they shared. After the potency of that kiss, the revelation didn't bode well for his phi-losophy on love. Hell, just because he found her at-tractive on every level didn't mean he'd automatically fall in love. Sex was always hot in the beginning. As time passed that wore off and companionship became the important factor. Like any other relationship, the physical passion would fade.

A car approached from behind them.

Lucas put his hand on her back and steered her off the highway into the trees. He wouldn't take any chances in case the driver was Devlin. There weren't many cars out after the big storm.

Demi stood behind a tree and he behind her. The car passed.

They resumed their trek on the highway for a few more minutes. Then another car approached.

Demi found another tree and they waited.

This time the car slowed and pulled over not far from where they stood. Lucas recognized Devlin in the driver's seat.

"That man is relentless," Demi said.

"You go deeper into the woods." She took Wolf and did as he said.

Lucas waited for Devlin to get out of the car and aimed his pistol. He shot and the bullet hit the door frame. Devlin bent for cover. He held his automatic weapon. Lucas could see the barrel sticking up as Devlin held it. He took aim and hit the top, sending it falling from Devlin's hand.

Getting back into the car, Devlin started driving. Lucas shot at him again as he passed, hitting his mark but not fatally. He thought he had struck Devlin's arm, given that Devlin jerked his hand off the steering wheel and swerved a little. He kept driving. Lucas watched until he disappeared from view.

They walked up the highway and Lucas saw snowflakes begin to fall.

Tired, cold and hungry, Demi shook off more snow from Wolf's blanket and checked on him. His cute face sprang into an open-mouthed smile. He'd done that each time she checked on him, as though having fun with a game of peekaboo. Seeing the lighted sign for the inn, a surge of gladness suffused her. It was dark now and the snow had begun to fall more heavily. Lucas repeatedly looked around and she could tell he watched out for them. She could focus on protecting Wolf, which she appreciated.

As they turned onto the paved road leading to a

parking area in front of the inn, bright lights welcomed them. Demi hadn't seen a sight that washed her with relief more than this. It was a large log structure with a gabled window perched over the double-door entry and white-trimmed windows along the first and second stories on each side. She could see a Christmas tree through one of the windows.

She couldn't wait to get settled into a nice warm room and order room service. She hoped they had room service.

She walked faster, nearly trotting toward the entrance while holding Wolf's head. Lucas chuckled and jogged to the front door to open it for her. She entered as Wolf began to cry. He had a soft cry, not a screech, but low toned. He also used his hands to get his mother's attention. She talked to him every time he did that. He so melted her heart. Lucas was beginning to melt it even more whenever she caught him watching. She could tell he was comfortable with his affection. Yes, he wanted to know his brother's son, but was the boy's mother another matter?

Inside, they stood in a small, wood-floored foyer with a desk. Piano music played somewhere in the back. There were no doors other than a wide-open archway that led into a living room. Clanking dishes and running water told her the kitchen must be to the right of that room.

Demi went to the desk with Lucas, taking in a grand double staircase of dark-stained wood and banisters with white vertical spindles. The two beautiful curving stairways flanked the foyer, rising to a large landing area on the upper level where the Christmas tree twinkled.

A slightly plump older woman with short gray hair and black-rimmed glasses appeared through the living room archway. "Oh, hello."

A man matching her age trailed her.

"What are the two of you doing out in this weather?" The older woman spotted Wolf. "Oh, and you have a youngster."

"We don't have any arrivals tonight," the older man said, sounding mildly cantankerous.

"Oh, stop, Edward. We have plenty of rooms." The woman waved her hand as though swatting at him.

"We just put away all the food, Gladys."

The woman named Gladys went behind the desk. "Shush, Edward. Let's put you in room…" She looked up at Demi, the baby and then Lucas. "Let's give them the west corner. You'll have lots of room and there's a fireplace and a nice tub."

"Heaven," Demi said.

Gladys began processing the transaction on the computer. "What brings you two here at this hour and in a storm like this?"

"The storm passed." Lucas handed her a card.

"The snow hasn't," Edward said.

Was he as grumpy as he sounded? He seemed harmless and even friendly underneath his elderly annoyance.

"We had car trouble," Demi said.

"We can get a tow for you." Gladys gave Lucas his card back.

"Don't bother, it's totaled. It caught on fire." Lucas glanced over at Demi with a secretive grin.

"Oh, my goodness. I am so happy you are all right."

Gladys gave him the key—a real key. The charm of this place was already working its way into Demi.

"Do you have room service?" she asked.

"We have a kitchen and prepare food for all three meals a day, but it's all put away now. There's a restaurant not far from here that delivers to us, though." Gladys produced a menu.

Demi took it, thrilled to no end. "Thank you."

"Have a good night."

"Breakfast starts at seven," Edward said.

Lucas led the way up the grand staircase and down the hall to their end room. Only then did Demi realize they'd be sharing it. She hadn't thought to ask for her own.

Lucas opened the door and let her go in first. A king-sized bed with a cream comforter that had a thick green stripe running across the foot end was to the left of the door. A white nightstand with a dark wood top was on each side. A counter with a microwave and coffee machine was to the left. There was a small refrigerator below. The bathroom was behind an old-fashioned sage-colored sofa that faced a fireplace and high-backed chair. The walls were sage green and trimmed in white. Tall windows flanked the fireplace, and a larger window was between a dresser with a television and the high-backed chair.

Demi removed the baby pack and a now-fussing Wolf. Lucas put the backpacks on the sofa and went to the large window, performing his sentinel role.

After removing her outer clothes, Demi prepared Wolf's dinner, holding him in one arm. Then she went to the chair and sat, feeding him with a bottle.

Lucas left the window and checked the taller, narrower windows. When he finished, he turned on the fireplace and sat on the sofa with the restaurant menu.

"Pizza?"

Anything sounded good right now. "Sure."

He took out his mobile and put it away. There must have been no service because he went to one of the nightstands and used the phone to order.

Demi looked down at Wolf, with his red hair and closed eyes, as he suckled the bottle. He'd been a real trouper on the long, cold walk here. He'd only started complaining when he got hungry. Maybe he'd grow up to be an outdoor person, like her.

Lucas finished ordering and sat down on the sofa and watched them. Wolf began making tiny grunting sounds, contented with a full tummy. He opened his eyes and met hers. Their bond was magical. She'd heard other mothers talk of it but hadn't come close to imagining what it would be like for real. Indescribable. Miraculous.

Wolf finished his dinner. She needed to get him ready for bed.

Standing, she walked to Lucas. "Will you hold him so I can get us ready for bed?"

Lucas looked up at her and then reached out to take the baby. He cradled Wolf in his arms, his size dwarfing the little one.

Demi dug into her backpack, which she had strategically packed to fit the most items. She found Wolf's pj's and a fresh diaper and set them on the counter. In the bathroom, she flattened a towel out on the vanity next to the sink. Before retrieving Wolf, she washed her face and got into her own pj's—she'd opted for pants and a top.

When she emerged from the bathroom, Lucas was at the counter with Wolf, changing his diaper and talking to him in a baby voice. She couldn't hear exactly what he said, something to do with fresh and clean for bed.

She stopped beside them and saw Wolf's big smile. He giggled and waved his arms.

"It didn't take long for him to latch on to you."

Lucas smiled with a glance at her. He finished dressing Wolf and lifted him, raising him high and then bringing a pudgy cheek down for a blow-kiss. Wolf squealed in delight.

"I am never going to get him to sleep if you keep that up."

"We can hang out for a little while." Lucas cradled the baby in one arm as though he'd held infants all his life.

"How are you so adept at handling babies?"

"Friends and family gatherings."

"You like them."

"Kids? Yeah, of course. What's not to like?" He offered his pinky and Wolf grabbed hold. "Yeah."

His sing-song tone contrasted mightily with all his brawn. Adoration suffused her. After that kiss, the whole spectacle warmed her much more, having more sentimentality and heat.

"You said you don't want to have kids."

"Not my own. It's easy to enjoy them when they aren't yours."

A laugh bubbled up and out of her. She used to think the same before Wolf came along.

"He'll have to sleep between us tonight," Lucas said in his normal man tone. Then, to Wolf, the sound changing again, he said, "Won't you? Yeah." He brushed his nose with the baby's, eliciting another raucous bout of giggles. "We can't have you rolling off anything."

The baby would serve as a barrier between them. Demi should be glad for that.

"Are you sure you won't roll onto him?" she asked.

"I doubt I'll get much sleep tonight anyway. I won't roll over on him." Lucas's voice reverted to the animated version for the last declaration. "No I won't."

"How did I ever miss this Jerry Maguire character you have in you?"

His deep chuckle rendered Wolf still. His eyes grew big and he stared up at Lucas as though the rich sound fascinated him.

I'm with you, pal. More than his voice fascinates me.

Demi had to endure another half hour of Lucas playing with Wolf before sleepiness finally took over and the baby conked out in his arms. She also had to endure the way Lucas watched the transition from play to sleep. He held Wolf until the phone rang, signaling their pizza had arrived.

Demi took Wolf from him and laid the baby on the bed while Lucas took care of the pizza delivery. She arranged a blanket around Wolf and leaned down to kiss his forehead. She wasn't accustomed to sharing him with anyone. No one else had been around. She had to admit to a little jealousy, seeing how smitten her son was with Lucas. More disturbing, though, was how Lucas bonded with him. Wolf could almost be his own son. Being his brother's son was close enough.

Lucas put the pizza on the oval wood coffee table and retrieved some paper towels from the counter next to the microwave.

It was after seven, and she was starving. She sat next to him on the sage sofa. He handed her a slice on a paper towel.

"I don't understand why you deprive yourself of having children when you love them so much."

He chewed a bite of his own slice and looked at her. After he swallowed, he said, "Eat."

"No, really. Why do you?" To make him happy, she bit into her pizza.

"I don't look at it like I'm depriving myself."

"But you are." He'd made the decision not to have them when it was obvious he adored them.

"I enjoy other people's kids. Why do I have to have my own to satisfy that urge?"

He called it an urge?

"Did you plan on having Wolf?" he asked.

She scoffed. "No. He was an accident. A very special one."

"Did you plan on having kids in general?"

She supposed she deserved the questions since she'd gone after him for answers on the same matter. "Actually, no. I hadn't given it much thought. Having them wasn't a top priority. Don't ask me why."

"But after Bo, you decided to stay away from marriage?"

"Marriage, at least for a while, and definitely not until I find a man I can trust. If I never do, that's okay with me."

"I don't believe you."

"Well, good, because I don't believe you, either."

And she didn't trust him, either. He didn't believe she'd stay away from marriage and she didn't believe he would, either. Where did that leave them?

Chapter 5

Early the next morning, Lucas woke before Wolf and Demi. He rolled onto his side and propped his head on his hand. Snuggled in a blanket on top of the comforter, the baby breathed evenly. Long, fine, dark-red eyelashes rested on his cheeks. Lucas didn't like how Demi's question bothered him. He did like kids. They didn't have a worry in the world and always gravitated toward fun and adventure. His favorite camping trips were the ones with big groups and kids.

Whenever he thought of having kids of his own, he also thought of how devastating it would be to lose them. He enjoyed other people's kids. He'd feel a lot stronger about his own. He knew people who'd lost a child. It changed them beyond compare. No parent should have to go through that, but the sad reality was, in life there was death. The only death he needed to suffer was his own.

After spending time with Demi and Wolf, though, he wondered if he'd made the wrong choice. He understood most people would not relate to his decision not to marry or have kids. He knew it was drastic. He also knew that he never, ever wanted to feel what his father had felt and lose touch with those around him, even his kids.

Lucas had needed his father after his mother died. He hadn't had his father. He didn't really have him to this day. His father was a quiet, solitary man. Successful, no arguing that, but detached from the rest of society. He functioned. He socialized. From the outside, no one would guess a depressed man struggled to survive day-to-day. On the inside a completely different man lived. He felt neither joy nor sorrow anymore. He'd lost too much. Money had meaning and nothing else. Money would not hurt him. Love would.

Lucas didn't live in isolation. Money didn't mean that much to him beyond being a necessity. He wasn't afraid of love, either. He just never wanted to be hurt the way his father had been hurt. It was a conscious decision.

He could just hear Demi argue with him. She argued with him a lot. That's why they butted heads so often.

"If you avoid love because you don't want to be hurt, then you're afraid," she'd say. Or something similar.

Once he fell in love, his well-being would depend on the well-being of the woman he loved. Who had control over something like that? Nobody, that's who.

Unless a person *chose* not to fall in love. He controlled his destiny.

Demi stirred, taking a deep breath followed by a long stretch. The comforter slid off her breasts, which stood out with the arch of her back. Even her modest pj top didn't minimize the shape of her perky chest. She had an athletic body, something that had always attracted him.

Her eyes blinked open. She turned her head and their eyes met, hers sleepy, and he was sure his were heating up.

"What are you doing?" she asked.

"Watching Wolf sleep."

She smiled softly and rolled to her side to look at her son. The motherly love that swept her expression left him no illusions as to what she felt for her baby. Their bond was powerful.

Feeling himself slipping ever deeper into this domestic bliss, Lucas pushed the covers off and got up. He busied himself making coffee.

Demi stayed in bed, waiting for Wolf to wake up. Once he did, she went about giving him a bath and dressing him. They'd go downstairs for breakfast.

Lucas put a cup of coffee on the side table by the bed where Demi was dressing the baby.

"Ah. Thanks."

He sipped his coffee just as four gunshots rang out from somewhere in the inn. He put down the cup and grabbed his gun. Demi had picked up Wolf.

"You stay here." He didn't think she'd put her baby in danger by trying to help.

She held Wolf against herself and nodded.

Lucas hurried from the room to the top of the stairs. There he stopped to listen as Edward pleaded with the gunman and his wife cried. Staying close to the wall, Lucas went down the stairs. From the foyer he couldn't see anyone in the living room. Going to the wide archway, he stopped at the wall and peered in.

"Please. Let her go," Edward said. "We don't want any trouble."

"Shut up old man."

Devlin. As if he needed any sign that's who'd shot up the inn.

The inn was the nearest place he and Demi could have sought shelter, especially on foot. Of course Devlin would case the place for them. Now he held the proprietors hostage, probably until they gave him the room number.

Lucas could see where this would lead. He stepped into view, catching Devlin's attention.

"I knew you'd come down here when you heard the gunshot, superhero wannabe that you are."

"Let them go, Devlin."

"Where is Demi?"

"She's in the room with her baby." Lucas saw no need to hide that information since he would never let Devlin past him.

"Go get her and bring her down here."

Demi held Wolf close, even though he was secure in her baby pack, an adjustable baby carrier. It was adjustable in all carry positions, but she preferred the front. She poked her head out into the hall and saw a young man doing the same from a room two doors down. Average in height, he had short brown hair and a lanky form. In lounge pants, he clearly hadn't intended to start his day early. An instant of recognition struck her.

"Vincent?"

What was Lucas's youngest brother doing here?

"Demi?"

Did he believe her guilty or innocent?

"Stay in your room," Vincent whispered. "Someone is shooting downstairs."

"I'm a bounty hunter, remember? Your brother is here, too." She lifted her right hand to show him her gun.

"Lucas? He found you?"

She had no time to explain. "You can't tell anyone."

"I won't as long as you don't tell anyone *we're* here."

We?

The shooting had stopped and she didn't hear anything, which worried her. Had Devlin already killed someone downstairs—that older couple who owned the inn? He'd have come up here looking for her, if so.

She had to go down there and she needed the element of surprise, but she could not take Wolf.

She walked down the hall to Vincent's room and saw her cousin, Valeria Colton, standing with the phone to her ear. Barely twenty years old, like Vincent, Valeria had dark hair and wore a nightgown that was visible under an open robe. When she saw the sexy lace, the reason for the lazy morning became clear to Demi.

The two must have sneaked away for a secret tryst. Valeria's father, Judson Colton, was dead set against any of his kids marrying a Gage and Valeria was still young enough for him to try to control. He'd already blown a gasket over his daughter Serena falling in love with Carson Gage, a detective with the RRPD. Then son Finn Colton, the chief of police, had gone and fallen in love with Darby Gage. And if that hadn't been enough salt in his wounds, his other son, Anders, had fallen for Elle Gage, also with the RRPD. He had to be close to giving up on the old feud.

"Will you watch my baby while I go check out what's going on?" Demi asked Vincent.

"Are you sure you want to go down there? Valeria called 911. They're sending the sheriff over."

In this isolated county, there weren't many who made up the sheriff's department. It would take too long for help to arrive.

Valeria said something into the phone and hung up. She walked over to Demi with a startled look.

"Demi?"

"Lucas found her," Vincent said.

"I'm so glad you don't have to hide anymore."

She didn't explain she still needed to hide. She had no time.

Valeria admired the baby. "Oh, look at this sweet face."

Demi took Wolf out of the carrier and Valeria took him into her arms, cooing and not as afraid as before.

"I'll be right back." Demi stepped into the hall. "I don't mean to sound unappreciative, but if you do anything with my baby to hurt him or take him, I'll hunt you down. Cousin or not," she added with a pointed look at Valeria. "And uncle or not," she said to Vincent.

Vincent smiled. "You don't have anything to worry about. We're going to get married on Christmas Eve whether our parents like it or not. We are planning to start a family. We love kids."

Enough to kidnap one? Demi realized paranoia made her think that.

"What's his name?" Valeria asked. "We heard you were pregnant."

"Wolf."

"Wolf. What a unique name. He'll be just fine. You be careful."

"All in a day's work." Removing the baby carrier pack, Demi handed it to the young man and then began moving down the hall, mouthing, *Thank you.*

Downstairs, she heard voices coming from the right of the living area.

"You're going to have to go through me first," Lucas said.

"All right," Devlin answered, and Demi feared he'd shoot him.

"Wait!" Demi recognized Edward's voice. "I'll go get her if you let my wife go."

"I'll let her go when you bring her down here."

Devlin wanted Demi and was holding Gladys hostage, most likely at gunpoint. Demi would risk too much by going in there, at least, she would if she entered through the archway.

"Please. Let me go now," Gladys said desperately.

Demi went to the front door. She took the handle and slowly pulled. When she had enough room, she slipped through. Pausing to listen, she heard nothing except Gladys's continued pleading and, with a sick feeling, hoped that drowned out any noise Demi made.

Outside, Demi ran toward the side of the inn, glad

for the winter boots she'd put on in a hurry. Leaping over short bushes and dodging trees, she reached the edge of the inn. Clearing the corner, she stopped at the edge of the exterior lights around the large patio. Keeping to the shadows, she made her way to the patio door, which was far enough along the back of the building to be beyond the living room.

Through the glass, she saw the dining area and, closer to the living room, Devlin holding Gladys at gunpoint and Lucas aiming his own gun at Devlin. Edward wasn't there and must have gone to find Demi.

She tested the door. It was unlocked.

Lucas faced her, so she stepped into view and waited until she saw his eyes shift as though looking at Gladys. He'd seen her but didn't let on.

He started talking to Devlin. Demi couldn't understand what he said, but his muffled voice came through the glass door. Sliding the door open, she stepped inside.

Devlin held Gladys with his arm hooked around her neck and his gun to her temple. She clung to his arm and made distressed whimpers. Edward had not returned. Lucas stared at Devlin but Demi knew he was aware of her approach.

Demi's top priority was Gladys. Demi had to be stealthy. She contemplated shooting him right then, but feared his gun would go off and he'd hurt Gladys.

Demi stepped forward.

Devlin began to turn his head. She wasn't sure what had alerted him, maybe a cool draft of air when she came in from outside. Gladys looked at Devlin, saw his distraction as he spotted Demi and shoved him.

Lucas was on Devlin in an instant, knocking his hand and jarring loose the gun.

Gladys wailed and ran for the front of the inn.

Demi kept her gun on Devlin, but now Lucas had him in a wrestling hold, Devlin gripping his wrist to prevent Lucas from aiming his gun at him. Lucas got in two punches, but Devlin seemed unfazed. His previous gunshot wound didn't seem to slow him down, either, indicating it hadn't been that severe.

Devlin dodged Lucas's next punch and delivered one of his own. Lucas crashed into a table, knocking a chair over and stumbling. Devlin roared in a crazed way and tried to take the gun from Lucas.

Lucas kicked Devlin's knee, forcing a yell from him and making him take an unsteady step back.

"Don't move!" Demi ordered.

Picking up a chair, Devlin hurled it at her. She leaped out of the way.

Lucas swung his gun toward Devlin's head, but Devlin blocked him and slammed his fist into Lucas's sternum. Lucas answered with a chop of his free hand and then delivered a hit to Devlin's head. Devlin partially blocked that. He staggered.

Demi had a clear shot and readied her gun. Just then, Edward appeared with a rifle. Devlin saw him and dove just as Edward fired, able to grab his own gun on the way. Devlin crouched behind the end of a buffet against the wall.

Tipping a table over, Demi took cover behind that.

Edward shot his rifle again, yelling, "Get out of my inn!"

Lucas appeared beside Demi. She peeked around

the edge of the table and saw Devlin making a run for the door where Demi had entered. Lucas rose and ran after him.

"Stop!" he yelled.

Devlin twisted and shot his weapon, forcing Lucas to take cover again. Lucas didn't remain long behind cover. He ran after Devlin.

Demi heard gunshots before she made it to the door. Looking outside, she saw Lucas chasing Devlin toward the front of the inn. Rather than follow, she went through the dining area and into the foyer. Hearing crying, she looked up to the open landing. Edward had his arms around his wife.

She felt bad for them and responsible for bringing violence to their magical world, but Demi had to make sure Lucas was all right and Devlin was no longer a threat. She opened the front door. Devlin had hopped onto a snowmobile and was racing away, zigzagging to avoid Lucas's gunshots. He didn't avoid them all, though. Lucas was a good shot and a few bullets sparked off the handlebars and chassis.

Demi closed the door and looked up at Edward and Gladys huddled together, watching.

"It's safe now."

Gladys sagged against her husband and cried some more. He rubbed her back after lowering the rifle and leaning it upright against the railing.

Jogging up the stairs, she stuffed her gun into her holster. "This is all my fault. That man is after me." She put her hand on Gladys's arm. "Are you all right?"

Gladys sniffled and moved back from her husband,

who kept his arm around her. She nodded. "Just had a bit of a scare."

Demi had to smother a smile. She sounded so sweet and innocent. A "bit of a scare" didn't come close to the terror she'd been through. Demi wished she could wrap her hands around Devlin's neck and rid the world of him right now. He'd caused more than enough grief for the people of Red Ridge. Now his evil had spread here, infecting this peaceful, kind couple.

Lucas came in through the front door, mouth and eyes in grim lines. He had to be frustrated, not being able to capture Devlin yet again. Devlin had a snow-mobile, though. Lucas couldn't chase him on foot.

"We need to go, Demi," he said.

"The sheriff will be here soon," Edward said.

"We can't stay." The sheriff might recognize her. "We've caused you enough trouble. I'm so sorry." She really did feel terrible for putting them through this.

"It's not your fault, dear." Gladys moved away from her husband to put her hand on Demi's arm. "You can't control what criminals do."

"Why is he after you?" Edward asked.

"I wish I knew." She couldn't go into any detail on that. "But I need to ask you not to tell the police we were here."

"Why not?" Edward asked, wary.

Lucas reached the top of the stairs.

"That shooter set me up for something I did not do. I can't explain or I might put you in more danger and I don't want that. Just tell them he was after someone he thought was staying here but they weren't."

"You're asking us to lie to the sheriff?"

Gladys elbowed her husband. "You poor dear. Of course we will."

Demi hugged the old woman, who clearly had a sixth sense about the decency of others. "Thank you." Demi eased away from Gladys and walked around them toward the hall.

She knocked on the couple's door. It opened to Vincent's anticipatory look and Valeria hanging back with Wolf.

Wolf saw Demi and made a high-pitched sound, his tiny arms reaching for her.

Demi's heart swelled with love.

"Is everything all right?" Vincent asked.

"The shooter got away," she said. "No one was hurt. Just had the scare of their lives."

Valeria brought Wolf to the door. "What if he comes back?" Her worried eyes met Demi's.

"He won't. He has to know the sheriff will be here soon," Lucas said from beside her.

Vincent handed Demi the baby carrier pack and she slid it on before taking her son from Valeria. She put him back into the carrier and kissed his forehead. Wolf pressed his hand on her chin, making grunting sounds of contentment.

She caught Lucas watching with soft eyes and turned to Valeria and Vincent. "Thank you again."

"He's a good baby." Vincent put his arm around Valeria.

"He's a happy baby," Lucas said.

"What are you doing here?" Vincent asked his brother. "Are you turning her in? I thought she was innocent."

"I'm not turning her in."

Demi glanced at him, still not so sure he meant that. He met her eyes and sent her an admonishing blink.

"I'm going to stay at his cabin until we can find proof," Demi said.

"That was Devlin who came here shooting, wasn't it?" Valeria asked.

"You're very insightful," Lucas replied. "It was. He knows we're on to him and is going mad that Demi won't take the fall for him like he planned."

Lucas sounded convincing, but Demi refrained from believing him completely.

"You have to promise not to tell anyone you saw me here," Demi said.

"We promise. Don't tell anyone about us being here, either," Valeria said.

"We won't, but I doubt it will matter anymore. I'm sure the two of you will have no trouble with your wedding—once the real Groom Killer is caught, that is." Demi had nothing but good vibes from these two. She could tell they were in love.

"It will bring the Coltons and the Gages together once and for all," Lucas said.

"That's a wedding I won't miss," Demi said.

"We'll be sure to invite you." Valeria beamed.

"There will be many other Colton-Gage weddings," Demi said. "There have to be others hiding their love just like you."

Valeria smiled and exchanged a romantic look with Vincent.

"Thank you for watching Wolf," Demi said.

"It was our pleasure. Gave us a taste of what it will

be like for us when we have our own," Valeria said, looking up at Vincent with adoration. Genuine love.

As Demi followed Lucas back to their room, she wondered whether she should have chosen another phrase. Genuine love? Did that even exist?

Funny how she'd thought the same about Bo, and he'd turned out to be nothing like what she thought.

How did anyone ever truly know when they found true love? Some people said they knew when they first met the person, but that had to be based on the newness of meeting them and not knowing them enough. On the other hand, she had met a meager few who'd said they'd dated for over a year, maybe three, and *knew* they were in love. Demi didn't buy it. She believed with all her heart that *nobody* knew—one hundred percent, no shred of doubt whatsoever—that they were in love.

Life wasn't designed that way.

People were born. People died. How nice to have someone to get from point A to point B with, but nothing in between was a certainty.

"You okay?"

She entered the room, realizing Lucas had opened the door and held it for her.

"Yes."

She walked inside, still in a daze. Maybe it was *her*. Maybe she had a more complex personality than others. Pickier about men?

Yes, now, but what about before she met Bo?

She had not been all that particular, not in great detail. She'd looked for men who attracted her physically, men she could relate to and talk to. What happened next she hadn't really contemplated. She supposed she had believed she'd *known* she was in love. Now she knew she had not been. That pretty much screwed up her perception on things.

"We have to get out of here."

Distracted, Demi saw him ready with both their packs. Of course they needed to leave. "Okay." Then clarity came back. "How are we getting to your cabin?"

"Any way we can."

"Does Devlin know where you live?"

"He might, but he won't get in." She met his eyes and couldn't dispute they had to get away. Besides, she could not put Gladys and Edward through any more trauma.

"How far is your cabin from here?"

"About ten miles."

"We can't walk."

"No, we can't."

"We can't steal a vehicle from this place."

Gladys and Edward were no longer on the landing. Demi followed Lucas down the stairs and found them sitting at a table, holding hands. They had righted the toppled furniture and were now likely waiting for the sheriff.

"I hate to trouble you more, but would it be possible to borrow a car?"

"The sheriff will give you a ride to town," Edward said.

"We can't wait for the sheriff," Demi said.

"But…why not?" Edward was clearly becoming suspicious.

"We're bounty hunters," Lucas said. "That man is someone we need to bring back to Red Ridge."

"Ah." Placated, Edward nodded. "Then you'll be needing transportation. I know I would like to see that man caught and put behind bars." He glanced at his wife. "For putting my pudding through what he did."

"You have a vehicle?"

"We have two. You can borrow the truck. Just get it back to me as soon as you can."

"We can do that. Thank you."

Lucas retrieved the truck keys from Edward.

Outside, Demi faced a new dilemma. Getting into the truck, she wondered what would happen once Lucas had her in his cabin. She'd be on his terms there. Would he turn her in to the Red Ridge police? While her instinct told her no, she could not rely on that. She had to know for certain, and the only way she'd do that was if she could prove her innocence.

Lucas could tell Demi was nervous about going to his cabin. She kept looking out the window and biting her fingernail. Once, Wolf reached up his hand and grasped her finger, effectively stopping another chew.

At his driveway, he stopped at his iron gate and entered the security code on the pad installed at the side.

"A security gate?" Demi asked.

"A security system." The gate was only part of it. "Devlin will not be able to get past this."

The gate parted in the middle as it opened. Lucas drove through and Demi twisted to watch it automatically close. He saw her follow the fence until she couldn't see it any more.

"There are cameras and motion detectors all around the house."

"Are you paranoid or something?"

"No. I just don't want any unexpected visitors. Works great for solicitors, too." He drove the mile to his cabin, a two-story square-log and dove-tailed-corner home with a covered porch that spanned the full width of the front. Two windows beside the single door lined up with the two on the second level. A bigger window on the west side had the best view of the Coyote Mountains. Although it was a small mountain range, beautiful rock formations rose up from the heavily forested land.

"Wow." Demi got out of the truck and gaped at the cabin.

With two bedrooms and a loft, it wasn't huge but definitely a decent size. He loved living here. It had the most important thing to him—outdoors.

At the door, Lucas let Demi inside first. She walked into the entry, a square area where he had a coat closet and a boot bench. He'd done the lower level all in gray-brown wood flooring. Straight ahead, the dining area was beneath an open loft. Demi took that in and then removed her boots. He did the same and set the security alarm before following her and Wolf into the main living area.

To the left, a center window went to the ceiling and two others reached about three-quarters of the way. Framed by wood beams, each was topped by four smaller framed windows and together they provided a picturesque view. Light-colored stone encased the fireplace and extended to the ceiling. He'd put the sectional so it faced the windows and the fireplace. His

sister Elle had helped him find coordinated area rugs
for the living and dining rooms.

To the right, the kitchen island had three tall chairs.
He'd done the counters in black granite and chosen
stainless steel appliances. Queenie's food and water
bowls were at the end of the kitchen island. He missed
her. He'd go into town and pick her up tomorrow.

Wolf began to fuss.

Demi bounced him as she wandered through the living room. "Why do you have so much security here?"

He'd wondered how long it would take her to ask.
Unfortunately, he didn't feel like explaining.

"It's remote."

She turned from the stunning view. "You're afraid
of wildlife?"

"No." There was no way around an explanation. "I
dated a woman who stalked me."

Demi walked back over to him. "Really? What happened?"

Reluctantly, he said, "I broke up with her and she
didn't like it." He watched her grow more curious.

"Why did you break up with her? Did you know
she was unstable?"

"It didn't feel right."

"Why not?"

She must know he didn't want to talk about it and
still she probed. She probably did that on purpose.
Knowing this topic made him uncomfortable, she half
teased him with her questions.

"It was getting too serious. She fell for me faster
than I did for her. I started to feel smothered."

"Nooo….you?" she mocked.

He was glad she was keeping it light. It made talking about it easier. "I told her I needed some space and she went off the deep end. She didn't believe me when I said I didn't love her."

"Did she pin the tail on the donkey?"

"Very funny. She wouldn't stop coming over and calling. She waited for me to leave the K-9 unit. When she came to my cabin, that was the last straw."

"Why didn't you call the police?"

"I am the police."

She lifted her eyes impatiently. "You know what I mean."

He had not intended to hurt her. He was careful not to hurt any woman. He usually made sure they understood his view on marriage. This woman had been different. He'd been more attracted to her than other women and hadn't given his usual speech.

"I didn't call because she might have been right about a few things," he said.

"That you're marriage phobic?"

"That I may have led her to believe we had a chance for something long-term."

"Marriage."

"Maybe."

"Did you love her?"

"No. That was the problem. She loved me and I didn't love her."

Demi angled her head and studied him as though doubtful. "Or were you afraid you *would* fall in love with her?"

When he'd first met her he had wondered if he could—or would—fall in love with her. "She began showing her possessive side pretty early on. No, I wasn't afraid of love with her. I knew it would never grow into that."

"I can't believe you'd go to all this trouble because a woman stalked you."

"She was an expert markswoman and kept threatening to shoot me in my sleep." That had convinced him enough. "Building the fence kept her from hiking up to my cabin and peeking into my windows. The security system was to keep her from catching me by surprise."

Demi contemplated him a moment, seeming more satisfied with the amount of information she'd received. "What happened to her?"

"She eventually stopped trying to get to me. Last I heard she moved away. I don't know where she went and I don't want to know."

"Aside from the stalking, is that how all your relationships end?"

"Some. Most are mutual. Some women have told me to get lost."

"The smart ones."

Wolf fussed more fervently and Demi had to address whatever troubled him. Before she turned, Lucas saw her disappointment. She knew those women who dumped him had done so because they refused to deal with his unconventional views on marriage and family. Lucas didn't want that to bother him, but it did. He didn't want to analyze why.

Chapter 6

Demi stirred, beginning to wake up. She reached over to touch Wolf and her hand came against the flat blanket. Popping her head up, she didn't see Wolf. Apprehension gripped her. She flew off the bed and looked around Lucas's guest room, which was upstairs, down the hall from the loft. She reached the railing of the loft at the same time she heard giggles bursting from Wolf.

Lucas held the baby high above him as he sat on the sectional. Seeing her, he lowered Wolf and held him normally. Demi went down the stairs and walked into the living room. His chestnut hair neat and stylish, Lucas had already showered and dressed in jeans and a dark blue button-up. He wore only socks on his feet.

"I heard him stirring. I thought I'd let you sleep. I changed his diaper and fed him breakfast." Lucas's dark gaze fell over her front. She wore a nightgown and felt undressed.

He stood up and came to her, handing over the baby.

She took him and, out of the blue, Lucas kissed her. She doubted he realized what he was doing until he'd done it. It was a quick kiss, like a good morning kiss.

Tingles spread from that brief touch. She suspected he'd experienced the same. He looked a little startled before he stepped back and walked into the kitchen.

"Coffee?"

"Yes."

"I need to go into town today."

Demi stiffened. "Why?"

"I need to go get Queenie. She's probably depressed by now."

That sounded like an excuse. "Is this when you turn me in? You tell the police where I am and they come and get me?"

He gave a long sigh. "I thought we resolved this."

"I don't trust you." She didn't trust anyone, really.

He moved closer and put his hands on her shoulders. Wolf's eyes moved to him and he smiled toothlessly.

"I'm going to get Queenie and I need to check in at the training center. I'm not telling a soul you're here. Okay, you don't trust me. I'll be back here in a few hours—with Queenie. You will be safe here, with the security and your experience."

Stepping back, he headed for the front entry and grabbed his jacket. "Don't go anywhere."

She didn't respond. Maybe she should make a run for it. He had acknowledged her experience. She did like that.

"Demi...?"

She was tired of running. She also did not want to walk with Wolf, to put him through that again. "I'll be here when you get back." She just hoped like hell he was being straight with her.

Lucas passed the police department and arrived at the K-9 training center. A large, warehouse-like facility with a brick and white-trimmed front facade, the center had an administrative area and a kennel. In the back was an expansive fenced area that included an enclosed agility course and an equipment shed.

Lucas walked from the rental vehicle he had just gotten that morning. He'd arranged for someone else to return Edward's truck. Inside the training center, the desk area teemed with officers and administrative personnel.

"Hey, Lucas." The dark-haired twentysomething woman behind the reception desk greeted him, her blue eyes sparkling behind brown-rimmed glasses. She was relatively new so he didn't know her name. "There's a puppy who's going to be happy to see you. Where've you been?"

Not everyone knew he'd gone in search of Demi Colton. "Working. Where's Elle?"

"In the agility ring."

He thanked her and headed for the rear of the building. Outside, he opened the gate to enter the agility ring, seeing Elle with Queenie. Tall and slender, his sister had her honey-blond hair in a low ponytail as she often did. She'd turned out to be a good K-9 cop despite her brothers' objections. Their approval had been important to her. Lucas approved. He just worried about her safety.

Her brown eyes looked up as Queenie finished a round on the course and barreled toward him. Her tan coat gleamed with health and her strides were long and smooth. She barked twice on her way.

Lucas braced himself for impact. The Belgian Malinois jumped for him. He wrapped his arms around her and endured her enthusiastic licks. Going down on one knee, he let Queenie find her footing, ruffled up the scruff of her neck and scratched her ears.

"I won't leave you like that again," he said. "I didn't need you this time, girl."

She gave a high-pitched yip, as though admonishing him. He chuckled and stood as Elle came over.

His sister hugged him. "Any luck?"

"No." He didn't like lying to her, but he couldn't risk anyone finding out Demi was at his cabin. Not only as a precaution, in case Demi was right and she would be arrested, but also to win her trust.

"Guess you should have taken Queenie."

"Guess so." He petted the dog's head and stood. "Where's Danica?" He hadn't seen his other younger sister. She could usually be found in the training center, since she was one of the unit's best trainers.

"She took the day off. She and Shane Colton had plans to do something."

"What about the rest of the clan? Where's Carson?"

"Where he usually is, at the police department. Vincent is either at the college or with Valeria Colton," Elle said.

"I thought she broke up with him months ago." He

knew full well the young couple was still together since he'd just seen them at the inn. But the last thing he wanted to do was mention that.

"She did, but rumor has it they're still seeing each other and planning a Christmas Eve wedding."

Their youngest brother had taken quite a shine to that Colton girl and caused a scandal when he'd proposed to her last winter. A Gage marrying a Colton? No way.

"So much for the Gage–Colton family feud over a poker game that cost our family some land," Lucas said.

Elle smiled. "A hundred years is a long time to hold a grudge."

"Yes, I suppose so."

Edmund Colton had begun developing the town in 1890 and gotten rich in the process. The Gage family had embarked on a competition to see who could make more money. Some years they did.

"Let's hope Devlin doesn't believe the rumors—or hear them for that matter."

"You're that sure Demi isn't the killer?"

He hadn't been certain where Elle stood on who the killer really was. He'd suspected she was on the fence and her question just confirmed it. "Yes, I think I am."

"I better get going." Lucas signaled for Queenie to come with him. "I'll see you soon, sister."

"That's good, brother." She turned back to the training area and headed for the kennels.

Lucas went inside and walked toward the front entrance. On his way a policeman spotted him and headed to intercept him.

John Williams was an older cop with years of experience behind him. Lucas had worked with him on a few cases. He seemed like a nice enough guy, except he was rather rigid when it came to criminals. If they were guilty, by God, they belonged in jail. He worked hard to put them there. Lucas respected that about him.

"You're back," John said, shaking Lucas's hand.

"John. Yes, just got back yesterday."

"I take it you didn't find her. I didn't hear about any arrests."

"We have enough reason to believe she isn't the Groom Killer."

"There's plenty of evidence to prove she is," John said. "I know some around here believe she's innocent, but there are others who aren't so quick to agree."

John's attitude enlightened Lucas about his stance on the matter. Lucas wasn't surprised. Williams was the kind of cop who required the evidence in hand before he'd be convinced.

"Finding a smoking gun would help. I've got to run. Good seeing you, John." Lucas started walking away.

"What if you do find that missing gun and it has Demi's prints on it?"

Lucas looked back. "Then we have our Groom Killer and we better find her."

John half smiled. He obviously liked Lucas's response. Lucas would do what was right. That was in his nature. John knew that about him. Everyone did. Integrity meant everything to him.

"Hey, Lucas."

Lucas turned before reaching the door and saw Officer Hunter Black approach. His reddish-brown hair waved as he jogged.

"I heard you were back. Any luck? I know you didn't find Demi, but did you get anything else? Any possible leads on Devlin?"

"No, unfortunately." He wouldn't explain how Devlin attacked and chased them. The owners of the inn had agreed not to say Lucas and Demi were there. They did not know Devlin was the one who had attacked. But Valeria had called 911. The fact that they were there might get back to the RRPD.

"There are a lot of people who want him caught. He can't run forever."

"No, we'll catch him."

Hunter nodded. "Men like him make me wish I'd have left Colton Energy sooner."

Hunter had quit his high-paying career at Colton Energy to escape the greed and takeovers. After his parents died when he was fifteen, he was taken in by a neighbor, Mae Larson, who'd turned out to be a criminal herself, along with her grandsons, the Larson twins. Hunter had good reasons for joining the force.

"There are some around here who still think Demi is guilty," Lucas said, voicing his frustration.

"Yeah, some do doubt Demi's innocence, but they're pretty much outnumbered by those who don't."

That was enough to be concerned about. What did the chief think? Lucas didn't want to ask.

"How's Layla doing?"

"Much better now that her father's apologized for trying to force her to marry Hamlin Harrington. He didn't know Hamlin's son could be the Groom Killer."

"*Is* the Groom Killer."

"Is. But we still need some hard evidence."

"I'll find it."

Hunter scrutinized him, tipped off to the level of Lucas's determination. "You're awfully supportive of a woman who, up until now, seemed more of a rival."

"I never had anything against her. We competed for bounties on occasion. We never really got to know each other."

"Now you do?" Hunter leaned in. "You holding out on me?"

Lucas shook his head. "I felt terrible for going after her as the Groom Killer, when Devin set her up all this time."

"Yeah. Innocent and on the run. Not a good place to be. Too bad you couldn't find her to let her know she's got nothing to worry about."

Lucas didn't mention why he didn't agree Demi had nothing to worry about. "What's Fenwick Colton going to do to save his company now?"

"I don't know. He has until the end of this month to come up with something. Layla is trying to help him. Not so much for him. She loves that company like it's her own. She'll do it for the family."

Lucas hoped she'd find a way, because if she did the K-9 unit and training center would be saved, as well. Fenwick funded the center. Without funding, the unit would not exist. Running a K-9 center was expensive.

The thought of losing the center presented another problem for Lucas, on top of catching the Groom Killer. Maybe he could think of a way to help Layla.

Demi looked out the living room window again. Still no sign of Lucas. The more time that passed, the more she worried that she should never have trusted him. She had showered and dressed in jeans and a soft gray knit sweater. She spent the morning playing with Wolf until he started to get tired and then put him down for his nap. While he was awake, she'd had something to distract her.

She paced to the kitchen and then back to the window. This time she saw Lucas driving toward the cabin. She waited to see other vehicles. Lucas stopped the rental and got out. His dog, Queenie, was in the passenger seat and jumped out after him. He opened the back and took out two grocery bags.

Still no sign of other vehicles.

Lucas entered the cabin. Queenie bounded in, stopped short when she saw Demi and looked up at Lucas for direction.

"Nobody else is coming," he said, closing the door.

Her whole body sagged with relief and a burst of humor because he'd read her so accurately. He hadn't turned her in.

"A girl can never be too sure." She took in how good he looked in his jeans as he turned and removed his jacket and slung it over a kitchen island chair.

Then he faced her and said to Queenie, "Go say hi."

The beautiful dog barked twice and trotted over to her. Demi crouched and greeted her. A well-trained dog, Queenie had poise but also an instinct for detecting good character. Demi scratched the most important parts and said, "Hello, Queenie, good to see you again."

Queenie's gold-tinged eyes twinkled with love between sweet blinks.

"You can baby her," Lucas said. "You won't ruin her."

Demi didn't speak to her in baby talk. As a free-lance bounty hunter, she had no K-9 and considered all the dogs at the center sort of like coworkers, much different than pets. Lucas had teased her for not talking to Queenie like a pet.

He crouched with her and scratched Queenie, who turned worshipful eyes to him.

Demi could feel their close bond and admired it for a moment. When Lucas looked up, his eyes captivated her. From soft love for his dog, they changed to something warmer for her. The attraction she had felt numerous times before and could always subdue now expanded.

He had also responded to the pull. Had he subdued this before, as she had? They had been intrigued by each other and had hidden it. She'd hidden it because she could not imagine becoming romantically involved with him. They butted heads far too often. Had they ever gotten along? His determination to beat her to bounties annoyed her and compelled her to best him. She had, many times, but he had also and just as often. She had often wondered if her being a Colton and his being a Gage had influenced his aggressiveness in that regard.

Why had he hidden his attraction?

"You never liked losing to me," she said.

"What makes you say that?"

"You didn't."

Queenie's eyes followed the back-and-forth talk.

"I was competitive," Lucas said. "So were you. You got angry if I caught the bounty before you."

"Only when you knew it was my bounty."

Chuckling, he stood. Queenie remained sitting. "Just because you called it your bounty didn't make it yours."

There he went again, riling her. She stood, too, and Queenie went to a dog bed in the living room and lay down.

Lucas must have enjoyed getting her going. He often did that when he won a bounty. She'd always thought he was gloating, but the light in his eyes and his affectionate tone now made her reevaluate. Had he been teasing her all this time? Teasing or not, she didn't like it. But she did like that he was attracted to her. She didn't want to like that. In fact, she grew uncomfortable.

"Easy. We both liked catching the bounty, that's all."

"You teased me on purpose." She felt slighted and her ire rose.

"Of course I did. You took me seriously and I found that endearing. You were so easy to make mad."

She humphed and went into the kitchen. "That wasn't very nice."

"You're getting mad again."

Opening the refrigerator, she realized she was, and over something silly. Why did she get so offended by him?

Because he was handsome. Because she had dreams about him. Because she'd thought he didn't feel the same about her.

Why was she even entertaining these thoughts? They were the least compatible couple she could think of.

Except for their reluctance to get involved with anyone. Sure, they had different reasons, his a lot more unreasonable than hers, but overall they both would have difficulty entering serious relationships again.

She almost flinched when he came up behind her and put his hand on her arm.

"I'm sorry. I adore you when you get mad."

Taking a bottle of water out, she faced him. "Adore me?"

"You were always so easy to set off, but what made it adorable was that you weren't aware I was teasing." He paused and added in a playful tone, "And that you were so easy to make mad."

He'd gotten in her face about how slow she was or that she thought she was a better bounty hunter but he proved every time that she wasn't. He had critiqued her methods, from being unable to track fugitives by their electronic transactions to questioning the wrong people. He hadn't smiled or laughed while he said those things, egging her on.

But his eyes had always had that sparkle, like they did now. His eyes had always been the thing that tickled her feminine senses. That had only worked to fuel her temper.

He hadn't been getting in her face. She'd taken insult over something benign. He'd kept that fact from her, that it had been benign. Then again, she shouldn't have been so naïve.

Realizing that made her even more uncomfortable with the chemistry they had together, chemistry that had stirred to new heights now that they were spending so much time together.

Had her naïvety allured him? She wasn't sure she

should be flattered. Demi didn't think of herself as naïve. Her quick temper had blinded her, most likely.

"Well, I'm not so easy to make mad anymore," she said with more sass than she'd intended.

He moved a step closer, a short step with smooth a movement that drew attention to his trim stomach and muscular arms and shoulders. "No?"

Did he have to do that? She could smell him now. And his chest beckoned her to run her hands over the hard plateau.

She shook her head.

"Are you sure?"

Seeing his eyes had a familiar light, she hardened herself to a warming reaction. Not anger. Far from it. "I've had a lot of time to work on it."

"I bet I could still make you mad."

"You just admitted to teasing me. Now I know."

He lifted his hand and brushed some hair off her cheek, the bob style swinging back down but not sticking to her skin. The touch sent tingles spreading from there and down her arms.

"I could find another tactic."

And he would. Lucas Gage had a confident personality. Until now, she hadn't realized he also possessed a lot of charm. She almost told him *this* tactic would not make her angry. Quite the opposite.

"Be careful. You might fall for me more than you want to," she said.

"We were talking about making you mad."

"Yes, and you have way too much fun doing that." She would not enlighten him that his flirty tactic would—and did—have the opposite effect.

He chuckled, that deep raspy sound she loved but had never admitted to loving.

"My secret is out." His voice caressed her just as his hand did.

She could think of nothing clever to say. She couldn't think. Not with him wooing her this way. He had to be aware that's what he was doing.

What if he wasn't? Or what if he was but couldn't or wouldn't stop himself?

His head lowered.

He was going to kiss her and she'd let him.

Oh, no.

Wolf's cry interrupted. Too happy to attend to him, Demi left the bottle of water on the counter and made her way upstairs to the second bedroom.

She changed him and sat in a chair in the bedroom to feed him. Lucas appeared in the doorway with a fairly large box. It was a crib. Gaping at him, she couldn't find the words to ask why.

"I went to the next town to buy it." He set the box down and proceeded to open the top. "I picked up a few other things we might need, too."

"You didn't have to do that."

"Diapers. Food. A playpen and some toys. A few others."

He'd gone to the next town so as to not raise suspicion, of course. If anyone in Red Ridge had seen him buying a crib and other baby items, they'd know he'd lied about hiding her at his cabin.

"You sure are proactive."

He looked at her. "It's just easier if I go."

"You're awfully excited about Wolf." He had to be. Why had he bought all that for Wolf?

"Excited? He's a great baby. I want him to be comfortable. And you."

As she continued to look at him without responding, she sensed him question himself. He had enjoyed picking up the things for Wolf. True, he probably did want Wolf and Demi comfortable while they camped out in his cabin, but most of what motivated him had more to do with Demi and Wolf than making them comfortable. Did he think she would just stay here and not go after Devlin—prove her innocence?

"Lucas, I'm going to dress up in a disguise and go into town to search for that missing weapon." She didn't know where she'd start, but she had to start somewhere and staying in this cabin would get her nowhere.

"I can do that. You don't have to worry."

Oh, yes, she did. She had to take care of herself and Wolf. "I can't sit here and do nothing, and there is only so much I can do on the internet."

"Then we both go under disguise. We start with Devlin's condo. What are you going to do with Wolf?"

Demi bit her lip, her ire still roiling. There was only one solution. "I can ask Brayden to watch him."

"No."

"You can go to him and tell him I'm here. He'll come here and no one will ever know."

"No, Demi."

"He's the only one I would trust."

He sighed. "Not a good idea. He would go against the department if he helped you."

"He's my brother."

"Half brother."

"He's my *brother*, Lucas." She would not back down on this. She could see him begin to realize that. And also that he was also helping her.

"Bring him here," she added "Call him. If you don't, I will. I'll wait until you're asleep and use your phone." No one would blink an eye about Lucas, a deputized K-9 bounty hunter, calling Brayden, a K-9 cop.

He grumbled from down deep. "You're impossible sometimes, you know that?"

She smiled. "Yes."

Chapter 7

The next day, Lucas arrived back at the cabin with the disguises Demi had requested. They'd dress up as hippies. He saw her watching him with more than idle curiosity. He wore lighter-colored jeans today and a dark Henley, and he caught her admiring his tall frame and lingering on his butt in the soft denim. After draping his jacket over the kitchen chair, he turned and took a moment to admire her. She had on a black sweater dress with tights and no shoes. She looked good in sweaters.

He petted Queenie's head and she stood from her sitting position and went to Demi for more attention.

Demi scratched behind Queenie's ears and then the dog went to her bed in the living room and lay down.

Lucas picked up the shopping bags and boot box he'd brought in from the rental. "I can't go to the next town for a while," he said. "People will start to talk."

She laughed briefly and went to sit on the sofa. "Can we go to Devlin's condo tonight? I'm anxious to get started."

"Sure. Police have already gotten a warrant and searched Devlin's home for the missing gun but didn't find anything."

"They might have overlooked something. Maybe more than a gun," Demi said.

They could hope, anyway. Lucas didn't think they'd find anything. Police had searched thoroughly. Finding nothing meant no judge would grant them another warrant. He wanted to start with Devlin's home.

"Have you contacted Brayden?" she asked.

"Yes. This morning. He didn't believe me, at first, that you were here, at least not willingly. He should be here in about an hour. I made him promise not to tell anyone." His conversation with Brayden had been strained to say the least. Brayden had initially attacked him, accusing him of wanting to turn Demi in.

"He won't." She lit up. The idea of seeing her brother made her very happy.

Lucas wouldn't mention how their talk had gone. He put the shopping bags and boot box on the big ottoman in the living room.

"What kind of tricks are you up to?" Brayden had asked, and a little later he'd said, "You and Demi don't like each other. Why should I believe she's staying with you? Unless you're forcing her?"

Finally Lucas had asked, "If I was going to take her in I would have done so by now."

That had placated Brayden enough to get him to agree to stop by in a couple of hours. Hearing a buzz from the control panel that indicated someone was at the front gate, Lucas realized Brayden had not waited for the decided-upon time. He was early.

"Ah!" Demi shrieked with glee and trotted over to the panel. "How do you work this thing?"

He brushed her hand away. "Let's be sure it's him."

No doubt it was. Lucas pressed a button. "Who's there?"

"Brayden. Where's my sister?"

Lucas set the gate to open. It would automatically close.

Demi rushed to the front door and went outside in the frigid air, hugging her arms and waiting to see Brayden's truck appear. It finally did.

Demi bounced up and down a few times, no doubt to keep warm.

"You can wait inside," Lucas said.

She ignored him and Brayden's truck came to a stop. He got out, tall and fit in jeans and a black Henley under a winter jacket, and walked to the front porch, his boots thudding on the stairs. His curly black hair didn't resemble Demi's original red hair, but they had the same blue-green eyes.

Demi threw her arms around him. "Oh, it's so good to see you."

"Hey, Demi. I've been worried sick about you. Shane got your texts but that's all we've heard from you. Why didn't you contact me?"

He looked injured. He and Demi were the closest of the Rusty Colton branch of the family.

"I didn't want you to try and find me. I knew Shane would tell you he heard from me."

"We've all been trying to find you." He looked around her at Lucas. "Some for not-so-good reasons."

Before Lucas could refute the comment, Brayden said, "Let's get you inside. It's freezing out here."

Inside, Queenie came to inspect Brayden, who reached down to pat her head. Lucas went about brewing some fresh coffee as Demi and Brayden caught up with each other. Queenie came into the kitchen with Lucas, sitting and watching his every move.

"When I heard you were wanted for the Groom Killer murders, I knew you didn't do it," Brayden said. "I was so afraid something would happen to you. We sort of went our separate ways after we grew up. Quinn, Shane, and I have gotten closer since all this started. It would have killed me if I didn't get the chance to get closer to you, too."

"How did you all get closer? Because of me?"

"No, a true-crime television director came to town to do some investigating for a miniseries on the Groom Killer case. We didn't want her to do it, at first, but after we started talking we got closer."

"He's going to marry the director," Lucas said. "Her name is Esmée da Costa and she has a son, so Brayden will be a father." Lucas didn't like the parallel. Demi had a son, too. Wolf wasn't his but he could be a father figure if he fell hard enough for Demi.

"How did you know that?" Brayden asked.

"People have loosened their tongues since they found out we've identified the real suspect and that suspect is on the run."

He noticed how Brayden eyed him suspiciously. Boy, were he and Demi ever related.

"You're getting married?" Demi beamed. "Oh, that's wonderful!" She hugged him again.

Brayden seemed to stiffen. He wasn't the social type, more of a lone wolf.

Demi moved back and Brayden relaxed. "Assuming I don't get whacked by the Groom Killer."

Demi swatted her hand in dismissal. "Devlin is no match for you."

"Except with his automatic rifle," Lucas said. "He just about mowed down Demi's cabin with it."

"Devlin found you?" Brayden shot a look at Lucas. "Did you lead him there?"

"I saw a stranger in town about a week ago who seemed to be watching me," Demi said.

She hadn't told Lucas that.

"I don't think Lucas led anyone to me," she added.

"I didn't. I was careful."

"Like you're being now?" Brayden challenged him. "Hiding Demi here until you can prove Devlin is the Groom Killer?"

"Brayden," Demi admonished him, but only mildly.

"Devlin came after us because the police are on to him."

"He must not like it that it looks like I won't be taking the fall for him," Demi said.

"Unless you're arrested," Brayden said. "The police have evidence against you, not Devlin." He looked over at Lucas, having voiced his main concern over Demi being with Lucas. Then he turned back to Demi. "Why don't you come and stay with Esmée and me?"

Lucas had to put his foot down on that one. "No. She's fine here with me."

Both Demi and Brayden faced him with a silent question. Why was he so adamant? Lucas didn't really know, himself. He needed to make sure she survived, for one. For another, he couldn't let any other man take over the job of protecting her, whether she would admit to needing it or not.

"Lucas does have some impressive security here," Demi said.

"I don't like it that you're here. Lucas was absolutely convinced you were the Groom Killer. The two of you don't even get along."

"Well, I know he's a good bounty hunter. He'll find Devlin."

"Yeah, but…"

"I didn't trust him, either, at first."

"But you do now, Demi? Why? Has he tried anything with you?"

Demi glanced at Lucas in a way that would tell Brayden something had occurred between them.

"He has?" Brayden started to move toward Lucas in a threatening way.

Demi took hold of his arm. "Brayden, stop."

He did and looked at his sister helplessly. "He wants you where he can control you in case the investigation on Devlin falls through. Don't let your heart blind you."

"Isn't that what happened to you and Esmée?" Lucas asked. Esmée had a son, too.

Brayden barely contained his anger, his mouth going tight. Lucas was sure that only his connection with Demi stopped him from going on.

"I need a favor from you, Brayden."

He calmed. "Anything."

"First, don't tell anyone I'm here."

Brayden nodded. "I wouldn't do that to you."

"Second, I need you to watch Wolf while I go in search of the missing gun Devlin used to kill some of his victims."

"I can find the gun for you."

Lucas almost audibly smirked. He remained silent and waited for Demi's half brother to be shot down.

"That is something *I* need to do, Brayden. I can handle it."

"I don't want you to put yourself in any danger."

"I've been in danger since this whole thing started. And don't forget, I'm a bounty hunter."

"A bounty hunter who's good in the woods, too." Brayden nodded. "It's just hard for me to let go after so much time not knowing if you were all right."

"I'm fine."

Brayden looked at Lucas once again. "He better not do anything to hurt you or have you arrested."

"I won't let him." She started to turn. "I want you to meet Wolf." Brayden led him to the bedroom where Lucas had put together the crib.

Lucas followed, Queenie on his heels.

Demi picked up Wolf and handed him to Brayden, who smiled down at the bundle and held him. Wolf's eyes opened briefly before he drifted back into sound sleep.

That kid was great. Lucas had no idea babies like this one existed. Wolf slept soundly and only fussed when he needed something. He was a happy baby.

His gaze shifted to Demi. Most of the credit had to go to her. She must be a good mother.

"Of course I'll watch him," Brayden said.

Lucas was glad for Demi that she would have someone she trusted to guard her baby, but he also dreaded having to deal with her brother, who he'd long known did not like or trust him. No surprise there. Brayden would have heard all about Lucas—from Demi's point of view.

Brayden had left with an agreement to return later. Demi sat on the sofa as Lucas walked toward her.

She indicated the bags and boot box that Lucas had brought back earlier. "What did you end up buying? Anything good?"

"I found this little boutique in Deadwood." He opened one of the bags to pull out a multicolored and striped Baja hoodie with a large belly pocket.

"Ooh, a drug rug." She took it from him and held it up to inspect the gaudy thing.

"The sales clerk said it's made with recycled eco-yarns and that it is environmentally friendly."

"And caters to hippie tree huggers. Nice."

He dumped the contents of another bag onto the ottoman.

Demi put down the hoodie and lifted a white, high-low boho dress with gray embroidery. Also among the items were a peace necklace and some bracelets, a suede vest with fringe and a long blond wig with braids swooping to the back over the rest of the hair that hung straight.

Lucas opened the lid of the boot box and showed her a pair of dark knee-high leather boots.

"Double nice."

Next he showed her sunglasses, handing her one pair.

"Are we going to draw too much attention to ourselves?" Maybe she should have come up with a different disguise.

"We'll draw attention to our clothes, not who we are." Lucas put on the hoodie over his dark Henley and then flipped the hood over his head. Then he slid on the second pair of sunglasses and stood before her for inspection.

"You look cool." He changed his pose as though modeling for her. She laughed.

"Go try yours on."

She took the dress, boots and wig, and went into the lower level bathroom off the living room. She had to hand it to Lucas. He had pegged her size. Most likely he'd checked before he left this morning. The dress was soft and fit to perfection. She began to wonder if he'd chosen this for selfish reasons. The bodice dipped a little low and the uneven hem rose above her knees in front. The boots were smooth and sexy.

She fitted the wig on her head and loved how the braids hung and clasped with a barrette at the back. The peace necklace might be a bit much, but the silver bracelets added a nice touch.

Leaving the bathroom, she saw Lucas holding her sunglasses. Laughing again, she took them and put them on, very aware of how he studied her.

"I should have gotten a red wig."

"Then people might recognize me."

"Yes, but you're so beautiful with long hair. It should be your natural color."

She went still with his compliment. He never said things like that to her. He thought she was beautiful? She didn't compare to the women he dated. She didn't spend much time on her appearance—hair, nails, clothes. Her job didn't allow for high heels.

"I'm not beautiful with shorter hair?"

"You are beautiful no matter what style of hair you have. You're beautiful in your nightgown."

Had he lost his mind? Why did he speak so freely to her? "You're not exactly homely yourself."

He grinned and a grunt of a laugh erupted from him.

"Anyway, I thought you preferred more of a porn star look in your women."

His grin fled. "Porn star?"

"Your girlfriends are all so…perfect and…" She didn't want to say empty-headed.

"You could look like any one of them," he said. "And I've seen your boyfriends."

Bo? Bo was handsome, as handsome as Lucas. Did he mean before Bo? She didn't date very often, not as often as Lucas did. She did prefer men who looked like Lucas but she looked for more than that.

"My boyfriends all had something I liked about them aside from their looks."

"What about that guy who still lived with his mother and didn't have a job?"

"He was between jobs, and his parents had money."

Lucas said nothing, just wore a slight grin that leaned toward mocking. He thought she was no better at dating than he was.

"You were engaged before Bo, too."

"I broke it off because it didn't feel right."

"None of them felt right. Is it possible for any man to feel right for you?"

The thought popped into her head that he could be right for her and shocked her. She put it aside as best she could.

"Bo isn't the only reason why you can't trust men, is he?"

"I trust the right men." He'd made it clear he considered her as beautiful as the women he dated, but Demi didn't agree. She had more earthy good looks. She couldn't believe he'd choose a woman like her to date. Maybe women like her were too much of a threat to his decision not to marry or have kids. Like the thought that had struck her, maybe he had the same suspicion—that he could like her, maybe too much.

"I think you deliberately date men you know will never feel right," Lucas said.

"I think you deliberately date women you know you'll never fall in love with," she countered.

"Touché." His grin turned more genuine. He moved closer to her. "That being said, what are we going to do about this?" He bent his neck and kissed her.

It was a warm, soft kiss. He kept it brief but that didn't lessen the flying sparks.

She could only stare up at him. What did he think he was doing?

"You see? That's a problem," he said. "You like me too much."

What? He'd done that on purpose? Teasing her again? Disappointment made her stomach turn. And then she chided herself for being disappointed. And then she just got mad.

"I *don't like* you." She pushed him back. "You're always *mean* to me!"

He smiled without malice. She didn't know how to take him.

"I'm never mean to you, Demi. Why have you not noticed that yet?"

Someone knocked on the door.

Brayden. Thank goodness. Lucas confused her. She went to the door and opened it to see her brother's smile emerge. He made her feel better just like that.

"Where's the little guy?" Brayden came in, looking from her to Lucas and then back to her. "You okay?"

"Y-yeah." She glanced at Lucas.

That was all Brayden needed. He marched over to Lucas and leaned close. "What are you doing with my sister?"

Lucas held his hands up. "Nothing. I didn't get a chance to tell her I liked her, too, before you came to the door."

Demi gaped at him. For a man who vowed never to marry he sure sent mixed messages. Was he not worried about what kissing her would do? Then she realized he was worried. That's why he'd asked her what they would do. He didn't want to fall for her any more than she wanted to fall for him.

Falling for him...

He must have kissed her to make her aware of the problem. Warn her. She could not, under any circumstances, *fall* for him.

"Demi?"

She focused on Brayden.

"I'm okay. Everything is okay. I need to find that missing gun."

Brayden hesitated, unconvinced. "I'll let it pass for now, Demi, but if he so much as—"

Lucas planted his hand on Brayden's chest and pushed him out of the way a little, nothing too forceful, just a message. "Relax. I'm on your side."

"Since when?" Brayden muttered.

"That's enough. Please. I'm up against murder charges, you two. Could you please get along?"

Judging by the look on both faces, their answer was no.

Devlin lived in the upscale part of town in a luxury condominium complex a few blocks from Main Street. He owned a unit two-story unit with a sizable balcony and two walls of windows with views of the Coyote Mountains. The guard at the gate let them in after they'd announced who they would see. Not much of a guard.

Now, well after dark, Lucas walked with Demi and Queenie toward the stairwell of Devlin's condo building, he with his hood up over his head, and she in her wig and sunglasses. Queenie would pass as a pet. He'd scoped out the security already. The guard did regular rounds and wouldn't be near here for another hour. Cameras might capture them entering the stairwell, but in disguise they wouldn't be identified and wouldn't be noticed until the morning.

On his way home yesterday, he'd stopped by and followed a guard into the control center. He'd used his credentials as a deputized K-9 bounty hunter to ask them some questions relating to the ongoing Groom Killer investigation. Queenie had been with him, and the guards had been all too willing to help as much as they could. Lucas had begun by asking each of them about the times of each murder and if they had seen Devlin. They said they'd reviewed video at the request of other officers and hadn't seen Devlin during the times the murders took place. Video surveillance had recorded him coming home late at night most nights, not only the nights when murders occurred. Lucas had asked if they had seen him themselves on those late nights and they explained that only two guards worked nights and the control center wasn't manned during the night but the recordings were reviewed every morning.

Lucas picked his way into Devlin's condo.

"Residue," he said to Queenie, who immediately set out to search for gunpowder residue scents.

The lower level was an open floor plan. A spacious kitchen had a gas stove in a kitchen island that faced the living room with a large leather sectional and a big screen television hanging above a gas fireplace. There was also a bathroom, along with a double door leading to an office. It appeared the bedrooms were all upstairs.

Demi searched the bookshelf in the living room while Lucas went into the office. The desktop computer had already been searched. Devlin had not used the computer during the times of the murders and there had been nothing found linking him to any of the crimes, other than communications with Hayley.

Lucas noticed a laptop case he hadn't seen before and had not seen reported in the reports relating to any searches. He saw Demi head upstairs for the bedrooms as he opened the case. He booted the computer and easily accessed the folders. He spent several minutes going through files, not finding much. Devlin didn't seem to use this computer for anything other than work. Then he found a file full of photos of Hayley. Nash Maddox, another K-9 cop, reported catching Devlin looking at a photo of Hayley. Hunter had found the room upstairs filled with all things Hayley Patton and a storage device that further proved his obsession.

Demi joined him in the office. "I found these in his nightstand drawer. She held a pair of underwear. "And this." She held a bra in her other hand. "Must be new since the condo was last searched."

"I found the photos Nash reported."

"No weapons anywhere."

"Let's wait for Queenie to finish."

Lucas hadn't expected to find actual weapons. Police had already searched his condo and Devlin wouldn't be that stupid. Lucas was more after anything Devlin may have left after the searches were conducted or something he'd forgotten and hadn't yet been found. Devlin may have returned to his condo while he was on the run. Police weren't watching the place like they had when he'd first become a suspect.

Queenie barked.

Lucas and Demi hurried upstairs to the room where Devlin had created a shrine to Hayley. Everything had been taken for evidence. Queenie sat in the closet looking up at the attic hatch.

Lucas dragged a chair into the closet and stood to open the hatch. He used his small flashlight to peer inside. As he turned in a half circle, he found a shoebox. Bringing that down, he gave Queenie her reward and put the box on the bed.

"There's gunpowder residue in here."

"How was this missed before?"

"Maybe it wasn't." Lucas opened the lid and found some receipts inside and some other pieces of paper. Notes. Also inside were several spent ammunition shells.

"Let's go through this at your cabin," Demi said. "We can return it if it ends up being real evidence."

They were already operating in secret, without the RRPD involved, so returning anything they might find seemed their best option.

Leaving the condo, Lucas checked the stairwell for any signs of people. No one moved up or down the stairs. He led Demi down to the ground level, Queenie at his side, and walked toward the rental. On the way, he noticed a car he hadn't seen when they'd arrived. As they neared, he spotted a man sitting behind the wheel. It was a different car than the one Devlin owned, but that didn't mean he couldn't find another one.

He kept his hand close to his weapon and saw that Demi had noticed the suspicious driver, as well. She veered away from the vehicle, taking a long route to the rental. There, she got inside and Lucas drove from the parking lot onto the street, heading toward Main.

The car left the parking lot behind them and now tailed.

Lucas drove in the opposite direction of his cabin. He turned onto Main Street and then drove around one block to let the other driver know they were aware of him following. That car kept going straight when Lucas drove back toward Main Street.

"I don't think that was Devlin," Demi said.

Lucas didn't either, which meant whoever had parked outside Devlin's house must have been a police detective on watch for Devlin.

Chapter 8

Lucas had to go into work the next day, so Demi would have the day alone with Wolf. She hadn't been alone all day since she'd left her cabin and was reminded of how lonely she had been. She found more Christmas decorations and entertained Wolf by putting them up. Garland on the mantel. A table centerpiece that looked old enough to have come from his mother. She and he shared that, as well. They'd each lost a mother.

How much of his determination to never fall in love had to do with that? He claimed it was how his father had suffered that had fueled most of his decision, but what about how he'd felt growing up without his mother? He'd grown up learning how family life was with only a father. He didn't really know much about what it was like to grow up with a mother.

Demi did. She couldn't imagine not having had her mother through her childhood and teen years. That had to have had some kind of an effect on Lucas.

She passed the front door on her way to the kitchen and saw the gate communications monitor come to life. The camera was activated by movement. A car drove by very slowly.

Demi stopped and walked to the panel to watch. She could see the bumper of the car through the trees. She saw nothing else, but the car seemed to have parked along the side of the road up from the turn into Lucas's driveway. The driver must have seen the camera.

What would they do now?

The motion detectors would set off an alarm if anything emerged from the trees. Lucas had explained the system would only pick up movement of something roughly the size of a human or larger.

Getting her jacket, she left the house with her gun and walked down the lane to the gate. Keeping out of sight of the road, she walked into the trees, her booted feet sinking into the shaded snow. At the fence, she could see the car. A dark blue sedan, the windows were tinted and the engine wasn't running.

She memorized the license plate number and went a short distance along the fence before she spotted a man walking off the highway and into the trees. He wore a beanie and sunglasses. He had the same build as Devlin, but his bulky jacket and hair hidden by the hat made it difficult to tell.

Demi took cover behind a tree and watched him look up at the fence. The twelve-foot-high iron barrier with coiled barbed wire would be a challenge to climb. He seemed to have decided the same and headed back toward his vehicle. When he made a U-turn on the highway and drove away, she jogged back up to the cabin. Lucas considered his property impenetrable but he had no motion detectors along the perimeter. Some wire cutters would take care of the barbed wire. Climbing twelve feet wouldn't be easy but it could be done.

Lucas entered the training center. If the agility course had cleared enough, he'd start with that. He took Queenie through the administration area, greeting coworkers on the way to the back. The dog tugged on her lead more than usual. She knew where they were going. Queenie loved the agility course. He also spent a fair amount of time training her in air-scenting to search for the lost or missing persons. She was an excellent tracker in missing-person cases. Ground and air were her specialties. She'd found Alzheimer patients before and responded to his verbal commands, answering with a bark and standing still at the location of something significant.

Noticing a couple of officers look at him, he wondered if he was imagining their suspicion. Lying violated his moral compass. Even though it was for the good, keeping Demi a secret bothered him. His fellow duty men stood for honor and justice. He hated betraying them. But there were some who would see Demi jailed based on hard evidence. He satisfied his morality with the fact that, if he let that happen, an innocent woman would be arrested.

Outside, he entered the fenced area and saw no one else in the arena. The snow had melted enough to do the agility training session. He'd do variable terrain later, an important part of practicing her expertise. No surface deterred her. She could track on gravel, dirt, vegetation or in urban areas. She could also pick out a criminal in a lineup by scent alone.

He might be a proud papa, but she really was an amazing animal. He sometimes thought she understood English—beyond his verbal commands.

Removing her leash, he gestured for her to sit beside him. She did and waited for his go-ahead. Spaced sixteen feet apart, four sets of obstacles made up the hurdles. On his hand signal, she began. The first was a plastic barrier painted like a brick wall. Queenie cleared that while he moved along beside her. She sailed into the group of white picket fences, wagging her tail when she finished and then the motion stopped as she approached the open frame. She leaped through and ran into a turn, easily maneuvering over a chain link fence. Next was a board jump.

At his voice command, Queenie jumped six feet over the first and lowest of the boards, which progressively grew higher until she cleared the last. With a quick and graceful transition, she reached the shrub jump and finished.

At his command she came to sit beside him. He gave her a few tiny treats with a "Good girl."

Next he took her to the catwalk. Queenie sat beside him again and waited. He signaled and she climbed an angled ladder to a platform and then waited halfway across for Lucas to give the go-ahead to finish down the other side.

Last was the crawl and then the A-frame. Lucas

asked her to sit before beginning each one, and when she completed her exercise, he rewarded her with a rub and a few pats.

"Good girl."

Queenie hadn't lost her edge. She completed the training like a pro and with a tongue-hanging smile as she came to sit before him. Lucas spotted an officer in uniform watching him from the other side of the gate.

A five-foot-nine dark-haired man with blue eyes, Brian Miller wasn't part of the K-9 unit. Something must have brought him here from the sheriff's office. Brian had a wife and two sons, and rumor had it that he lived beyond his means and preferred to go out with his friends rather than spend time with his family. He didn't strike Lucas as one of the best examples of a good cop.

Lucas took Queenie out of the training area. The sun had sunk lower in the sky, but at least it was clear.

"Weather cleared up nice," Brian said. "A little cool."

Lucas wondered if he went for the small talk to alleviate the pressure of what he'd really come here to say. "Yeah, it sure did. What brings you by?"

"I heard you got a lead on where Demi may have gone. Something about a cabin deeded to a woman around the same time she vanished?"

"I checked out all new rentals and purchases in a fifty mile radius from Red Ridge and checked them all. Just got back."

"What about the one with the deeded cabin? Dead end?"

"Yes." He hoped this man that he barely knew wouldn't keep asking questions.

"I checked that out, too. The woman's name was stolen. Did you know that?"

Great. Lucas wondered if anyone would uncover that. He already had. That's why he'd driven there to find out if the woman was Demi. "Yes, but she wasn't Demi." There would be no way for him to learn it had been Demi at the cabin unless they did fingerprint or DNA analysis. Lucas didn't think there were enough believers in Demi's guilt left to go to those lengths.

The cop stared at him, doubting. "Why didn't you turn her in?"

"She wasn't Demi."

"But she stole someone's identity."

"She wasn't Demi," he repeated more sternly. This guy wasn't a threat to him. He was a rookie, probably trying to make an impression on his boss by reaching. What did he think he could do?

Ordinarily Lucas would not have let a person guilty of a crime go free. Identify theft made a lot of people suffer unnecessarily. But Demi had not harmed anyone with her theft. He told himself not to feel bad about deceiving everybody.

"The woman's identity she stole was a deceased woman," Lucas said.

"So you just let her go?"

"I never apprehended her. It wasn't her I was looking for."

The cop eyed him in that distrustful way again. "You think Demi is innocent. Everybody thinks she is. She isn't."

Lucas didn't argue, hoping Miller would calm down and let him get on his way. At his side, Queenie sat and looked up at him with soft, blinking eyes as though she understood.

To his dismay, and maybe Queenie's, Brian's face reddened and his mouth twitched. His brow lowered a fraction and his gaze hardened.

"Her name was written in blood at your brother's crime scene," Brian almost sneered.

How could Lucas get rid of this kid? Miller had to be five years younger than him. "Devlin could have done that to throw off investigators."

"What about her necklace and that witness?"

"Devlin could have planted it and the witness had a rap sheet a mile long." Not to mention witnesses had a tendency to end up murdered after they made those claims. The policeman also had to know that another witness had confessed to being paid to lie by a man who sounded like Devlin. But that was all circumstantial. Lucas and Demi needed hard evidence proving Devlin's guilt.

"Did you really come here to give me a hard time because you aren't convinced Demi is innocent?" Lucas asked.

"The evidence…"

"Was planted. Go back to work. Come, Queenie." Lucas walked to the door.

"You're making a mistake." The rookie cop followed. "A murder weapon was found at a property belonging to Devlin but who's to say Demi Colton didn't plant that while on the run?"

"Give it up, Brian." Lucas walked with tile-eating strides through the building.

When Demi heard Fenwick Colton had arranged a public meeting at the Red Ridge Police Department K-9 Center, she insisted on going. Everyone would be there and she knew it would be a risk, but she had to know what Fenwick had to say. His daughter, Demi's cousin Layla, had gone through a lot because of him. Devlin's father, Hamlin Harrington, who'd been engaged to Layla as part of a plot to save failing Colton Energy, would be there, as well. Why had Fenwick asked him to attend? It might have something to do with the Groom Killer case, given Hamlin was Devlin's father.

Lucas had argued against her going, but she came up with an ingenious disguise—to go with Lucas as his newest flashy girlfriend. They would say they were having dinner right afterward. She'd used makeup to change the appearance of her eyebrows and lips, and already had brown contacts and a silky, long black wig. With fake diamond jewelry and extra padding to appear bustier and fuller in the butt, she didn't look anything like herself. She wore a sexy black dress and high heels. Look out, Mrs. Doubtfire!

The next problem was finding someone to watch Wolf. Brayden would attend the meeting along with all the other officers. The natural choice had been Lucas's brother Vincent and his secret fiancée, Valeria. They had been happy to oblige.

Demi wondered if he'd given in to her insistence on going with him because he wasn't completely convinced she'd be arrested even if everyone found out she was back in town and living with Lucas.

Lucas kept looking at her. As they walked to the front doors of the center, she caught him eyeing her breasts and legs. He'd probably taken a good look at her rear, as well. Her ire flared because he preferred women who looked like this false version. Demi was no model. She was attractive but she did not dress like an advertisement for beauty.

They reached the front doors and Lucas held one open for her, his head tilting as his gaze found her cleavage. The bra she wore pushed it up with the padding underneath and to the sides of her breasts. When his eyes lifted, she narrowed hers in warning.

He grinned and put his hand on her lower back as they walked inside. Passing through the administration area, they reached the large conference room where everyone had gathered. Policemen, policewomen and all of the K-9 officers sat on rows of chairs. Even Dr. Patience Colton was there, pretty, with dark hair and dark eyes, and dressed in her veterinarian's coat. Before Demi had gone on the run, she'd brought in an abandoned dog that had been injured and Patience had fixed the poor creature up. Demi had found a good home for the pooch. She found the veterinarian nothing like what the rumors said. Daughter of Fenwick Colton and a member of the richest of the Colton clans in the area, she worked hard and treated people as equals.

As Dr. Colton glanced over the crowd and saw her, Demi forced herself not to tense. Would Patience recognize her? She seemed to look from Demi to Lucas as though taking notice he had a new girlfriend. She looked away without any indication of recognition. She stood next to tall and muscular Nash Maddox, a K-9 cop with sandy blond hair and hazel eyes who frequently glanced over at the doctor with a telling intimate connection.

Demi didn't think she'd ever seen so many Coltons and Gages in one room together. The fate of the K-9 center united them. Could it be that this would finally end the hundred-year-old feud? The Colton ancestors had blamed the Gage ancestors for cheating in a poker game, which had cost the Coltons a lot of land. While those ancestors were long gone, fights over land and property and a general pervading animosity continued, passed down the generations.

Dark-haired and serious, Detective Carson Gage stood next to his half sister, Elle. Tall and curvy, her medium-length hair was freshly combed and shiny and, like most in the room, she wore jeans. Carson saw Lucas and gave a nod of greeting. Demi had never noticed him to be overly chummy with his half siblings. His girlfriend, Serena Colton, wasn't there. She and Demi had gotten close before she'd gone on the run. Serena lived out at the Double C Ranch. She surmised that Elle had grown closer to Carson since she was seeing Anders Colton, the foreman of the Double C Ranch.

Lucas's father, Edson Gage, wasn't there but he had no reason to be. He had no ties to the K-9 center, just a lot of old money.

She recognized a few other of the attendees, like Micah Shaw. His father had been a regular at The Pour House, her father's bar. Micah had always been in love with Bea Colton, another daughter of Fenwick Colton, and Demi wondered if they'd finally be able to get married. He chose a seat near the front.

She searched for Hamlin Harrington and found him sitting by himself in the front row. With a full head of brown hair, he was handsome at sixty. In a dark suit and tie, he didn't look around at anyone except Layla, who stood next to Officer Hunter Black off to the side of the seating area and front of the room.

Demi spotted Brayden standing beside her other half brother, Shane. Shane took no notice of her, but Brayden's brooding gaze said he didn't like that she was here with Lucas. He had to know it was her in disguise…or did he?

He walked over. "Lucas," he greeted. "Kind of strange, you bringing your new girlfriend here."

"Talk to her about that."

Brayden stood beside Demi, glancing around as though checking to make sure her cover passed muster. "I wouldn't have recognized you if I didn't know you were staying with Lucas."

"Good." No one stood or sat close to them so she wasn't concerned anyone would overhear. Lots of people talked among themselves, as well.

"Are you doing all right?" Brayden asked.

She knew what he meant—was she all right with Lucas.

"Yes." She glanced at Lucas and their gazes met briefly. They were *too* all right. Excessively, heatedly, *too* all right.

"If he hurts you in any way, I want to know about it."

Lucas sent Brayden his answering disdain with just the slide of his eyes.

"Be nice to each other."

"I'm serious, Demi. If you need another place to stay, you can stay with me. You're my family and Gages haven't shown much appreciation toward that."

"That's changed over the last year," she argued with a harsher whisper.

"Maybe so, but your future is on the line."

"Lucas won't let anyone take me off to jail." She again met Lucas's eyes, and as seemed to happen every time they looked at each other, a warm spark tickled her.

"I won't." Lucas looked directly at Brayden, who met the defiance with distrust.

Finn Colton entered the room and headed for the front podium. The chief of police had thick, dark-blond hair and blue eyes, and had captured the heart of Darby Gage, Bo's ex-wife. Demi hadn't experienced any awkward confrontations with her. After she'd discovered Bo's true nature, she wished she'd had the opportunity to talk with Darby. While she'd been in hiding, Demi had learned that Darby had taken over Bo's German shepherd breeding business.

The microphone whined as Finn reached the podium and said, "Welcome everyone." He moved back a bit from the microphone. "As you are all aware, the K-9 center is in need of new funding by the end of the year. Fenwick Colton is here today to give you an update." With a grim face that promised whatever Fenwick would say wouldn't be good news, Finn turned to his right. "Uncle Fenwick?"

Finn was the son of Judson Colton, the ranching side

of the family. While they had money, they did not have as much as the Colton Energy clan.

Dressed in an expensive medium-gray suit and purple tie, Fenwick walked regally up to the podium. Thin and not very tall, he had to adjust the microphone.

"Thank you for coming," he began. "As many of you know, I have been working to secure alternate funding for the Red Ridge K-9 Unit." He looked over the crowd like the dauntless corporate shark he was. "I feel obligated to let you know where that stands as of today. Hamlin Harrington had agreed to donate enough funds to save the unit. However, as you also know, given the circumstances surrounding his son, Devlin, that deal has fallen through."

A rush of anxious murmurs crossed the crowd.

"What happened with Layla's wedding to Hamlin?" someone called out the question.

"I cannot ask my daughter to marry a man she not only doesn't love, but would do so on monetary conditions. I'm sorry. I don't want the K-9 unit to be shut down, but at this point I don't see any other way."

Another rash of murmurs and whispers spread.

"Does Hamlin know his son is the Groom Killer?" someone else asked.

"There's no evidence to prove that," Finn said from his stance a few feet to the left of the podium.

"There is against Demi Colton," another officer countered.

Demi tensed as a wave of murmurs swept the crowd.

"When I spoke with Hamlin, he indicated he did not know about his son's murderous ways," Fenwick said. "And it is with a heavy heart that I bring you this news." Fenwick ran a finger beneath his eye and Demi wondered if he was tearing up.

Fenwick? Crying?

"This K-9 center was very important to my late wife. I'm afraid I will disappoint her. My company is in financial trouble. We've tried everything and it's fallen through. I am helpless to save this K-9 center. He wiped his other eye. "I am very sorry."

Apparently he *was* genuinely sorry.

The murmurs grew louder. Demi could hear the emotion in the exchanges even without hearing what was said.

"Are we seriously all going to be without jobs after the end of the year?" Brayden asked.

Lucas didn't respond but Demi could see the news had him concerned.

Demi caught sight of Layla Colton. She had left the seated crowd and stood before her father, talking in what seemed a soothing way. Fenwick wiped his eyes again and leaned down to kiss her cheek.

Why had she backed out of the marriage? Layla struck her as someone who would do anything to save Colton Energy. If she didn't marry Hamlin, where would she and her father get the money they needed?

"Can I have your attention, please?" Finn Colton had returned to the podium.

The murmuring and increasingly loud talking died down.

"I know this comes as bad news, but I want you to know we're doing everything we can to save this unit. In the meantime, I have an update on the Larson case that not all of you are aware of."

Demi perked up at that. Twin brothers Noel and Evan Larson had the worst reputations anyone in Red Ridge could have. The pair of thugs engaged in many criminal activities ranging from smuggling automatic weapons and drugs to money laundering and murder, but Noel was the more aggressive of the two.

"As many of you know, we had a lot of circumstantial evidence against them, but nothing that would prove their criminal activities, especially murders. After finding a stockpile of illegal weapons at their grandmother's house, however, and the threat to Officer Hunter Black's life, we've arrested them. We've also arrested Mae Larson for her involvement. We've had one witness come forward just yesterday. Prior to this, any who crossed the Larsons or did business with them were too afraid to talk. This witness claims to have seen Noel Larson shoot a man over a drug deal. We are in the process of gathering more evidence and information on the man who was murdered."

A round of cheers erupted. The Larsons had gotten away with crimes for too long.

"In addition to that, we've informed Mae Larson of her charges and she's agreed to testify against Noel and Evan to reduce her sentence."

Another, louder set of cheers filled the room.

Mae had taken Hunter Black in as a teenager after his parents died. It must have come as quite a shock to discover she worked with the twins. Looking at Hunter now, Demi didn't notice any reaction, but he might be good at concealing his emotions in public.

Demi saw Elle looking at her. Was she suspicious

or just curious about the new girl Lucas had brought? Elle headed over.

Uh-oh.

Lucas glanced at Demi as though sensing the same.

Elle came to a stop before them. "Hi, I'm Elle, Lucas's sister."

"Hi, I'm Chelsey." Demi changed the sound of her voice so it was lower.

Elle studied her again and then looked at her brother. "You sure get a lot of girlfriends."

If Demi was his girlfriend, she would have been worried. Lucas went through girlfriends like socks.

"I keep hoping he'll meet someone who works for him."

"Is that even possible?" Demi asked.

Elle fell into another close study of her. "You seem familiar. Have we met?"

Demi should not do much talking. Even disguised, her voice, or something she said, might give her away.

"No. I'm not from here. I get that a lot, where people tell me I look like someone they know."

"Huh." Elle looked from her to Lucas.

Demi felt certain Elle had figured it out. If she had, who else would? Demi searched the crowd. Most were busy talking. The topic of the meeting had distracted them.

But then Elle returned her gaze to Demi and took in her large breasts before meeting her eyes.

"Any more luck finding Demi?" she asked Lucas.

"Not yet."

"Demi?" Demi asked. "Who is that?"

"She was wanted for murder, but Devlin is the

Groom Killer, not Demi." Elle looked over at Lucas. "One would think she would know that by now."

Lucas said nothing and Brayden sort of grinned.

Elle knew.

"Don't worry. I won't say anything," Elle said.

Demi checked the crowd again. "What if someone else recognizes me?"

"I didn't recognize you. I saw you with Lucas and took a guess."

Other people could make the same guess.

"I don't think she has anything to worry about anyway," Brayden said.

"Yes, she does."

Demi followed Lucas's gaze to a cop she didn't recognize. He stared at her and Lucas with a set brow. When he started toward them, Lucas put his hand on her back.

"Let's go."

She couldn't have agreed more.

Chapter 9

Lucas closed the door to his cabin after Valeria and Vincent left. They said they had spent the evening watching *G-Force* and Wolf had loved it. Lucas found that humorous because Wolf was too young to comprehend a movie. He pictured the little guy fascinated by the colorful screen and moving guinea pigs dressed in special ops gear.

Now he faced Demi holding Wolf in that sexy costume of hers. While he missed her red hair and green eyes, the dark wig and brown eyes had a dramatic effect on the shape of her face. And those breasts...

She looked up. "He's aslee—" She stopped abruptly when she saw him.

He cleared his throat and scratched his head.

"Um..." Demi turned. "I'm going to put him down."

Lucas followed, magnetized by the sight of her and more. The *more* part he wouldn't and couldn't address.

At the door, he leaned against the frame and watched her gently put Wolf into his crib. She covered him and then stood there looking down.

Pushing off the doorframe, he joined her and saw Wolf's sweet, innocent face in peaceful sleep. His tiny hand rested atop the soft white blanket. He had Demi's red hair and green eyes. Lucas couldn't see much of his brother in the boy, but he'd probably grow into that. He wondered if he'd remind Lucas of Bo as a kid. That would bring back a lot of good memories.

When he turned to Demi, her eyes rose from checking him out. He supposed they'd both done their fair share of that tonight. The more time he spent with her, the more difficult it became to remain aloof. How far would this attraction go? It seemed to have generated its own power source. What had begun at her cabin had simmered and gradually intensified.

Ever since he'd seen her come out of the bathroom in her sexy getup, he hadn't been able to keep his eyes off her. Now that they were finally alone, he couldn't control his desire. The urge to touch her was too great.

Facing her, he did what came naturally. He slid his hand to the small of her back and pulled her against him. Her hands curved over on his biceps and her eyes drooped with responding warmth, which only encouraged his baser instincts. He felt them rev into a low roar and did nothing to restrain the inner beast.

He pressed his lips to hers the way he'd been wanting to ever since he'd kissed her that first time. She moved her mouth with his and the kiss quickly escalated to a deeper taste. Her hands glided over his shoulders and crossed behind him. He held her firmer to him, and continued to satisfy the need to devour her.

When she moved her hips against him, he unzipped the back of her dress and let it fall. The vision of her, now clad only in her stuffed bra, panties and high heels, only heated him up more. He took in her pushed-up cleavage. Unbearable.

Lifting her, he carried her across the hall to his bedroom. Setting her on the bed, he stepped back and removed his shirt, shoes and jeans, making quick work of it.

He went to her and she moved back on the bed as he climbed over her. Kissing her more slowly now, he didn't bring his body down yet. The anticipation killed him.

Moments later he could not contain his passion and kissed her the way he had in the other room. He heard her shoes fall to the floor and then she ran her bare foot up his calf, her legs widening as she did.

He left her mouth to groan in pleasure and met her feverish eyes. Rising up a little, he unclasped her bra. The material parted and the stuffing fell away. He paid no attention to it and put his mouth around the tip of her right breast.

She arched her head back and moaned, moving her hips against him.

That's when he realized he could have her right then, and it would be so hot he would go out of his mind. Lose control. He had experienced nothing like this with any other woman.

A shot of fear arrowed through him.

He lifted his head and stared down at her. She regained some coherence and opened her eyes.

"What are we doing?" he asked.

"It's okay." She lifted her head to press another kiss to his lips.

He felt the extreme fire swirl again and lifted higher. "I'm serious, Demi. What is this?"

"It's sex."

She could have sex with him even when she didn't trust him. He'd have been all right with that if he hadn't had this inner struggle going on right now.

"I don't think it's a good idea." He got off the bed and stood.

Demi propped herself up on her elbows and caught sight of the stuffing on the mattress. Hurriedly reclasping her bra, she scooted off the bed.

"I get it. I'm not one of your supermodels so I'm not safe enough to have sex with?"

What was she saying? Did she honestly think he wasn't attracted to her? "What do you mean, one of my supermodels?"

"You prefer beautiful bimbos to smaller-chested average women like me who can actually form thoughts." She rolled her eyes in what appeared to be self-reproach.

Knowing her, she hadn't liked making the comparison. She never said anything bad about anyone. Demi might have a temper but she treated people with respect. Lucas was a little taken aback that she might be jealous of any woman who could snare him, even temporarily.

"Demi—"

"Stop. I'm going to sleep now." She left the room.

He doubted either one of them would be able to sleep for some time.

The next morning, Demi didn't speak to Lucas, despite his trying. She couldn't believe she felt inferior to the women Lucas dated. As she lay awake the previous night, she'd realized her lack of trust in him was to blame. He would never love her if he had his way, but he had to feel the sexual energy between them. Sexual energy didn't mean they'd fall in love, but there was more to the energy than just sex. That was the part she doubted. She felt there was more, but did Lucas?

He sat at the dining room table with the phone and dialed a number on speaker. He had said he was going to call Layla today. Why, she didn't know. What could Layla do to save the K-9 center? She wasn't going to marry Hamlin and she was in love with Hunter Black. At least Hunter wasn't a Gage. Marrying him wouldn't alienate her father.

Layla answered and Lucas introduced himself. They exchanged some small talk and then Lucas asked if there was anything any of the K-9 unit could do to help.

"Unless you can raise millions by the end of December, no."

"I could ask my father."

Edson Gage was wealthy but would he donate money to a Colton?

"I already did," Layla surprised Demi by saying. Meeting Lucas's eyes, she saw his surprise, as well.

"He said if my father sold him some land of his choosing, then he would. He saw it as a way of settling the old debt, the property lost in a gambling bet. I couldn't agree, of course. If my father knew I even went to Edson with such a request, he would be absolutely livid."

"I'll speak with my father," Lucas said.

"You would do that?"

"I would do anything to save the K-9 center."

"My father needs help with Colton Energy. At first I thought my father mishandled funds and I was furious. But it turns out that wasn't the case. I don't understand how the company fell into such financial disarray. It was so strong before all the chaos broke out in this town. It's as though there's been some kind of accounting error."

"Maybe there was," Lucas said.

Layla fell silent for a moment. "I've looked over the books many times and didn't see anything amiss, but maybe I missed something."

"It's worth another look."

"Thank you." She sounded sincere. "And thank you for calling. I appreciate that. More Gages and Coltons should talk."

"Enough of them are planning to marry. I can't imagine it will be long before we're all having family events together."

Layla laughed. "From the looks of things, I have to say you're right." Lucas looked over at Demi and she had a terrible feeling he thought—or feared—she'd be part of that—with him.

He wasn't falling for her, was he? Demi entertained the possibility. What if she let down her guard and tested this out? What if she gave them a chance as a couple?

And risk ending up with another man like Bo? Risk ending up the way her other serious relationships had ended?

After Bo, she'd promised herself she would be sure the next time she fell in love. Unlike Lucas, she hadn't turned her back on love. She just needed to be certain it would last. According to Lucas's mantra, love never lasted. She sure hoped he wasn't right.

Edson Gage lived a comfortable life on the money he'd inherited from his parents. He invested in select ventures, most of which had something to do with development. Lucas wasn't close with his father, but growing up there had been happy times.

After driving up the stately lane that led to the house, Lucas stopped on the wide driveway and got out. He walked to the front door and entered without knocking. His father lived alone except for a cook and a housekeeper. A fortysomething German woman with a stack of towels in her arms greeted him.

"Your father's in the library, Lucas."

He thanked her and headed through the large, old-style, dark interior to the living room where the far wall of windows had double doors leading to a stone patio. His father had a putting green set up in the back, although it was now covered in snow. The upper level was open with a soaring ceiling above where he stood. The wide stairway led up from between the living room and kitchen, a portion of the hall open. The library overlooked the living room from a Juliette balcony.

There wasn't enough room for seating on the balcony, just a view.

Lucas headed up the elegant staircase, passing the open railing and reaching the double doors leading to the library. He spotted his father standing with an open book in his hand, reading by windows that had a view of his fifty-acre property. The mountains weren't visible today; gray clouds had set in for another storm.

Tall, with always shrewd and unfeeling icy-blue eyes, Edson Gage exuded an aura of power without trying. Lucas respected him for that. He'd had his world torn apart more than once and still he persevered. Fenwick Colton was on the brink of destruction, but destruction had never touched Edson, at least, not financially, not detrimentally so. Destruction had only come to his heart. He still had a head full of dark hair and the silver-rimmed glasses gave him a dash of sophistication to go along with his dominating presence.

"Lucas. I wasn't expecting you so soon."

"I'm early."

"I haven't heard from or seen you in a while. What have you been doing?"

"Looking for Demi Colton."

"Ah, that murderous vixen. And have you been successful?"

"She's innocent." Lucas hadn't had a chance to talk to his father about that and wasn't sure if his brothers or sisters had. "Detectives have uncovered Devlin Harrington's obsession with Hayley Patton, which gives Devlin a motive to have murdered her fiancé—Bo. And the witnesses who've claimed to see Demi at the crime scenes were paid to do so by Devlin."

"I won't get into the details with you, Lucas. I'm a man who requires evidence. If you believe she's innocent, I trust your judgment so long as you can produce evidence."

His father could have been a judge. "I'll get the evidence."

"What brings you by?"

"I want to talk to you about the K-9 center. It's in trouble."

"Fenwick can't come up with the funds required. I've heard."

"Layla told me she came to see you."

"Layla Colton." His father smirked. "She actually thought I would bail Fenwick out."

"She said you wouldn't do it unless you got something in return."

"That's correct. The land taken from our ancestors. That's all. But Fenwick will never agree."

"What if he does?"

Edson's smile had little to do with warmth. "He will not, Lucas. I admire your gumption, but Fenwick is not amenable to friendly relations with we Gages."

"I don't see how he can keep up those old hostilities, given that so many Gages are going to marry Coltons."

"He doesn't care about any Colton from Rusty's loins."

Lucas walked farther into the library, dwarfed by floor-to-ceiling bookshelves and not liking the mahogany desk and ornate chairs and rugs. The only thing missing was dust floating in the light.

"If you could make peace among the families, would you?"

His father closed the book and walked to the shelf, returning it to an empty space. Then he faced his son. "I don't care about making peace."

His father didn't care about much since he'd lost his last wife.

"Is that because you still have something against the Coltons?"

"I've always thought the Gages should have gotten back their land, but it's a fight that is so old that it hardly matters anymore. That said, if I had a chance to get back what was lost, I would. One for the family."

Hence his offer to Layla.

"Layla can never ask Fenwick to do that."

"She can. The question is whether Fenwick will see reason."

"A lot of people will be out of jobs without the K-9 center."

"I've considered that. You'd keep your dog and you go independent after they close the center."

"I don't want to be an independent bounty hunter."

His father contemplated him a moment and walked over to him, stopping with a sigh. "I'll let Fenwick state his own terms. If they aren't a slap in my face, I'll give it serious thought. And so you don't think I'm not thinking about my kids, I believe this deal will be one example of how we can unite the families. Fenwick has to put his ego aside and want the same. He has to want the families to get along, to let the century-old feud die with the ancestors who created it. "What happened when Layla came to see you?"

"I gave her my terms and she said her father would be livid if he found out she came here."

"She came to your house?"

"Yes."

"What else?"

"She left in a huff. Frankly, I don't know what else she expected. Did she really think I'd donate the money and not get anything in return?"

"Fenwick's first wife was instrumental in starting the K-9 center and keeping it going. When the money ran out, he funded it in her memory."

"I have no sentimental weakness for the K-9 center, Lucas. As I've said, I require something in return and I believe if Fenwick agrees to a deal, it will work to end a foolish feud."

Lucas could not argue that. "Layla will want the center to stay connected to her father, since he wants to keep honoring his first wife's wishes."

"I would be agreeable to funding the center for a specified period of time and turn it back over to Fenwick. He has to make me an offer."

That might be enough to keep the center running in the short term, but Lucas wanted more than short term. He also respected his father's strategy.

"How do you know there will be Colton-Gage weddings?" his dad asked.

"Things I've heard."

"Who?"

"You must know about Anders Colton and Elle."

"She hasn't talked about marrying him."

"Of course not. The Groom Killer is still free."

His father nodded and seemed to think that over. "Any progress?"

"I'm looking for evidence to prove she's innocent."

"She isn't your bounty. Why are you helping her?"

Not able to predict his father's thoughts, he said, "Like I said, she's innocent."

"Have you been in contact with her? You used to be sweet on her in high school."

How had his father noticed that? And why had he never said anything? And moreover, had Lucas been that transparent? As a young man, probably.

Edson grinned. "Another Colton–Gage union in the making?" he asked in a nonconfrontational tone.

"No." Lucas smiled back and shook his head.

He wouldn't allow any rogue cop to arrest her. Finn, the police chief and Demi's cousin, didn't believe she was guilty. He would support that…wouldn't he? Maybe he'd keep her behind bars until the missing gun was found.

As far as his father's insight went, Lucas and Demi seemed headed for the bedroom whether their minds agreed or not.

"Catching the real Groom Killer will bring the Coltons and the Gages closer," his father said. "Colton–Gage weddings will, too. A deal with the Coltons to right past wrongs will cement it."

"I don't see how you can say that. The property was lost in a poker game."

"A game that we've all been told by our ancestors the Coltons cheated to win."

"And they maintain they didn't."

"That doesn't matter anymore, Lucas."

It did if Fenwick viewed Edson's offer to bail him out as blackmail. He'd lean more toward Colton–Gage weddings bringing them all together. Red Ridge would be filled with the sound of church bells as soon as Devlin was captured.

Lucas didn't argue with his father. Maybe he'd get lucky and be right. He stayed a little longer, making small talk about other things, and then left.

Outside he saw a car with a driver across the street. Devlin following him again? One of these times he wouldn't get away. As though aware of this, the driver pulled out into the street when he saw Lucas pass his own car and head his way.

Chapter 10

Demi had all the receipts they'd found in the shoebox in Devlin's condo strewn over the living room floor. They'd already gone through them and hadn't found anything of significance other than a few receipts for flowers Devlin had purchased—for Hayley? Maybe he'd imagined giving them to her. Lucas had saved all the photos on a USB device and they'd gone through those, as well. They'd found nothing different from what had already been analyzed by the police.

A chilly draft passed through the room with the shift of wind outside. A fast-moving storm spit down snow and cold. Lucas had lit the gas fireplace. Wolf was snug and warm in his crib and Queenie lay curled beside Lucas on the couch. Demi watched him a moment, his focus intent on the computer screen. The quiet, aside from an occasional gust and the flames in the fireplace, gave her a sense of hominess she hadn't experienced before. She'd had fleeting feelings like that with Wolf, but she'd still felt alone, or at the very least, that something important was missing. Reflecting back now, she had often wondered what would have happened had Bo not turned out to be someone she didn't know and they'd actually worked out. They would have been a family.

She also wondered if the reason she'd given him that ultimatum—to either change or it was over—was because she feared a future with him, that she didn't trust him. Maybe Lucas was right. She didn't trust anyone.

"Come look at this."

Demi abandoned what had become a futile search for anything new that detectives might have missed. Glad he hadn't noticed her drift off into deep thought, she got up and went to the sofa, where he sat with his laptop. She took a seat next to him, leaning in to see the screen and finding her shoulder pressing against his side. She flinched with the zap of awareness and moved back.

"Careful, I bite." He grinned.

He did not bite. As soon as she thought that, she smiled and hoped he couldn't see her delight. He was a nice man, much nicer than her original impression. Before his arrival at her cabin, she would never have had a thought like that. When she realized how much she warmed with that knowledge, and what it might open up for them, she stopped smiling.

He didn't bite? Her sentimental thoughts earlier must have made her vulnerable.

He pointed to the screen. "It says here that a witness

saw Devlin walking on the sidewalk in front of a gas station a day before one of the murders."

She read that part of the report. "That doesn't seem significant."

"There's a pawnshop next to that gas station."

She turned to look at him. Pawnshops sometimes sold guns, although the legitimate shops didn't sell stolen guns and didn't accept guns from minors or anyone who lived outside of their state.

"Might lead to something." How clever of him to have thought of that. "What's it called?"

"Nigel's."

Nigel's. "There's a receipt from that store." She went to the receipts and shuffled through them until she found the one. Then she held it up to Lucas, looking at the date. "He went there a few days before the missing gun was used to kill."

"We'll check that out first, and then I want to get inside Devlin's place of employment."

"How are we going to do that?"

"I brought home some janitor uniforms."

She took in his pleased look and the sparkling dark eyes that melted her. "You're getting good at this."

Another gust pattered snow against the windows.

"For a fast-moving storm it sure isn't in any hurry to pass," Demi said, still vulnerable and needing the distraction.

"Yes. But we're warm, safe and dry in here."

Like a family.

He stretched his arm over the back of the sofa and continued to look at her with that sparkle. She eased against him more and turned to watch the fire.

"So this is what living like a family feels like," he said.

Whoa. Her defenses shot up. Why had he said that? Surely he didn't mean it. He had to be teasing her again.

"How does that make you feel?" she asked as casually as she could.

He took several seconds before he said, "Nice."

She looked at him, her face near his. "Really?"

"Yeah." He grinned. "But I'm sure I'll come to my senses in the morning—after the storm passes and there isn't a fire burning."

Oh, there was a fire burning. Just not the kind he meant.

Demi entered the pawnshop with Lucas and Queenie the next afternoon. She'd opted for her favorite pair of skinny jeans that had beads on the back pockets. She wore that with a gray sweater that flared at the waist and high-heeled boots. The sexy girlfriend again. Lucas wore black jeans with a white button-up and tactical boots. He looked good in anything. She'd sneaked peeks at his rear a few times, as well as his profile, square jaw, sloping nose and that thick, reddish-brown hair and those dark eyes that sometimes smoldered when he looked at her.

A run-down brick one-story in an area near Rusty's bar, Nigel's would have been an ideal place for Devlin to buy guns. If they could trace where he purchased them, maybe they could follow his steps and gather more evidence against him.

The pawnshop had posters and paraphernalia hanging on the walls. Glass display cases lined the sides and back, and a row of shelving ran down the center. The dirty light-tan linoleum floor had to be about thirty years old. Queenie looked up at Lucas, who gave her a hand signal. The dog went right to work. Before coming here, he had presented Queenie with an article of clothing from Devlin's condo to let her know that scent was the one he wanted her to search for.

Appliances lined the front and blocked the barred windows. A multitude of items ranging from clothes to toys filled the shelving, and in the display cases more valuable things like watches and jewelry gave testimony as to how they'd gotten here. People hard on their luck or battling addiction may have traded their possessions here.

She walked with Lucas toward the back. A short, bald clerk with a round stomach stood behind the counter, blinking his eyes until they opened wider. He must have been very bored before they arrived.

"Can I help you?" He saw Queenie sniffing the rows of the shop. "Is that your dog?"

Demi went to the counter with Lucas, who handed the man the receipt and a photograph of Devlin. "We'd like to ask you a few questions about a purchase this man made. Do you recognize him?"

"Your dog won't go to the bathroom in here, will it?" The clerk took the photo and the receipt, looking at the photo first.

"She's well trained," Lucas said. "Do you recognize that man?"

"He does look familiar." The clerk examined the receipt and then looked at the photo again. "Yes, yes. I do remember this man. Angry fellow." He looked up at them. "He tried to buy a gun and when I refused, he argued. He offered to pay twice its worth. When I again refused, he grew very angry. I almost called the police. I had to threaten to."

"What did he buy?" Demi asked, catching a glimpse of Queenie heading to the back of the shop where the office must be.

The clerk looked at the receipt again and then went to his computer and clicked the mouse a few times before he entered a number. "Ammunition. Lots of ammo." He printed a page and handed it to Lucas. "The same caliber as the gun he wanted to buy."

Demi met Lucas's glance when she saw the caliber of the ammo was the same as what had killed the victims.

"I hear on occasion about black market deals. I make it my business to, so I know who not to sell to. In this part of town, a man can't be too careful. I would lose my livelihood—which isn't much—if the law came snooping around to see if I've made any illegal sales or sales to criminals. I know who the local criminals are and I added Mr. Devlin Harrington to that list after he came here."

"Where would he have bought a gun if he bought it on the black market?" Lucas asked.

Queenie came to sit beside Lucas, indicating she had found nothing linked to Devlin. Demi hadn't expected her to and she didn't think Lucas had, either.

"Who else? Those Larson twins or one of their lackeys."

It couldn't have been the Larsons. None of the guns recovered from them matched the missing weapon.

"If he didn't get the gun from them, who would he go to?"

"Could be a guy I know of who sells guns, but not on the same scale as the Larsons. His name is Slater."

After leaving the pawnshop, Demi waited at Lucas's cabin while he tracked down Slater using computers at the police department.

Valeria stayed, agreeing to watch Wolf tonight after Lucas found Slater. They made a light dinner and Demi ate while she also fed Wolf. Lucas had said he'd grab something on his way to the police department.

"I hope we didn't ruin any plans you had tonight." Demi didn't mean to infringe on Valeria's love life.

"Vincent is studying late tonight," Valeria said. "I get so tired of having to sneak around."

Demi imagined it had to be hard to find time to spend together. She joined Valeria on the couch, having just put Wolf to bed. "I know the feeling."

Valeria smiled at her quip. If anyone had to do any hiding, it was Demi. All those months had been difficult. Having Wolf had eased some of her loneliness and fear of the future.

"Looks like you're sneaking around with Lucas, too."

"Only until Devlin is caught."

Valeria's smile changed, softening into something knowing. "I see the way he looks at you, and you him."

"How?" Like he's afraid of falling in love?

"Like the two of you have already…" Valeria wiggled her eyebrows. "You know."

"We haven't." Demi feared she'd answered too defensively.

"Well, it looks like you will soon, then."

"Lucas isn't my type."

Valeria moved back as though stunned. "He's a great-looking guy. And you're beautiful. Aside from that, you're both bounty hunters. You must have a lot in common."

"Lucas doesn't want to get married or have kids. There was a time when I might have preferred that, too, but now, with Wolf, I want a family."

"Everybody wants a family, even people who decide not to have kids. They still have each other."

"Lucas doesn't."

"Well, that is just plain stupid for him to say that. What's he afraid of?"

"Falling in love."

"Then maybe you should make him." Valeria eyed her pensively. "How do you feel about him?"

Demi didn't think she loved him, but she *could*. And that was the part that frightened her.

"You've known him for a long time. You seem to get along. Aren't you at least attracted to him?"

"I'm probably too attracted to him."

"Well, I know he's attracted to you. It's so obvious. He might think he'll never fall in love, but if it's the real thing, there will be no escaping it. That's how it was with Vincent. I wanted to finish school and start my career before I got married and had kids. When I met Vincent, those plans went straight out the window. I knew after our first date that I could fall madly in love with him. It just happened. And when it's mutual, there is nothing like that feeling in the world. Nothing will stand in your way—or, I should say, love's way."

The more Valeria talked, the more apprehensive Demi became. "I don't want to fall in love with Lucas. I don't trust him."

"And how could you, after Bo and how he treated you?"

Bo wasn't the only one. Men in general were not to be trusted, not in the early stages of a relationship. Anything could happen. A woman didn't truly know a man until she'd been with him for a long time. Worse, Demi had no idea how long that would take. How long before she felt comfortable in trusting a man... Lucas?

Valeria put her hand on Demi's knee. "Don't worry. If it's meant to be, it will be."

Demi thought she might have turned white. Even if she dug her heels in, would she be drawn inexorably to Lucas?

Valeria laughed lightly and briefly. "You should see your face. I can't wait until Devlin is caught and Red Ridge has weddings again. There will be one every Saturday for a long time."

"Starting with yours." *Please make her stop talking about Lucas and falling in love.*

Valeria lifted her yes dreamily. "Yes." She put her hand on her chest just below her neck. "I want my wedding to be perfect." She looked at Demi. "I wanted it to be the event that brings the Coltons and the Gages together again, but in the past year, so many Coltons and Gages have fallen in love. Vincent and I decided we want to have it at The Grange."

The Grange was an old farmhouse outside of town

that had been converted into a bed-and-breakfast. It had a barn that could be rented for events like weddings.

"Round tables with Christmas-candle centerpieces. A *huge* Christmas tree. Prime rib dinner and country music. My bridesmaids will wear red dresses with white flowers in a bed of evergreen as their corsages." Valeria sighed. "I go crazy with impatience sometimes. Do you know I have all my invitations ready? I'm going to personally hand them out, since we'll have to wait until the last minute to announce our wedding."

"Does your father know?"

"He doesn't know we're going through with the wedding." Her face fell with obvious disappointment.

"He'll come around." How could he not, with all the Colton–Gage weddings there would be when Devlin was finally either dead or behind bars?

"We could have a double wedding," Valeria said. "I mean, if you want to."

The girl had thought she saw Lucas giving Demi smoldering looks and now she had them getting married—in less than a *month?*

She'd clearly wandered off in fantasyland a little too long.

But she did get Demi thinking…

Lucas had returned home and brought Demi with him to confront Slater. He lived near the house she and her mother had lived in with Rusty, before her mother left him. Lucas parked on the street with the car lights off, while Queenie sat with ears perked and nose working through a crack in the window. Slater's house was lit up and several people stood in the garage around a keg of beer. Music thumped from inside and the voices of people laughing carried out into the night.

There was a loveseat and a rocking chair on the decaying front porch. Kids' bicycles, a discarded cooler and bags of trash decorated the yard.

Demi couldn't stop Valeria's words from repeating over and over. Valeria wanted a Christmas Eve wedding. That was less than three weeks from now. What if Lucas did fall in love against his will? What if she did? She imagined them standing at the altar with Valeria and Vincent. He'd be handsome in a tuxedo and she'd be in a white wedding dress, one that resembled what she had dreamed of before all her relationships had tanked on her. She hadn't thought of that dress in a long, long time.

"What are you thinking about?"

Jarred back to the now, she gaped at Lucas.

"Must have been good." He grinned. "Now you have to tell me."

He deserved to hear what she'd been thinking. What he didn't know was that it would wipe that teasing grin off his face.

"Valeria thinks you and I are destined to get married." She smiled when his grin vanished in an instant.

"Why would she say a thing like that?" He sounded scared, which only made Demi's smile bigger.

"She sees the way you look at me."

"The way I—" His brow shot low. "And how is *that?*"

"She used the word *smoldering.*"

He just continued to look at her.

"That wasn't what I was thinking about. It's what made me think about it, but it isn't what I was thinking about."

"I'm afraid to ask."

"I bet you are, but you're going to hear it anyway. I was thinking about the dress I used to dream about wearing on my wedding day."

"You were…" His brow lifted in befuddlement.

"It's made of silk and has a V'd bodice with lacy shoulders and sleeves, and a long, beautiful lacy train that tapers up the back."

"Sounds pretty." His voice was stiff.

She had to continue. "Valeria said you and I could share the altar for their Christmas Eve wedding."

As he continued to stare, Demi couldn't stop smiling.

"You're saying that on purpose."

She laughed. "Yes, but it's all true. And frankly, I think you need to hear more things like that."

"More things like what? That you want to get married?"

He didn't say *to me* and she was glad. "More things like talk of love and everything that comes with it."

"Says the woman who can't trust men enough to get married."

"I was thinking about that, too."

"Oh, no."

"Oh, yes. I wondered at what point should a woman—namely me—start to trust a man she's with."

"Probably longer than three weeks." He nodded smugly. Christmas Eve was in less than three weeks.

She laughed again. "You and I have known each other for years."

The smug look cut to a blank one.

"Since when are you the one who does the teasing?" he finally asked.

"Who says I'm teasing?" She was and she wasn't. She couldn't explain why his anti-love attitude bothered her so much, but she could explain why she had to let him know what she'd been thinking. She found him very attractive, always had, and spending this time with him had changed her opinion of him. While she didn't welcome the feeling, she *was* falling for him. Part of her intended to get him thinking along similar lines.

But that was enough for now. Time to change the subject. She looked out the window. "I can't believe my mother and I used to live here."

He cleared his throat and adjusted himself on the driver's seat. "Here?" He seemed slow to move from such a romantic topic to that.

She pointed behind the house. "About two blocks that way."

"You grew up here?"

She turned to look at him. He still seemed tense. "Don't tell me you didn't know."

"Well, yeah. I knew you were Rusty's daughter. I—I guess I never thought of you living in a place like this."

She had never heard him stutter before. Maybe she had gotten him thinking. How would that change anything between them? Demi couldn't wait to find out.

Then what he'd said registered. Would he have had an issue if she had grown up *in a place like this?* Feeling her temper flare, she breathed a few times and let it pass. "My mother left him when I was young. She did all right supporting us and raising me. Our house wasn't anything special but it didn't look like that." She indicated the party house. "It was small but clean and maintained."

"That's why I never thought of you as the wrong-side-of-the-tracks kind of girl." His tension faded and Demi knew he'd fallen into relaxed conversation with her.

"As you said, I'm Rusty Colton's daughter."

"You're also your mother's daughter."

She smiled. He sure could be charming when he tried. She scrutinized him, the slight crinkle at the corners of his eyes and the now-happy light in them. He wasn't trying.

"Lucas Gage, is that natural sincerity I hear?"

"I've always been sincere."

Her temper had been easily triggered and he'd played with her. Why had she never seen that before? Even now her ire rose. Why had he teased her, deliberately made her angry?

"Like when you teased me?"

"I don't know if I'd call that sincerity."

"No, it was mean."

"I wouldn't call it mean, either. You were too easy to set off."

So he had done it because he knew he could and enjoyed it? Well, she wouldn't let him do that ever again! She could recognize his tactics now.

"Easy." His deep, low voice touched her most sensitive areas, challenging her control.

He had just read her reaction. He had known he had triggered her again. She held back her temper the way she always practiced.

Then she remembered a time when he hadn't teased her. That had been after she'd saved his life. Before they'd gone their separate ways, before and one else had intruded, he'd thanked her. The way he'd thanked her had been unmistakably sincere and she had seen more than friendly warmth in his eyes.

"Atta girl."

He had read her reaction again, her control of her temper. With a low growl, she softly swatted his shoulder—equally playful, getting him for the first time.

He chuckled, the deep sound doing more to put her off-kilter.

"You better watch it or I'll keep talking about my wedding dress and Valeria's invitation."

His laughter faded but she sensed he hadn't tensed with the mention of weddings this time. Instead, she found herself caught by his gaze. His smile slowly vanished and he seemed just as caught. Endless seconds passed. She savored each one. A minute wasn't a long time but it felt like several. She didn't want this feeling to end.

He turned away first, his brow creasing above his nose.

The magic fled. He'd shut himself off. Demi looked out the passenger window into the darkness, too-familiar disappointment arresting her.

"That's Paulie Gains. The other one is Slater."

She turned to the party house and saw two men walking toward an old, beat-up truck. One was shorter than the other—Paulie. He wore a puffer jacket and black jeans with a beanie on his head.

"Paulie is the one who said he saw me running from the bar where Bo's body was found," she said, remembering the bitter taste of injustice.

"Police think Devlin paid him to say that. They couldn't prove it, though."

She hadn't heard about that. Glancing at him, she wondered if that was what had changed his mind about her. Likely it had been a combination of many things, that included.

"They're on the move," Lucas said.

She watched with him as the two men got into a truck.

"How do you know the other man is Slater?" She saw him use a small pair of what must have been night-vision binoculars.

"Finn sent a photo of him. He's got a rap sheet like Paulie." He lowered the binoculars. "Get down so they don't see us."

She slouched low, as he did, hearing the truck pass.

Lucas started the truck and made a U-turn, turning on the lights and following. He stayed far enough back to avoid notice. Slater turned a corner and a few seconds later, they followed. Demi saw them turn into a trailer park.

Parking down the street, Lucas got out and opened the back for Queenie. Demi got out and walked beside Queenie and Lucas. They headed down the first street and, at the second intersection, Demi spotted the pickup truck. Queenie trotted ahead and began inspecting the truck. At the back door of the crew cab, she sat and barked once.

Lucas opened the door and she hopped in while Demi checked the trailer. The drapes were shut. Music played but at a reasonable volume and she didn't hear anyone talking.

Queenie came out with a single black-leather glove. Lucas praised her and took the glove.

"Devlin was in this truck at some point," he said.

"What now?"

"Let's go have a talk with Slater and Gaines."

That seemed a bold move. They'd just waltz up to the trailer door and announce themselves?

"Gaines isn't going to tell the truth. He said he saw me kill Bo." In fact, if he recognized her, he might panic.

"If he doesn't he doesn't. Let's cover every angle."

Of course that's what she wanted, as well. Demi wasn't afraid of the danger in approaching these small-time criminals, and if it lead to finding Devlin, it would be worthwhile. At the door, Lucas knocked.

Talking inside stopped, leaving just the sound of a nineteen-eighties rock band, guitars jamming and heavy drums thumping along with a screaming singer. Several seconds later, the door opened to an unfamiliar face. The man was tall and skinny with longish uncombed hair and eerie light-blue eyes with shadows beneath.

"I'm Deputy Gage and this is my partner, Chelsey. We'd like to ask you a few questions."

"What for? I ain't done nothin'," the man said.

"We aren't here about anything you might have

done, you or your two guests. We're looking for Devlin Harrington and we were told he may have bought a gun from Slater."

The man glanced back and Demi saw Slater give a nod. The man stepped aside and allowed them in, eyeing Queenie as she went to work. She inspected the small living room and kitchen and started down the hall.

"What's your dog doing?" the man asked.

"Searching for scents of Devlin," Lucas said.

The three seemed to relax, as if understanding that they weren't going to be busted for gun trafficking.

"I didn't sell Devlin any guns," Slater said. A dark-haired man with dark, thick stubble, he was in pretty good shape and of average height. He wore a leather vest with a chain peeking out. What little of his arms was exposed revealed he was also tattooed.

Gaines sat beside him. Shorter than the other two, he had the look of a man who spent too much time running from the law. Skin blotchy and wearing sunglasses, he appeared to watch.

"When is the last time you saw him?"

Slater thought a moment. "He stopped by my house about three weeks ago."

Three weeks ago he must have purchased more guns, namely the automatic weapon he'd used at Demi's cabin.

"Did he ever talk about the guns he owned?" Lucas asked.

Slater gave a nonchalant shrug and a shake of his head. "Naw."

"Where he hid them?" Lucas pressed. "Where he disposed of them?"

"He never said anything to me."

Lucas turned to Paulie. "What about you? You and Devlin are good friends. Did he ever mention anything to you?"

"First of all, we aren't good friends. And he never said anything about any guns."

"Why did he stop by to see you?" Demi asked Slater.

"It was a social visit."

Demi grew frustrated with the vague answers.

"What about you?" Lucas asked Gaines. "When is the last time you saw him?"

"Three weeks ago, like Slater says."

Was that another lie?

"I don't know him," the other man said. "I just rent a room here."

The trailer must be Gaines's.

Queenie emerged from the hall and came to sit beside Lucas. He bent to pet and praise her and then straightened. "Thank you for your help."

Later, at his cabin, Lucas talked with Demi about the lies Slater and Gaines had told. How could they get one of them to talk? Lucas decided to keep a watch on them in case Devlin upgraded his violent weapons collection or he turned to friends for help. Not working and not being able to access his money due to the risk of capture, he had to be struggling by now. Who better to turn to than fellow criminals?

While Demi prepared dinner in the kitchen, Lucas played with Wolf. The kid was amazing. Lucas never would have believed anyone who told him he'd latch on to a baby, but Wolf's lovable personality had captivated him with his open-mouthed smiles and the tiny sounds he made that had to be laughter. The little tyke crawled toward him and Lucas kept backing up, also on his hands and knees. Wolf let out a cackle. Drool dribbled down his chin, making Lucas laugh.

"All right, all right, stop stealing my son away from me." Demi bent to lift Wolf, smiling.

She might be joking but Lucas didn't think it was all in jest. He stood and followed her into the kitchen, where she had just finished putting something in the oven.

He also knew she hadn't been completely teasing when she told him what she'd been thinking about. Sharing Valeria's desire for a Christmas Eve wedding, the details of her dream dress. He'd been so shocked at the time he hadn't been able to react.

But his reaction had sunk in. He hadn't shied away from the idea. In fact, the first thing that had come to his mind was how beautiful she'd look in a dress like the one she'd described. His next thought was to wonder what had made him trip all over his words. If there was any woman he'd like to see walk down the aisle looking like that, it was Demi.

"Why are you so afraid of me getting close to Wolf?" he asked.

"I'm not."

"You aren't fooling me, Demi." She'd had boyfriends she'd gotten close to, but she'd always backed out of the relationships. "Is it because you don't trust me?"

"You're Jerry Maguire."

The character in the movie, not a real person. Jerry Maguire had loved the boy in that movie but not the woman, or so he'd thought. Was Demi afraid he'd get close to her son and then leave? *Would* he leave, or would she be the one who left? And why was he even thinking about who would leave whom? They weren't in a relationship.

Or were they?

Wolf fussed as Demi tried to give him a bottle. He reached for Lucas and cried.

"Let me hold him." Lucas reached out.

Demi reluctantly gave him the baby, who immediately stopped fussing. With a frown of disapproval, she handed him the bottle.

He took it and Wolf looked up at him as he suckled.

"Don't worry, Mommy, you're irreplaceable. We've just had a good afternoon together."

"The only thing I worry about is how you're going to be able to walk away when this is all over."

She went about cleaning up the mess she'd made making dinner, leaving him to wonder, when *what* was all over?

Chapter 11

A few nights later, Lucas and Demi disguised themselves as janitors to sneak into Harrington Incorporated. Lucas had scoped the place out and duplicated a couple of badges. He'd said he piggy-backed into the building the night before and used a computer to access the security software that created badges. He'd almost gotten caught, but finished before the guard returned from the bathroom.

Entering through a back door, he led her to the basement, where the facilities department was located. All the janitorial supplies were in a storage area. He took a trash can on wheels and she rolled a cleaning supply cart. They went to the elevator without running into anyone. Devlin's office was on the top floor. Riding up, she glanced at Lucas. In a Harrington Inc. white button-up with his badge hanging around his neck, he did not look like a janitor. Maybe she knew him too well, maybe she'd been spending too much time with the sexy man, but he looked more like a doctor or a cop—the cop that he was.

She'd left her hair dark and put on a baseball cap to go with her Harrington Inc. white button-up.

On the top floor, she followed him into the hallway. Most of the lights had been turned off on this floor. Someone worked in an office. The door was open across the cubicle space and Demi heard someone tapping on a keyboard.

"Burning the midnight oil," she said.

"At least it isn't Hamlin."

Devlin's father couldn't be called a slacker. He'd built a successful green energy corporation where his son worked as an attorney. Well, up until now. Hamlin would have to find another sleazy lawyer.

Devlin's office was conveniently open. The office looked clean. It would be good if the janitors had already been there—unless the late-night worker had seen them. The janitors wouldn't return if they'd already cleaned, so if that worker saw Demi and Lucas he might sound an alert.

Too bad they hadn't been able to bring Queenie. Her nose would have been busy in here.

Lucas went to the computer and Demi went to the bookshelf, not seeing much there other than legal books. She opened a credenza drawer and went through the contents. Most everything was electronic but Devlin did have some things that were in files. Nothing sprang out as suspicious.

"I've accessed Security's badge records."

Demi abandoned what she was doing to go stand beside him. "Did you hack in?"

"Devlin has access."

Not surprising, since he was Hamlin's son, but why would he want access?

"He left early from work on all the days the victims were killed in the evening and came to work late the next mornings. Zane Godfried was murdered the morning of his wedding. Devlin didn't come in to work that day, but he did come to work on Saturdays regularly."

"What about email traffic?"

Lucas navigated with the mouse and a few minutes later said, "No email traffic during the times the murders took place."

"We can use that against him."

"It's still not enough."

"Well, there's no gun here."

"He hasn't logged in remotely since he's been on the run and he hasn't used his badge to access the building."

"All useful enough. Let's get out of here."

Glad to have taken the time and the risk to do this, Demi pushed the cleaning cart out of the office. The other office light was still on but the sound of typing had paused. They made it to the elevator without incident and rode to the basement. There, they returned the cart to the storage area. Lucas eyed the security camera in the hall.

She heard a radio crackle and a voice but couldn't make out what was said. Seconds later, a security guard appeared around a corner in the plain white hallway, talking into his radio. He saw them.

The stairwell was before the elevator. She and Lucas had to get to the main level to exit the building. The guard passed the stairwell.

"Good evening," he said as he neared.

"Hello," Demi said.

"Janitors all left for the night." His gaze lowered to their badges. Their pictures matched them but the names did not.

"What are you doing down here?"

"We're new, just finished up," Lucas said.

"Why don't you come with me." The guard stepped aside, indicating they should start walking down the hall.

Demi glanced at Lucas, who kept a blank expression and started walking.

"What are you doing down here?" the guard asked again.

"We returned our cleaning supplies to the storage area," Lucas answered.

"I don't recognize you."

That's because they weren't the people named on the badges. Demi reached the stairwell and made a dash for it.

"Hey!" the guard shouted.

She heard Lucas right behind her as she pushed through the door, banging it against the wall as she ran through. She took two or three stairs at a time, Lucas behind her and to her right.

"Stop! Both of you, stop!" The guard chased them.

Up on the first level, Demi shoved the door open and ran down the hall, Lucas running beside her.

"I've got intruders!" the guard yelled into his radio.

Demi reached the back door and burst through. Her feet and Lucas's thudded on the pavement as they raced through the parking lot toward the rental. Demi ran with all her strength, determined not to be detained by the Harrington's security guards and then transferred to jail.

Lucas reached the driver's side as she ran to the other and got in.

Lucas raced away and she saw the guard had stopped chasing them and was still yelling into his radio.

"That was close," she said.

"Too close."

Both of them caught their breath and then Demi turned to look at Lucas. He glanced her way and she smiled.

"Seeing that makes the risk worth it," he said.

While he gave her tingles by saying that, she didn't understand. "What risk?"

"What we're doing isn't exactly legal."

She hadn't thought about the risk he took with his job. He could lose a lot and yet he helped her anyway.

Later the next day, Lucas changed focus and dug into Slater's background. He'd talked with Slater's parents, who revealed he'd just broken up with a woman, given Lucas her name and shown him a photo. Apparently his parents were quite disappointed with him and would do anything to make him straighten out his life. If that meant going to jail, then so be it.

Lucas had assured her that if Slater could help them in the Groom Killer case, he'd either help arrange for a lighter sentence or be excused from sentencing with some counseling or other probationary requirements.

Lucas walked to Slater's ex-girlfriend's house in the rough part of town, Demi beside him. She'd brought Wolf with her this time. Lots of women had babies and she didn't resemble her old self much, anyway, even when not in disguise. She looked fabulous in another pair of skinny jeans with a white sweater that the baby carrier covered for the most part. Wolf gazed up at her in rapt fascination, taking in every feature. Demi saw him and smiled before she planted a little kiss on his nose that got him giggling.

Damn kid sent shards of warmth spreading through him. How would he ever walk away from the little boy? He could very well be like Jerry Maguire and keep seeing Demi just to keep Wolf in his life. One big difference, though. He knew he was attracted to Demi, while it had taken Jerry much longer to realize his own feelings in the film.

Slater's ex-girlfriend answered the door, eyeing Demi and the baby and Lucas. She had long, dark, straight hair, her blue eyes were shadowed and she had a ring in her nose. Lucas could see inside the house. Two other women sat in a messy living room with the television playing a violent movie. Gunfire, racing cars and music blared.

The woman turned her head toward the other two. "Hey, turn that down." Slater's mother had said her name was Tracy.

One of the women turned down the volume as Tracy faced Demi and Lucas again.

"We don't buy anything from door-to-door people." She pointed to the No Soliciting sign.

"We aren't selling anything," Lucas said. "We're here to talk to you about Slater."

"We broke up. I can't help you." She started to close the door.

"Wait." Lucas put his hand on the door. "We're investigating the Groom Killer case and are trying to locate a gun Slater sold to Devlin Harrington. We think he stashed it somewhere."

"Gun? I don't know about any guns. He hung with Devlin, though. Always thought that was weird, a guy as rich as that befriending Slater."

"We think so, too. What can you tell us about them?"

"I don't know about their friendship," Tracy said. "Slater wouldn't talk about him. He did sell drugs for the Larsons, though. That's why I broke up with him. You might try their grandmother, Mae. She might know something about where guns are."

Maybe so, since she had already enabled her sons to stash guns in her basement and that had led to their arrests. But what would she know about what Devlin would do with a murder weapon? Nothing, most likely, but could she reveal something else that would point them in the right direction? Or would she reveal more about her boys?

Mae Larson had been released on bail and had been no help to Demi and Lucas. If she knew something she wasn't talking. She wasn't talking about her boys, either, despite everyone being aware she likely had a lot to say that would benefit the case against them.

On another stakeout of Slater's house, Demi rested her head back against the passenger seat headrest, missing Wolf. Valeria and Vincent were staying the night at the cabin. It was already after ten, and Demi and Lucas wouldn't be back until late. She loved how her baby's cuteness drugged Lucas. His cuteness drugged her. He was going to grow up to be a successful, wholesome man. Lucas must see that, which made her nervous. One glance across the car and she knew why. His clean-cut profile radiated smart, sophisticated handsomeness. His muscular build made her imagine more carnal heat.

Thankfully, Slater emerged from his house. At this hour he had to be going somewhere clandestine.

Like last time, they ducked and waited and then followed. Slater went to the same trailer as before. After he went inside, Lucas parked down the street.

"There's a different vehicle in front," Lucas said.

Demi saw the Subaru and didn't recall seeing it there the last time. "Let's get a closer look."

They got out and walked to the trailer. Demi followed Lucas along the side and peeked through the open slats of the plastic blinds on the kitchen window. Three men gathered around the table, Slater one of them, Paulie another. Slater sat and the other two stood. Money changed hands, and Paulie took a big envelope from the third man. Slater had a gun in front of him on the table.

Paulie dumped the contents of the envelope onto the table. Bundles of money tumbled to a standstill. Slater inspected the amount and then leaned over to pick up a duffel bag. The visitor unzipped it and parted the opening. Demi could see packages of white powder inside.

"It's a drug deal." She moved to allow Lucas a glimpse.

"Let's bust them." When Lucas faced her, his gaze ran down the front of her.

She'd dressed as his girlfriend again, just in case. His appreciation of the false version of her once again disturbed her.

"Do you prefer this?" She swept her hand down the front of her oversized boobs, visible between the sides of her jacket.

"I prefer what's underneath."

Without time to berate him more, she removed her gun from the thigh strap hidden by the black skirt. What did he mean? Underneath her disguise as one of his hot girlfriends or clothes in general?

Lucas reached the door first and waited for her. "Use your gun for protection. Let me handle the bust. You're supposed to be my girlfriend, remember?"

She nodded, not liking how the idea of being his girlfriend appealed to her and dressed as someone she wasn't.

He turned the knob and kicked the door open, charging in and yelling, "Police! Put your hands where I can see them!"

All three turned startled faces toward them, Slater still holding the money and the stranger holding a bag of drugs.

Demi covered where Lucas's pistol didn't aim, which landed on Slater. He watched her intently as she moved toward him. At the table, she picked up his gun and put it into her coat pocket, never shifting aim.

Lucas went to the stranger and patted him down, then did the same with Paulie.

"Maybe now you'll admit you knew it was Devlin who paid you to say you saw Demi Colton at my brother's crime scene," Lucas said into Paulie's ear.

Paulie's eyes rolled toward him, guarded and tense.

Lucas read them their rights and called for backup. Demi worried whether anyone would recognize her, but she wanted to hear what Slater and Paulie would have to say now.

Lucas had gotten her into the observation room where Paulie was being questioned by the chief, Finn Colton.

Lucas stood next to Demi with his arms at his sides. He'd decided not to be the one to interrogate Paulie so he could be with her. He also told her he thought maybe Paulie would open up to someone else. Lucas could be intimidating, but Demi thought that would work in his favor rather than against. She was grateful that he stayed with her, though.

So far no one had recognized her. On the way in, one officer had eyed her too long for her comfort but he didn't confront her. Now, inside the observation room, she was away from prying eyes.

Facing charges for drug dealing, Slater had readily started talking when offered a reduced sentence. He admitted to selling Devlin the same type of gun that had been used in certain killings—the same model she and Lucas fought so hard to find. It was another crucial big step toward proving Devlin was the Groom Killer. Slater also told of his dealings with the Larson twins, detailing specific drug and gun deals he'd orchestrated for them. With the Larsons in jail for threatening a cop, he'd felt safe enough to do so in exchange for immunity.

Now she wanted to hear Paulie confess that Devlin paid him off. So far he was refusing to cooperate and had only said *someone* paid him. Another witness had said he recognized Devlin's voice.

"You'll get a stiff sentence for drug trafficking," Finn said. "If you tell us the truth about who paid you to say you saw Demi running from Bo Gage's crime scene, we can help you out with that."

"Maybe I should just ask for a lawyer."

"That's your choice. We'll pursue the maximum sentence in the drug case."

Paulie began to fidget, biting his lower lip and tapping his fingers on the table. "I don't know who paid me, like I told you before."

"Another witness already confessed to being paid by Devlin Harrington to say he saw Demi near a crime scene. That leads us to believe she isn't the killer, that Devlin is."

Finn waited patiently.

"I can't say what isn't true."

"I can understand if you're afraid, with Devlin on the run, but you're going to do time for drug trafficking no matter what. The only difference will be the amount of time. We can arrange to reduce that time if you cooperate now. And if you're in jail, Devlin won't be able to get to you."

"I might get off with probation."

"Not with the amount we caught you with." Finn

explained what he'd be able to do for Paulie if he co-operated.

Paulie fidgeted some more and then finally said, "Devlin did pay me."

Demi closed her eyes and let her head fall back in relief. Beside her, Lucas took her hand and gave her a squeeze.

"He left the cash for me, but I saw him walking away from the back of the gas station. He must have waited for me to get the money. He didn't know I saw him, but he sent me threatening text messages that said he'd kill me if I told anyone I was paid."

"We won't let that happen to you. Bail will be set at about fifty thousand. Don't post bond and stay in jail until we can find him."

"How long will that be? What if I go to trial before you find him?"

"We'll find him." Finn stood.

Lucas turned from the one-way glass and faced Demi. "We're getting closer. Now we just need to find that missing gun."

"We'll keep looking."

"I'm determined."

"After these two confessions, will I be arrested?"

"I don't see any reason to until Devlin is brought in. Most likely they'll want you to stay in town in case they need to question you."

Available for questioning was kind of a fine line. He hadn't committed to *not* arresting her.

"Don't worry. Let's get out of here." He took her hand and opened the door, checking the hall before leading her down the white hallway toward the exit.

On the way, Lucas spotted John Williams, who must have heard that two drug dealers had been hauled in. He intercepted them before they could reach the exit.

"How'd the interview go? John asked.

"Slater confessed to selling the same model of weapon used in some of the killings—the missing weapon—and Paulie confessed to knowing it was Devlin Harrington who paid him to say he saw Demi Colton running from the crime scene."

"That's compelling," John said.

He didn't seem convinced, even still. The man was hardcore when it came to the arrest of criminals, more on the side of guilty until proven innocent.

"Still don't have the gun, though. Just because some low-end drug dealer says Devlin paid him to say he saw Demi doesn't mean Devlin's the Groom Killer."

"It's enough to pursue him as a prime suspect."

"Maybe you're hiding Demi." The officer's offensive gaze moved to Demi, checking her out with lowering and lifting eyes.

"Have a nice day, John." Lucas took Demi to the door, glancing back to see John scrutinizing her, but he didn't feel the man was a threat.

Lucas walked with her toward the rental car. "I think you're safe to dispense with the disguises, Demi."

She stopped at the rental. "If Finn wants me available for questioning, that means he isn't completely convinced I'm innocent."

"He doesn't think you killed anyone, Demi. Besides, the cops who want to arrest you don't have the authority. And I'm beginning to think that if you were more out in the open, Devlin would stop trying to kill you.

You become more of a threat when no one believes you're guilty and when you are no longer running."

She thought he might have a point. She'd take a risk going public, but it could have a positive effect. And she wouldn't be running anymore. That, above all else, tantalized her.

Lucas opened the passenger door for her. She faced him, uncertain. Then she began to notice how close he stood. He had his arm on the top of the door and sort of leaned toward her, a light in his brown eyes and his mouth slightly upturned. The entire picture made her feel he enjoyed his ability to read her.

Or was it the disguise?

She decided to test him. Putting her hand on his chest, she inched closer. "Do you like me in this disguise?"

His eyes smoldered and lowered to her chest. "You do look great."

"Is this the type of woman you prefer?"

"I wish you'd stop that."

"Stop what?" She pressed her body against him.

"That...and...saying that." He'd clearly become uncomfortable with how she deliberately tried to turn him on.

"Do you want me to dress like this all the time?"

"No." He no longer seemed uncomfortable.

"Why not?"

"Demi, it's not the fake boobs that get me. It's what is underneath that sexy dress and all that makeup. It's your green eyes and your red hair. I liked your red hair longer, but you look really good with it shorter, too."

Demi didn't feel like egging him on anymore. No, rather, she felt like staying right there against him.

"Could have fooled me."

After looking into her eyes for several hot seconds, he put his finger beneath her chin. "Do you need some reassurance?"

"No." He'd made it sound as though she was insecure. But wasn't she? When it came to him…maybe.

He touched his lips to hers.

Demi sucked in a much-needed gulp of air, closing her eyes to sensation. He kissed her softly and just on the lips, making love with utmost patience.

When he at last ended the sweet contact, she gazed up at him, wishing they were somewhere more private.

Then she noticed someone watching, looking over Lucas's shoulder. It was that cop they'd run into earlier, John Williams, the disbeliever.

Chapter 12

"He doesn't have any power."

Brayden had stopped by to check on Demi and they'd talked about Paulie and Slater, how Slater's confession had led to others coming forward to give statements about the Larsons. They'd be in prison for the rest of their lives.

Lucas noticed how Brayden tolerated him more now. Maybe he could see Lucas meant no harm to Demi. If he had intended to take her in, he would have done it by now. Lucas wondered if the Gage–Colton feud had had anything to do with Brayden's reluctance to trust him or with it having taken him so long. If Lucas had to guess, he'd say no.

"He doesn't need any power if there's enough evidence to arrest me." Demi sounded worried. She'd been in hiding so long she must be finding it difficult to decide when it was time to come out.

"I won't let anyone arrest you."

"I won't, either," Lucas chimed in. "No one can get to you here."

He met Demi's look and felt her concern and also something else. Looking at him seemed to calm her, as though she had begun to trust him. Today she was just in jeans and a short-sleeved purple T-shirt, but she was as sexy as when she dressed like one of his girlfriends. He hadn't realized he chose women like that. Maybe he cared more now about the kind of woman he took as his girlfriend. Maybe Demi made him care more.

When she softened even further, Lucas refocused, seeing Brayden hadn't missed their exchange.

"There are a lot of people who don't think you should be arrested," Brayden said. "They outnumber those who would. Even if one of them did manage to arrest you, there wouldn't be enough to keep you. The bribes alone cast enough doubt as to whether you were the one who wrote your name in blood and left a necklace at the scene. It's obvious you're being set up."

"I've tried to tell her that."

"Don't be afraid, Demi," Brayden said. "From what I can tell, it's just Williams and Miller who want you arrested."

Lucas nodded his agreement. He hadn't noticed anyone else taking the conservative road. "I'll have Finn talk to them. Would that make you feel better?"

"Not if Finn is on the fence, and he seemed like it the other day."

"Finn is a reasonable man," Brayden said.

"That's what makes him such a good chief," Lucas added.

"Exactly why you need to come clean. People are starting to suspect you found Demi and are lying," Brayden said to Lucas. "Some noticed her at the meeting and didn't believe you'd bring one of your model girlfriends there. I think you better just be honest now."

"They think I'm in disguise?"

"They already know you changed your appearance. They know Lucas went looking for you at that cabin that was in another person's name. And look at you. You're beautiful. Just what a guy like Lucas needs to sweep him off his feet."

"Ha, ha, very funny," Lucas said.

"I'm not the only one who noticed the way you look at her. Elle. Shane. Even Finn said something."

"What did Finn say?" Lucas asked. He hadn't revealed any of that when they'd stood in the observation room.

"He asked why you brought your new hot girlfriend to the meeting. I said I didn't know. Maybe you had plans for right after. Demi dressed well enough to make that believable."

Demi folded one arm in front of her and bent the other to nibble on her thumbnail.

"Think it over." Brayden walked closer to her. "Can I ask you something outside?"

She came alert, pulled from her inner musings. Lucas didn't say anything, just watched them go out onto the front porch. He noticed Demi had left the door ajar and moved there.

"It seems like you and Lucas are...you know... getting along pretty well."

"We are."

"He's still treating you good?"

"Yes, Brayden. You don't have to worry. I think it's time everyone forgot the old Gage–Colton feud and started planning more parties together."

"There will be plenty of those as soon as Devlin is captured."

"Yes."

"I just want you to know that if you're happy with him, then I'm happy for you."

"Thanks, Brayden."

Lucas heard sounds like they hugged and walked away from the door before Demi came back inside.

After Brayden left, Lucas made dinner while Queenie followed Wolf on a crawl around the living room. She'd been protective of the baby ever since meeting him. Demi half imagined the dog picking Wolf up like a puppy if he ventured somewhere too dangerous. Watching that distracted Demi from her worry. Placing trust in others didn't come easy for her, even her own half brother's judgment.

Sitting on the floor with her legs bent to one side, she waited for Wolf to crawl toward her, his big openmouthed smile telling all about his fun. When he reached her, she lifted him and planted a loud kiss on his soft cheek. Queenie stuck her nose to the spot as though participating in the kiss. Demi laughed and petted the dog's head.

Lucas chucked as he served two plates of steaming potpie. He'd made chicken potpie from scratch, filling the cabin with a delectable aroma and making her tummy growl. Demi sat on the couch and put

Wolf on her lap as Lucas brought over two mugs of iced root beer.

Earlier, he'd lit a flat-based candle and put it on the big ottoman. Now he turned on a compact stereo and played contemporary country music. The candle, the music, the homemade dinner…was he romancing her?

"I've had more elegant dinners than this with men," she said.

"You'll never have a better chicken potpie than this." He scooped up some food and ate a bite.

"Why not the dining room table?" She raised a forkful and blew to cool it before putting it in her mouth.

Wolf's tiny hand grasped what he could of her wrist.

"I'm trying to sooth you. This is more relaxing."

She eyed him, seeing him meet her look and appearing nonchalant. She could see he didn't mind romancing her; in fact, she didn't think he could resist. His motive was to relax her but he enjoyed being with her and doing all of this for her.

"You know I won't let anything bad happen to you, don't you?" he asked.

She finished chewing and swallowing, not sure how to reply.

"Why don't you start working on your trust issues like you did your anger issues?"

Wolf made a sound and patted his hands up and down on his legs. She put a small amount of cream from the potpie on her spoon and put it to his mouth. He opened and she let him taste.

"It's not you I don't trust." Not when it came to whether or not the police would arrest her. If she was to be arrested, she would be arrested and he wouldn't be able to stop that.

"I'd go on the run with you if the police proved me wrong and *did* try to arrest you."

That was so sweet. Did he really mean it? She felt herself shy away from trust as she always did. What if she tried letting go with him? Took a chance? Would he run off when Devlin was captured and charged with the Groom Killer murders? Her heart said he would. Her gut had a braver reaction.

He stopped eating as he became aware of her looking at him. "Do you believe me?"

To her amazement, she did. "Yes."

"Do you trust me?"

That seemed important to him, which went against his anti-marriage and –family ideology. A man like that wouldn't care about trust. He wouldn't be involved long enough for that to be an issue, would he?

"Can you trust me?" he asked. "Or how about this— you just trust me for tonight."

That she could do. "All right. I trust you."

His entire face smoothed into warm satisfaction and before she could process his intention, he leaned in and kissed her.

Wolf's grunts and batting hands drew them apart with brief laughter.

Demi put Wolf to bed and returned to the living room, where Lucas was reading a book, an action thriller. Queenie lay curled at his side on the couch, sleeping. A fire flickered in the fireplace. It had begun to snow again. Aware of her movements, he wondered if she picked up the remote and began changing channels because she needed something to do or if she was in the mood to watch something. He'd picked up this book for something to do but nothing he read registered. He kept wondering why he kept kissing her. He never thought about the consequences first, he just did the deed. Kissing her felt incredible.

Closing the book, he stood. "I'll go make the rounds before it gets too bad out there."

Demi looked up and said, "Okay. Be careful."

When he put on his winter jacket, Queenie jumped off the couch and came to sit before him, ready to go to work. He put on a hat, a headlamp and gloves and left the house. Snow fell without wind and a little more heavily than a flurry.

Queenie had quickly caught on to the command "Devlin" and knew what to search for. He followed her down the driveway. Queenie had Devlin's scent now and he used that to help him search the perimeter to make sure he hadn't tried to breach the wall or had already breached the wall. The motion sensors would go off if someone made it closer to the house.

Nose to the ground, Queenie trotted along, reaching the front gate and covering that thoroughly. When nothing signaled a find, she trotted along the fence line.

This was the path they took every night now. She'd pick up on Devlin's scent if he'd been in the area over the last twenty-four hours.

Snowflakes twinkled in the beam of his headlamp. Only his boots sinking into the snow broke the utter silence, that, and Queenie's occasional snort. She had stealthy footsteps. If anyone was on the other side of the fence, they wouldn't know she was there.

Near the edge of his property, Queenie suddenly stopped and faced in the direction of the cabin. She woofed softly and sat, looking at him.

"Good girl." Apprehension flared, though. She'd picked up on Devlin's scent—inside Lucas's property.

"Go, girl. Show me." He ran behind her through the trees. She kept her nose low, tracking the scent.

At the clearing, he could hear the alarm going off inside the house. As he neared, a shape came running from the back.

Queenie barked and raced for the man.

Lucas drew his weapon and ran as fast as he could. The man had a weapon, as well. Lucas shot first, forcing the intruder to dive.

"Don't move!" Lucas shouted. "Move an inch and I'll blow your head off!"

Queenie had reached him and stayed a few feet back, teeth bared and growling. Lucas reached the man and saw it was Devlin.

"Throw your gun."

When Devlin hesitated, Lucas fired at the ground next to his head. "The next one will hit you."

Devlin threw his weapon.

Lucas moved to his side. "Hands stretched out to your side."

Devlin complied. "You got nothing on me."

"You're trespassing and you aimed a gun at me. Were you going to break into my house?"

"You shot at me first. I carry a gun for protection."

Lucas wouldn't argue. He brought Devlin's hands behind his back and cuffed him. "I finally caught you."

"You can't prove anything."

Maybe not, but he had Devlin and he was going to jail. "We have other evidence against you. And don't forget the inn."

That got Devlin's head turning. "I'm not the one who killed all those people. Demi Colton is!"

"Who said I was talking about the Groom Killer murders?"

Devlin didn't have anything to say to that. What could he say? He didn't know what evidence they had and Lucas wasn't going to tell him. Devlin had hacked Layla Colton's text messages and emails. They also had proof that he'd photoshopped pictures of her and her junior analyst to make them look sexual.

Demi must have called 911 because he heard sirens. Jerking Devlin upright, he forced him toward the driveway, reading him his rights on the way.

Demi came out onto the porch in her winter wear, holding Wolf and disguised as Lucas's girlfriend. She must have opened the gate. The sirens quieted but flashing lights blasted the snowy night.

Officers Williams and Miller exited a police car. Demi might not be aware of their suspicion of her and he wasn't sure anyone would figure out who she really was. He pushed Devlin toward the police car and the two men.

"We received a report of an intruder." Both men stopped and stared in shock at Devlin. "Devlin Harrington?" Miller queried.

"He tried to break in," Demi said. "The alarm went off when he cleared the trees."

"So he didn't actually break in." Miller scrutinized Demi.

Lucas explained his version of what had happened.

"Looks like we can arrest you for trespassing then," Williams said, taking Devlin from him.

"What's your name, for the record," Miller asked Demi.

Demi froze and didn't answer. This wasn't Finn. These were two officers who didn't believe her innocence.

"This is Chelsey, my girlfriend," Lucas said.

"How are you?" She flaunted her fake boobs and smiled.

"You look like…" Miller started toward her. "Are you Demi Colton? You sound just like her."

In front of and to the side of Williams, who held him, Devlin smiled wickedly. He must have thought things were about to go his way again.

"It is her," Devlin said. "She changed her appearance."

Demi glanced nervously at Lucas.

"We're taking her in with this one." Miller stepped forward again.

Lucas stepped in Miller's way and planted his hand on the man's chest. "Now hold on right there. You aren't taking her anywhere."

"I knew you were harboring a criminal!" Williams said.

"All the evidence points to her," Devlin reminded everyone—as if anyone needed reminding.

"Nobody is taking her in. You have the prime suspect in cuffs." Lucas nodded toward Devlin. "Right there."

"You can't stop us from arresting her, Lucas." Miller tried to go around him but Lucas now grabbed a handful of his jacket.

"Yes, I can stop you and I will. I'm ordering you to stand down. We'll meet with Chief Colton tomorrow morning. He has the final say as to whether the warrant for her arrest is still in force." Lucas paused. "Unless you'd like to explain to him why you went against my order? I'm the one who found her. I'm the one who decides what to do with her, and right now, I've just captured the prime suspect in the Groom Killer murders and until he's questioned, nothing changes here."

"It doesn't matter that you found her. You *hid* her. We have as much right as you to take her in," Williams said.

"You'll have to go through me." Lucas opened his arms. "Do you think you can take me down?"

Queenie came to stand next to him, hackles rising, teeth bared on a low growl.

Miller backed off, stepping back. Williams seemed more undecided, although he eyed the dog warily.

"If you don't show up in the morning, we'll be back." Williams tugged Devlin around, and he smirked at Demi before Williams took him to the police car.

After he was stuffed into the back of the cop car, Williams and Miller took him away.

Lucas went to Demi. She held Wolf protectively, still watching the taillights disappear through the storm and into the trees. Queenie sniffed the ground where everyone had stood.

"I can't believe he's caught," she said.

"It's about time. We still have a long way to go, though. We don't have enough to charge him with murder." Lucas feared he'd be charged with misdemeanor trespassing and let off with a fine. Since he hadn't reported the attempted murders Devlin had committed—at Demi's cabin and at the inn—to protect Demi from discovery, he couldn't arrest him for those crimes. He could, however, make sure Gladys and Edward were brought in to identify him as the one who attacked them. That would give the inn owners justice and keep Devlin in jail while they continued their search for a murder weapon.

More than anything, Lucas wanted Devlin charged with the Groom Killer murders. All of them. The confessions made by Slater and Baines definitely made Devlin a suspect, but they wouldn't want to take him to trial with only their words against Devlin's.

"Come on." He put his hand on Demi's back. "It's cold out here." The snow was picking up, reminding him of the blizzard he'd weathered with her and looking forward to being snowed in again. This storm wouldn't be as bad and likely wouldn't strand them, but they'd be cozy, just the two of them—plus Wolf and Queenie, of course.

Opening the door, he let Queenie in first and then Demi. Queenie shook the snow off her fur and went to her food and water.

"Everyone is going to know I'm here," Demi said as she removed her jacket. "Are you sure Finn won't have me arrested?"

Lucas took the baby so she could remove the rest of her winter gear. "I'm ninety-five percent sure. Stop

worrying. And I thought you were going to trust me."
Wolf began to fuss, so Lucas rocked him.

She smiled slightly, amorously, and he realized she
finally believed him.

Wolf cried more earnestly. The only time he fussed
was when he was tired or hungry.

"He's actually crying in your arms? At least I know
he still needs me."

Lucas handed the baby back to her. She bounced
him gently and walked toward the stairs, saying, "Let's
get you back to bed."

Demi cuddled Wolf until he quieted and his eyes
drooped closed. Then she got up from the chair and tucked
him in. Checking the window for the third time to ensure
it was locked, she made sure no one could see through
any cracks in the blinds and then left the room with a superhero night-light chasing enough of the shadows away.

Lucas stood from the couch when she entered the
living room and met her halfway. He put his hands on
her arms. "Are you all right?"

Warmed all over again by his protectiveness, she
nodded. He made her feel safe.

"Don't worry about tomorrow."

That would be impossible. She yawned. It was late.

"Why don't I make some tea?"

She wouldn't get to sleep easily tonight, imagining
what Finn would say. "Sure. I'm going to go get comfortable." She went back to the guest room and silently
changed into her demure nightgown. Also putting on
a robe and slippers, she returned to see Lucas already
had two steaming cups ready.

She sat on a stool at the snack bar, listening to the low volume of a television program about a Maine cabin restoration.

"I never dreamed you'd be the kind of person who'd settle down."

She eyed him as she sipped from her cup. "I didn't plan on having a baby this soon."

"But it suits you. Sort of. Stay-at-home mom versus the fiery vixen bounty hunter I knew? It's weird."

Before she'd become a fugitive, she'd have been offended by a comment like that, especially from Lucas. "Yeah? Well, I never expected you'd become daddy material."

"Daddy material?" He all but balked at that. "Yeah, Daddy versus antifamily, alpha male bounty hunter. Now *that's* weird."

"Hold on a second. I'm not a daddy."

"You are with Wolf. Don't even try to convince me otherwise. You're great with him."

"He's a great kid."

Don't go there. She did not want to think of him as Jerry Maguire. He didn't even look like him. He more resembled a rugged doctor in some romantic movie.

Lucas chuckled. "You didn't even get mad."

"Mad? About what?" Then she realized. "I'm a forced stay-at-home mom." She chuckled now. "You can't fool me anymore, Alpha."

"You used to get mad at me when I teased you like that."

"Ever since you told me you were teasing, I have no reason to get mad."

"I think having Wolf settled you down."

"And I think you meeting Wolf may have settled *you* down."

And there it went. The magic vanished just like that. There would be no taming a man like him.

His phone rang and he looked from it to her. Who would be calling in the evening?

He answered and turned on the speaker, which she appreciated. It showed he wouldn't hide anything from her.

"Lucas. It's Finn."

Something must have happened.

"Devlin got away."

"What? How?"

"He took Miller's gun and forced Williams to stop driving. He shot Williams and Miller and ran."

Damn it! Lucas should have taken Devlin in himself rather than allowing two officers he knew weren't convinced Devlin was the murderer do it.

"How are the cops?" Lucas asked.

"They didn't make it. Devlin shot them both in the head. They died almost instantly. Officers who responded to a 911 call reported that to me."

Lucas raked his hand through his hair as Demi gasped, unable to process the horror. Devlin had murdered Williams and Miller. They could have arrested Devlin and hopefully coerced him to confess to the Groom Killer murders, but Devlin had gotten away and it had cost yet more lives.

"Devlin killed two of our own." Lucas banged his fist onto the snack bar surface. "I want him behind bars. Now."

Chapter 13

Lucas sat on the couch with his laptop, reviewing for the umpteenth time all the reports on the Groom Killer case. Queenie lay beside him, snoozing. Demi held Wolf and fed him with a bottle. He'd offered to feed him but she'd refused. She'd held the baby all evening and he began to suspect her possessiveness, as though she was threatened by Wolf's connection to Lucas. The little guy finished eating and the next call of nature came.

Lucas put his laptop aside. "I can change him."

"No, no." Demi stood, putting the bottle on the side table. She took Wolf to the bedroom.

Lucas followed, now convinced she felt threatened. In the guest room, he watched her go about the task. Queenie trailed behind him.

"You'd rather change him than let me near him, huh?" he asked.

She glanced back. "No. I can take care of him just fine."

"I'm not saying you can't. I can help out, that's all. I like him."

"I *know* you like him." She sounded annoyed.

"I won't take him away from you." Lucas walked to the changing table. Queenie stayed sitting in the doorway.

Demi ignored him and finished the job. Lifting Wolf, she held him again and rocked him in preparation for bedtime.

"Any luck going through the reports?" she asked. Devlin killing two cops proved him a murderer and had taken more suspicion off her, but they still needed evidence linking him to the Groom Killer murders.

He wasn't fooled. She wanted to avoid any discussion about her insecurity.

"No. The buried gun got me thinking, though."

She looked up as Wolf's eyes began to droop, looking up at his mother with each drowsy blink. Lucas could not fathom how she could think the boy would ever stop worshiping her.

"How so?"

"Devlin buried one of the murder weapons in his back yard."

"Allegedly. There were no prints, remember. I could have just as easily buried it there." Her voice was mocking when she spoke the latter sentence.

"He might have buried the other weapon. Somewhere." Lucas reached out for Wolf. "Come on. Hand him over."

Demi eyed him, but gently placed Wolf in Lucas's arms.

"I can't go a day without holding him." He looked down at the boy, eyes closed and sleeping peacefully. His tiny chest rose and fell with each breath and he felt soft and warm.

"Someday you'll have to," Demi said.

He looked up, caught off guard by what she meant. Of course there'd come a day when they'd part ways. He wouldn't be able to hold Wolf every day. But Wolf had become more than a piece of his dead brother. He'd become a part of his life.

"He makes me think about what it would be like to live with him every day, to be a family."

"Well, we both know you can't do that, right Lucas?"

There went her sharp tongue, temper triggered.

He couldn't say anything. He'd made his own decisions. He had to live by them. Why, then, did he now feel as though he would miss out on something important? The idea of living with Demi and Wolf every day appealed to him on a certain level, on the level of witnessing Wolf grow, of loving the boy. Demi would be part of that and he wondered if she'd be the biggest part. They could have another baby. Be a family.

While his mind rejected these thoughts, his heart forged ahead. This was how being part of a family felt. He liked it. He remembered when his mother had still lived with the rest of the Gages. He'd been so young. And then all of that had been taken away. He and his siblings had to fend for themselves from then on. Their father had gone through terrible grief he never fully recovered from.

He still couldn't get the memories of how his father had suffered out of his mind, but somehow Demi had breached the wall he'd erected. He refused to put himself in a position where he risked going through the same. Happiness meant avoiding life's biggest tragedies. He loved his work. He loved his friends and family. He loved the outdoors. But none of that would touch him the way love for a woman and her baby would. That kind of love brought men to their knees, made them weak.

"I knew it."

Demi's disappointed tone stirred something in him. Denial. A rebuttal for her assertion. But wasn't she right? He couldn't—no, *wouldn't* open himself up to loss like his father had suffered. Right then he realized there was a difference. He *could* open himself up to love. Wolf had shown him that. And now Demi. She had always challenged his thinking, but now she challenged it in a much more personal way. He had begun to feel strongly about her, despite trying not to. Probably early on, when he'd first met her, he'd recognized he could have these kind of feelings for her. Maybe that's why he'd never acted on them.

"You're too afraid," she said.

Wasn't she? That they were both afraid didn't matter. Lucas couldn't fight his urge to see what this all meant, the heat whenever he kissed her, his connection to Wolf.

Demi left the guest room, Queenie getting out of

the way in time and looking up at Lucas as though chiding him.

He walked out into the living room with Queenie on his heels, watching as Demi picked up Wolf's empty bottle and took it into the kitchen. Tomorrow might bring a new revelation but he wouldn't think about that now. He'd been all right with living single, but that was before he'd spent all this time with Demi and Wolf. Now he didn't know, and he had to.

"Go lie down, Queenie."

Queenie went to her bed and did as asked.

Going to stand behind Demi at the sink, Lucas put his hands on her hips. She dropped the bottle. Water ran for several seconds before she shut it off. Then she turned.

Lucas put his hands on the edge of the counter on each side of her.

"What are you doing?"

"I think I'd like to prove you wrong."

She angled her head. "Wrong?"

"That I'm not afraid."

"Oh, you are afraid, Lucas. Of love."

"Not any more than you are."

Her head straightened but she said nothing.

"Let's see what happens." He slid his hand into her hair, his thumb caressing her cheek.

"What if I don't want to see?"

He grinned. "You do. We've been dancing around this ever since your cabin."

She met his eyes and he saw her uncertainty, her lack of trust. He couldn't tell her she could trust him beyond this. He couldn't promise to be with her for the rest of their lives and he doubted she'd expect that. She could trust him to be honest about this, though. He was ready to take this to the next level and he sensed she was, too.

To ease the stiffness, he lowered his mouth to hers. As before, that's all it took to get the fire ignited. She moved her hands up his chest and looped her arms around him. Her body pressed to his. She fit him so well.

He kissed her awhile longer, until they both breathed faster, then he lifted her and carried her the old-fashioned way up the stairs, down the hall to his bedroom.

Placing her on the mattress, he undressed, watching her do the same.

She pulled the covers back, presenting her bare backside, and crawled between the sheets.

Naked, he went to her, getting hotter as her eyes lowered and took in the sight of him. He got onto the bed. He wouldn't rush this.

Lying beside her, he began kissing her and running his hand down her body, her smooth and curvy body. She did the same, exploring, satisfying curiosity they'd long kept under wraps.

She rolled onto her back and he moved on top of her, still determined to take his time. He kissed her, soft and slow. Her bareness against him worked against his patience.

When she opened her legs, he lost control.

She put her hands on his butt, urging him on.

He proved and found her. Slipping inside, he moved back and forth. She made breathless sounds. He hoped she was as close as he was. So much restraint stole his usual stamina. Thrusting faster, he watched her close her eyes and dig her head back into the pillow with a cry.

He thrust harder and came with her.

Collapsing on her, he caught his breath and said, "I'm embarrassed."

"Don't be. It usually takes me longer, too."

"I guess we can call this a resounding success."

And, oh, what to do with that…?

Life had a way of changing one's perspective. Demi had to fight to keep a smile from bursting free several times the next morning. Witnessing Lucas struggle over the amazing sex they'd had last night exhilarated her. She ignored the deeper problem of what this meant for her future. She tried not to think about that. She'd stay in the now.

She hung some ornaments on Lucas's tree, the few she'd brought with her from her cabin. Christmas music played on the television. Lucas had a sound bar and a woofer that enriched the tunes. Lucas had gone on another patrol with Queenie, and Wolf was down for a nap. The weather had turned snowy again.

Finished with the ornaments, she went into the kitchen to bake cookies. She and her mother used to do this and it had become a tradition. She had just begun forming balls of dough when Lucas entered, bringing billows of snow in with him. Queenie trotted into the living room and shook, sending droplets of moisture and snowflakes flying.

After he finished removing all his outdoor clothes, Lucas came into the room. Their eyes met and locked.

Demi could feel the heat spark between them. She smiled and he looked away, bending to pet Queenie and tell her she was a good girl.

"Baking cookies?" he asked as he straightened.

"Family tradition."

He walked over to the kitchen island and sat. "You and your mother?"

"Yup. Thought I'd pick it up again for Wolf." Wolf was too young to eat cookies, but Lucas wasn't.

He fell quiet and she suspected he'd drawn that conclusion, her reference to family and all.

"You seem pretty happy today," he said.

"As opposed to other days?" Cops weren't chasing her to arrest her, only Devlin—to kill her.

"Are you okay with what happened last night?"

"Of course. Why wouldn't I be?" She put a batch of cookies into the oven.

"My stance hasn't changed on settling down."

He seemed to need to convince himself more than anyone. "I don't expect you to settle down, not with me." That almost felt like a lie, despite their intimate relationship being so young. She had always been a rational woman. At this stage of their relationship, she could not and would not project the future.

He said nothing, but she could see he lacked conviction. He thought Demi needed commitment from him. Her heart did, but as she'd told herself earlier, it was too soon for that.

Wolf began to fuss, waking from his nap. Demi went to get him. As she emerged into the living room, she saw Lucas look at them, in particular, Wolf.

"Did you have a bad dream?" she asked a still-fussing Wolf. "*You?* My happy baby?" Wolf quieted and became riveted on her face, tugging a love-filled smile from her. "Who would have ever thought I'd have such an even-tempered kid?"

"Surprised he isn't an angry child?" Lucas chuckled and came to them. "Must be Bo in him."

"Maybe. Hopefully Wolf won't grow up to be something of a Loki."

"You thought Bo was a god of mischief and strife?"

"If I was being generous."

"He wasn't always like that."

Demi wouldn't know about that.

"When we were kids he was always the one who helped others, a good friend and brother."

"What changed him?"

Lucas didn't respond at first. The storm picked up in intensity. Demi heard a strong gust pelt snow against the windows. Low gray clouds dimmed the interior of the cabin.

"I don't know. Maybe life didn't turn out the way he expected. Maybe he wanted more than he had. Maybe he met the wrong people. Lost faith."

Lost faith in the goodness of mankind? Demi could believe that. She could believe that's what made many men deviate from an honest path.

"What happened to Devlin?" she almost quipped, going to turn on a couple of lights and loving how cozy it was in the cabin, the smell of cookies beginning to waft from the kitchen.

"His is more of a mental health issue."

Anyone who obsessed the way he did over a woman had to have a few nuts and bolts loose in their minds.

Wolf made a gleeful sound and reached for Lucas as he often did now. Reluctantly, Demi handed him over.

Lucas seemed hesitant, as well. He held the baby and looked down at the angelic, raptly curious face. Wolf waved his little arms as though trying to touch Lucas.

Lucas lowered his face and Wolf flattened his hand on his cheek, then patted it a few times. When Lucas chuckled, Wolf went still at the deep sound. He clumsily touched Lucas's mouth as though trying to figure out where the sound came from and why, which only made Lucas laugh again.

"You're going to be the death of me, kid."

Yes, and Lucas would be the death of her, Demi thought, and moreover, her heart.

Early in the morning, Lucas woke to Queenie growling and what sounded like a muffled explosion. Groggy, he wasn't sure he heard an actual explosion or if that had been part of a dream. Queenie's growl hadn't been, though.

Sitting up, he became aware of Demi in the bed beside him. She'd come to bed with him last night, surprising him at first, but then, why wouldn't she after their night together? Part of him wondered if she'd done it on purpose, as though pushing his limits to see if or when he'd break. Did she hope for something meaningful to develop between them? Love? Marriage? More kids?

He dressed in jeans and a sweatshirt and walked out into the living room, the concept of him a father and husband clashing with his old ideology. He could definitely love Wolf. He refused to let his mind travel into the realm of loving Demi.

Queenie waited by the door. He put on a jacket, boots, and a hat and gloves and went outside with a flashlight and his gun tucked in his jeans. Queenie trotted with her nose to the ground. She headed for the back of the cabin.

Lucas followed her but stopped abruptly along with her when a loud explosion cracked the silence.

"Queenie, heel."

His dog immediately came to stand beside him. Cautiously he proceeded forward. As he came close to the property edge, he saw flames. Someone had blown a gap in the fence.

Seeing a figure moving, he drew his gun. A man ran from the cover of a tree.

Lucas ran to chase him. The man leaped over licking flames.

"Queenie, stay." He would not have his dog in the line of fire.

Jumping the flames, Lucas ran after the stranger. His boots sank into snow as he followed footprints. Then Lucas heard the unmistakable sound of a snowmobile starting and racing away. That had to be Devlin.

He stopped chasing and turned to head back to his property. He should call police but that would draw attention to Demi. He wished she wasn't afraid of being arrested. He also wished he'd stop trying to win her trust and do what he should have done when he'd gotten her into his cabin—not hide her and go through the proper channels. He supposed it was too late for that, anyway, since he'd broken into Devlin's condo and his place of employment without a warrant.

Reaching the broken section in the fence, he and Queenie jogged back to the front of the cabin. Inside, he found Demi up and dressed.

"What happened?"

"Devlin blew up a section of the fence in the back."

"Wha…"

"He drove off on his snowmobile. You try and get some rest. I'm going to stay up with Queenie and keep a watch."

"I won't be able to go back to sleep now." She folded her arms and walked across the room. "That's been established." More than once.

She walked back toward him and crouched to pet Queenie, who looked up at her. Demi had developed quite a bond with his dog.

"Queenie heard something."

"I heard her growl." Demi kissed the top of Queenie's head. "Thank you."

Queenie gave her three gentle licks on her chin, which made Demi laugh lightly and wipe her face. Still smiling, she went to the kitchen to wash her hands.

"I'll have the fence fixed this morning, as soon as I can get a hold of someone."

"A lot of good that will do. What if he blows it up again?"

He went to her, putting his hands on her shoulders as she dried her hands. "I'll be ready."

She lifted her head, putting down the towel. With her face so close and so pretty, eyes flashing trust he'd never seen before, he didn't think. He just kissed her.

He seemed to do that a lot with her, act without thinking. Lifting his hand, he held her soft chin and deepened the caress. Kissing her felt phenomenal.

Turning between his arms, she slid her hands up and over his shoulders. Unable to resist, he held her closer, running his hand down over her rear. If this kept happening he'd have an issue he wasn't prepared to handle.

Breaking the kiss, he withdrew, seeing her startled look change into understanding. She must know why he'd pulled back.

Demi wasn't going to let Lucas off that easy. She felt his passion and she saw his fear. Somehow he had to be shown love wasn't anything to be afraid of. He had to be shown his fear had no real foundation. She followed him to the couch, where he evidently intended to spend the rest of the early morning studying police reports.

Demi began undressing on her way over to him. At first he didn't notice, so adept was he at pouring his attention into distracting, therapeutic work. When she removed her shirt, to reveal she was not wearing a bra, and threw it to the floor, his eyes lifted.

She smiled and slid her jeans down her hips, stopping at the ottoman to step out of them and her underwear. By now Lucas was a rapt viewer. His gaze went down and up, his mouth slightly open, his fingers still poised above the keyboard.

Liking this way too much, she stepped around the ottoman and then over his knees, straddling him. Putting her hands on his chest, she pushed so he leaned back and then she lowered herself onto him.

"Demi…"

His voice sounded deep and gruff, full of warming desire. That only fueled her purpose.

Leaning closer, she kissed him, slowly moving her lips with his. He moved his hands up her back and down to her rear, fully engaged and satisfying her further.

Moving back, she unbuttoned his shirt first, indulging in the feel of his chest for a while. He returned the favor and cupped his masculine hands on her breasts. She unbuttoned and then unzipped his jeans.

Seeing he wore no underwear, an involuntary "Mmm," came out of her.

Parting his jeans to expose him, she rose up and then positioned herself at his tip. Bracing herself on his muscular shoulders, she sank down onto his stiffness.

Tingles drowned her senses and she had to stay still for a moment, not wanting this to be over too fast.

He apparently had other ideas. He began pumping his hips, bouncing her gently up and down.

She couldn't take it. She cried out and ground on him as an orgasm built.

"Lucas." She met his upward thrusts and came apart.

A low, lustful groan came from him and he followed shortly after.

How in the world could he not see how good they were together? He must see, but he denied it.

She lowered her forehead to his as the sensations gradually eased and she caught her breath.

When she reached a less intense state of mind, she kissed his mouth again. He kissed her and then they took turns kissing each other. She grew so hot she thought she'd come again just with him kissing her.

Unexpectedly, he lifted her and put her onto her back on the couch. Pushing her knees apart, he found her sweet spot with his tongue and worked magic on her. Seconds later she had the most incredible orgasm she'd ever had in her life.

When he finished, he moved up her body and lay on top of her, kissing her deeply. Then he let his head rest to the side of hers.

"Why did you do that?" he asked.

"I felt like it. Why did you do what you did?"

"I could tell you weren't finished." He lifted his head to meet her eyes.

"That was amazing." She smiled up at him. "How did you get so good?"

"I've never done that with anyone."

Wow. He hadn't? She felt special and was sure he didn't mean to make her feel that way.

"Are you trying to trap me?"

"You're the one who kissed me first."

Unable to argue, Lucas said nothing, just continued to look into her eyes, maybe trying to figure out his feelings.

Let him figure away. She felt like she'd made progress with him. Whether that progress would win her a prize—him—she didn't know and wouldn't for some time. But that was okay with her. She wasn't going to attempt any predictions. And she also would not think about what she'd lose.

Chapter 14

Mae Larson still lived in the same house where she had married her husband some forty-plus years ago, not far from The Pour House. Lucas welcomed being busy and not alone with Demi at his cabin. He couldn't believe they'd made love again. Even more, he couldn't believe she'd so boldly come on to him—and how much he'd enjoyed that.

Where did all that confidence come from?

Then he realized Demi had never lacked confidence. She only lacked trust in men. Trust that might be a practical and justified defense mechanism, especially when it came to him.

Mae opened the door with narrowed, suspicious eyes moving from Queenie to Lucas to Demi, disguised as Lucas's girlfriend.

"What do you want?"

Mae must not have recognized Demi, Lucas noticed. She had recognized Lucas, though. "We'd like a word with you regarding your grandsons' friendship with Devlin Harrington."

Her expression smoothed now that she understood they hadn't come to talk about her sons' arrests for possessing illegal guns and threatening an officer. He'd get to that after she agreed to talk.

"May we come in for a few minutes?" Lucas asked.

After brief hesitation she said, "I'm allergic to dogs. That thing has to stay out here."

"Stay, Queenie."

Queenie sat. She wouldn't move from the porch until he came back outside.

Mae stepped aside to allow them in. Lucas entered ahead of Demi. The interior of Mae's home hadn't seen any updates in decor in a couple of decades. Pictures of her husband and their kids, along with those of their grandkids, cluttered one wall of the living room.

Lucas remained standing in the entry with Demi.

"What do you want to know about Devlin? My grandsons talked about him on occasion. They were at least acquaintances."

"Did Evan or Noel ever talk about buying guns from them or anyone who worked with them?" Lucas asked.

"My boys never sold any guns."

So she'd deny that, even after Noel and Evan Larson had been arrested for selling guns and evidence had been found on burner phones and hard drives.

"Aren't you facing some charges yourself?" Demi asked. "For letting them store the guns here?"

Mae swatted her hand.

Did she think she'd get off? Her grandsons sure seemed overly confident of that.

"You'll go to prison for your role in what they did," Lucas said. "No lawyer in the country will change that."

Mae's brow lowered and creased. "I didn't sell any guns."

"You helped them," Demi said.

"There are witnesses coming forward to testify against them now that they are in jail," Lucas said. "You could reduce or eliminate your jail time if you also came forward with what you know."

Mae wrung her hands in front of her, clearly undecided as to what to say.

"We know you love your grandkids, Mae," Demi said. "But they've done a lot of illegal things and now they're going to go to prison. Nothing you say will change that, especially if other witnesses are coming forward."

"What witnesses?"

"Slater, for one."

Recognition made Mae's head draw back.

"Several other small-time drug dealers."

Mae wandered to the wall of pictures, almost a shrine to her family. "I heard Evan joke once that Devlin bought a gun so he could use it on Hayley, since he was so taken with her and with her not wanting anything to do with him."

"Did Devlin talk about Hayley with them?" Lucas continued with his questioning.

"Not that I ever heard, and they didn't tell me, but I assumed so since Evan cracked that joke." She turned to face them. "Devlin liked my grandsons. He liked the way they lived."

"Did Devlin ever tell anyone where he stashed his guns?" Lucas asked.

"Evan and Noel didn't tell me. They didn't tell me much about what they did. They needed a place to store their inventory and I agreed to help them."

"Did you know they were dealing in illegal activities?"

She didn't respond.

"Will you come to the station and give your statement? We can see about lightening your charges if you agree to testify against them."

"Testify against them!" Mae passed an indignant look to Demi and Lucas. "I wouldn't testify against my own grandsons! You said if I gave you information I could lessen my sentence."

"I said if you came forward with what you know. That includes testifying to what you know, but first we would need your statement."

Mae covered her mouth with her hands.

"Think it over, and remember, if you don't testify, you're facing serious jail time."

"Did Devlin ever say anything else to Evan and Noel about Hayley?" Demi asked.

"They laughed about all the pictures he had of her and once they said Devlin would follow Hayley and wait for her at the K-9 center. He'd watch her train the dogs and things like that. I found it rather disturbing."

She found that disturbing but not the evil things her grandsons did?

"But nothing about what he did with his guns."

She shook her head. "Not that I'm aware."

After they left, Lucas made a call to Finn to let him know Mae might agree to testify for a lesser sentence. He'd get the team ready to take her statement.

"Where would Devlin have hidden the other weapon?" Demi asked as she walked with Lucas and Queenie.

Lucas wished he had a better idea.

"He buried a gun at his property."

"No prints. You can't assume he was the one who buried it."

"No, but what if he buried another one somewhere else? As obsessed as he was over Hayley, maybe he hid it somewhere that meant something to him, something relating to his fantasy world that revolves around her."

She'd had a good idea. What would Devlin do with the guns if he wanted to have an impact on Hayley? If he'd given up all hope of ever winning her love, then maybe he'd try to punish her in some way. Or maybe he'd just get his rocks off hiding them in her environment. Home? Work? Somewhere the two of them went that meant something to him?

Dressed as his girlfriend again, Demi slipped into Hayley's home behind Lucas. He'd just picked the lock. With Hayley at work, they wouldn't be interrupted while they searched her place. She'd just moved into a small apartment not far from the training center. She had an electronic photo album that flashed pictures of Bo and her, and several of just her, posing for selfies. A large black-and-white painting of her hung above a white trim fireplace.

"She likes herself," Demi said.

Lucas glanced at the painting and grunted with brief humor. "She does seem like a confident woman. Good trainer."

"Yes, she does seem nice, but do you think she really loved Bo?" Demi searched a shelf while Lucas went through a built-in desk.

"She seems like she did."

"She seems nice, too, but she talks a lot of smack about people."

"She did say you killed her fiancé because you were jealous."

"Of course she did." Demi shook her head. "She knew I broke up with him, didn't she?"

"Don't know." He also sounded like he didn't particularly care.

She moved on to the spare bedroom, Lucas joining her and tackling the closet.

"Not your type, huh?"

He stopped in the act of looking at the shelf. "Hayley? I've never been attracted to her."

"Your brother was."

"My brother liked blondes."

"I wasn't blonde."

"Redheads are a brand of their own."

A brand? "You like redheads?"

He walked over to her. "Why are you asking me all these questions?"

She didn't really know. Maybe it was all the hot sex they'd been having. "Yes or no?"

"I like redheads." He left and went into Hayley's

room. Demi followed but didn't search. The guns weren't here.

"Did you ever meet a woman you thought might be the one?"

He turned from the closet. "No."

"Not even close? What happens when you meet someone? Are you only interested in physical connections?"

He thought a moment, putting his hands on his hips and looking across the room. Then he met her eyes again. "There was one woman. I met her about six years ago. She was in college, going for a chemistry degree. Smart. Pretty. We had a good time together and I liked talking with her."

"Tell me the best thing you ever did with her."

"We went on a ski trip. She wasn't a very good skier but we had fun, talking on the lift rides and leisurely runs down the slopes. We talked more at the ski lodge and later at the hotel room. She had an interesting family and wanted to become a college professor."

"Teaching chemistry?"

"Yes."

"She must have been smart." So, he liked smart women? Demi had gone to college but her degree had been natural resources with a minor in criminal justice. Did Lucas even know that about her?

"What happened?" she asked.

"I found out later that she didn't like skiing or any other outdoor activities."

"Is that when you broke up with her?"

"I didn't break up with her. She broke up with me.

She got tired of being outside all the time. She was more of a bookworm."

Demi would have thought he was the one who always did the breaking up. "She doesn't sound like she looked like any of your other girlfriends."

"I didn't date fashion divas all the time."

"What did some of those women do for a living? How did you meet them?"

"I didn't meet any models in South Dakota," he said. "Mostly I met them on the job. At restaurants. Through the victims of some of the fugitives I hunted, family members or friends. Also through my father's company, people who worked for him or associates of his."

That sounded normal. Maybe she had exaggerated on the bimbo part, but he still picked women who were ill-suited for him, whether he realized it or not. "There's hope for you yet." She smiled at him.

"Let's get out of here." Lucas headed for the door.

She trailed behind. "Why did the college student break up with you? Was it really because she didn't like the outdoors?"

Out in the hall, he walked beside her. "She wanted to move in together, to take things to the next level, I said I wasn't ready for that. We dated a little more and eventually she told me we felt stagnant. She wished me well. I wished her well and we parted ways."

"Did she catch on that you weren't interested in love?"

He didn't respond, seeming to travel back in thought to that time.

"Did you ever tell her that?"

"We had a conversation about it." Outside the apartment building, they headed for the car. Lucas checking the surroundings. He put his hand on her lower back. At the car, he opened her door.

She didn't get in. "Tell me about your conversation."

His eyes squinted slightly under the bright sky. "She asked if I'd ever been in love. Married. And I told her no and that I didn't believe in any of that. She asked why and I told her pretty much what I told you."

"That you were afraid your heart would break?"

He grunted as though she joked. "No. I preferred to be single and not start a family. I saw what that did to my father and I don't want to end up like him."

"Yes, but not every woman dies in a relationship, Lucas. Don't you see how flawed your logic is?"

"Flawed or not, that's the way I want it. A woman doesn't have to die to cause drama in a man's life."

Cause drama. Did he actually think *women* caused the drama? "Men can cause drama just as easily. What if you did get married and you were the one to break a woman's heart? Better yet, what if you ended up happy for the rest of your life with a woman?"

"Demi, we've been over this."

"What did that woman tell you after you explained your flawed thinking?" Demi asked regardless.

He didn't answer and Demi knew whatever she'd said had gotten to him.

"Tell me."

After a few more seconds of hesitation, he finally answered. "She said she felt sorry for me."

She smiled again, broader than before.

Back at the cabin, Demi sat on the floor, laptop in front of her crossed legs, going through Devlin's photos of Hayley again, searching for some clue as to what Devlin might have done with the missing gun. There may not have been prints on the weapon found buried, but Demi had no doubt whatsoever that Devlin was the one who'd buried it. If he'd buried that one, why not bury others? Right now she concentrated on photographs.

There were several shots taken from afar. Clearly Devlin had spied on her, stalked her. Hayley coming out of her home. Hayley at the supermarket. Hayley going to work. Hayley at work, training dogs. How had he accessed the training yard? The photos were taken outside the perimeter fence. He must have hiked in from the side or back. In some photos the edge of the equipment shed was captured. The center used the shed for storing things like a riding mower and snow removal equipment. Devlin must have used it for cover, so no one saw him drooling and sickly ogling Hayley.

She came across another photo of Hayley smiling, with her hand on the chest of a K-9 cop. They appeared to be flirting. Devlin had taken several of her with the man, the two of them sharing dinner at a local restaurant, him dropping her off and kissing her. More at the training center. He seemed to spend a lot of time watching her there.

The training center.

"Lucas?"

He turned his attention from his laptop.

"Come look at these."

He stood and stepped to where she sat on the floor. He sat beside her, one leg bent up and the other stretched out beside her and the laptop. He rested his arm on his knee and Demi grew distracted by the sexy pose.

"What is it?" he asked.

She pointed to the photo of Hayley with the K9 cop. "The training center. Devlin took several pictures of Hayley there."

"How? Where did he hide to stay out of view?"

Demi scrolled through the folder of photos until she found one that showed the corner of the equipment shed.

"That would be a good spot," Lucas said. "Only the facilities workers use that shed and it's far enough away from the building and the fenced-in training area to serve as cover."

"If any workers approached, he could move to the back and hide in the trees back there."

Lucas took control of the mouse and looked through all the pictures she'd just seen. "So, what are you thinking? Where would he hide guns if he decided to hide them at the training center?"

"Maybe he buried them there, somewhere on the grounds. In the training area?" Under where Hayley's feet had stood with that K-9 cop?

"He'd have a hard time getting in there."

"Somewhere around the equipment shed then." Maybe he'd memorialized the burial site.

Lucas thought a moment and Demi gave him time. "I'll take Queenie there tomorrow."

"We should look for other clues, too, like maybe Hayley's computer."

"If you keep showing up there, somebody is going to recognize you."

"I'll take my chances. I'm getting good at my disguises." Besides, she wanted to go with him in case he did find something. She could clear her name. If Queenie found the guns and they had prints on them and the bullets matched the ballistics testing, she could stop sneaking around and trying to avoid detection.

"I can see there's no point in arguing with you." Lucas's eyes sparkled with affection as he looked at her.

What did he see? Her enthusiasm must show, her determination and earnest anticipation of clearing her name.

Slipping his hand behind her neck, he leaned in and kissed her.

She kissed him back, a now-familiar tingle spreading like a sweet wildfire through her body. He must have the same reaction, because he deepened the kiss with heavier breathing and pulled her closer with his hand on her lower back.

After several seconds, he finally withdrew and she looked up into the heated passion darkening his eyes. The urge to have more of him overwhelmed her. If they were back at his cabin, she had no doubt where this would lead. Straight to his bedroom.

"Have you ever felt like this before?" she asked, not really thinking before the words came out.

"No."

The question sobered him. He immediately stepped back, the spots where his hands had been going cold.

Chapter 15

Lucas let Demi in the back door of the center. It was close to the end of the normal work day. This time she was dressed as a janitor again, hair up in a ponytail and wearing thick-rimmed glasses. No makeup. She hadn't worn makeup before Bo was murdered and worried someone might recognize her face. She kept her head down as she made her way through the office space. She started with Hayley Patton's desk. Lucas had managed to get hold of the passwords for her. She easily logged on to the computer, pretending to clean the desk surface.

She checked email and files and found nothing of significance. She hadn't expected to. Devlin would have been stupid to try and harass her with a trail of emails.

After emptying the trash, she found another unoccupied desk and proceeded to hack into Miller's account the way Lucas taught her. What she stumbled upon startled her. Miller and Williams had been in contact with Devlin. They'd arranged to meet. No wonder they were so convinced Demi killed all those grooms. Had Devin paid them? Then why had Devlin killed them? Perhaps for the same reason he'd killed that witness he'd paid to lie. Or simply to stop them from arresting him. The latter would be plenty of reason for a madman to kill. Devlin did not intend to be arrested. He'd gone to great lengths to prevent that—namely in how he'd framed Demi.

"What are you doing?"

Demi flinched and closed out the open email. She began wiping the desk, looking up to see Hayley standing there. "Cleaning."

"What were you doing on that computer?"

"Nothing."

"You were looking at something." Hayley moved around to inspect the screen. "What was it?"

"Nothing."

Demi put the cloth on her rolling cart and bent to empty the trash.

"You stay right there." Hayley marched off.

Grabbing a wig from the cart, Demi headed toward another desk. Dare she risk being caught again, by Hayley and whoever she'd gone to fetch?

She found a private desk in the corner. If she stayed low, she wouldn't be seen. She removed the overalls she wore, now in jeans and a white T-shirt. She put on her blond hippie wig and dug out another pair of glasses from the pocket of her overalls.

* * *

Lucas took Queenie from the enclosed training area after pretending to do a session. He could see the shed from there. It was far enough away from the enclosure that if any gun had been hidden there, none of the dogs would have alerted anyone.

"Come on, girl." He had already let Queenie smell Devlin's shirt and gave her a command. He unleashed her and away she went, trotting along the fence line. She veered away from the fence, not far from the shed, and zigzagged across the ground. She caught on to something near the shed and trotted from there toward a neighboring warehouse. At the edge of the gravel parking area, she stopped and sat, waiting for him.

That's where the trail ended. He went to Queenie. "Good girl." She took her treat. Devlin must have parked here when he'd come to spy on Hayley.

Now Lucas took out his gun and let Queenie smell that. She'd know to search for weapons now. "Find."

Queenie trotted back toward the shed. She didn't deviate. She went straight for it. When she reached the front double doors, she stopped and sat.

"Hey, bro, what are you doing out there?"

Lucas walked to Queenie and stopped, seeing Detective Carson Gage standing inside the training enclosure with Lucas's sister Elle, a fellow K-9 officer.

"Just doing some tracking training with Queenie."

"That's an odd place to be doing that," Elle said.

"Maybe not. I haven't trained her around building structures in a while.

Elle lifted her head speculatively and Carson just stared at him like he'd lost a marble or two. Why not take Queenie to a building outside the center? He could hear them both thinking.

Queenie moved to the doors of the shed and sat again.

"Huh," Elle said. "Did she find what you asked her to find?"

"Don't know yet." Lucas preferred to search the shed alone, without onlookers, but he apparently had no choice or his actions would seem suspicious. Unless this developed into something concrete, he'd rather keep it under wraps. He didn't feel like answering any questions, like why he'd chosen this particular shed to search. Then he'd have to explain how he'd illegally obtained Devlin's absurd library of Hayley pictures.

He used the key he'd gotten from the facility manager's office and unlocked the shed.

"How do I get my own key to the outbuildings?" Carson said.

"You ask," Lucas said. Except he hadn't asked. He'd *borrowed*.

Queenie entered the shed and maneuvered around all the equipment, nose to the floor. It was a sizable shed, maybe twenty by twenty feet. The dog zeroed in on something in the back. In a corner, she pawed at a stack of boxes and then sat.

Outside, he heard Carson and Elle talking about the upcoming Christmas party the K-9 center had planned for the weekend before Christmas. Their voices faded.

Lucas went to the doorway and saw them disappear inside. No one else was out in the training yard. Looking up, he saw clouds had gathered, gray and low and a chilled breeze moved his hair. Snow would arrive any minute now.

Returning to Queenie, he began lifting boxes until he reached the one she'd pawed. He opened that and discovered nothing more than extra heavy-duty work jackets and pants.

Queenie whined and pawed the wood floor.

"Okay, girl." He slid the box aside and examined the floorboards. All appeared to be in place. Finding a pry bar in a tool chest, he returned to the corner and began prying planks up. Queenie moved into the corner with her nose down, pawing at a different plank.

Lucas forced that one up.

Queenie began barking as the light dimmed inside the shed, not the kind of bark that alerted him to a find. Someone had entered the shed and closed the doors. She lunged just as someone knocked him over the head with something hard. He fell to his side, dizzy but conscious enough to see Devlin kicking Queenie aside and keeping her from biting him. Queenie whimpered.

"I'm going to hurt you for doing that!"

Lucas rolled out of the way of another enraged swing. Devlin's crazed eyes were wide and inhuman. He pulled out a pistol. One of the doors to the shed hadn't closed all the way. Had he planned to kill him quietly so as not to arouse attention? Now that that had failed, he'd resort to shooting.

Hearing Queenie growl, Lucas gave her a hand signal to keep her from lunging again. He would not have her hurt. He just had to be faster than Devlin with a gun. Problem was, Devlin had a gun in his hand.

After hacking into William's user account, Demi navigated through emails, finding the one with Miller and Devlin arranging to meet and forwarding it to her own email. She opened a browser and checked the favorites Williams had selected. One was for his personal bank account. She opened that and saw he'd saved his login information to easily access it. She opened his account and looked through his deposits over the last several weeks. She saw his regular payments from the RRPD, and then there was one for ten thousand around the time Devlin had gone on the run.

She printed a copy of that statement. Now she had to make it to the printer and then go find Lucas.

Standing, she heard Hayley explaining that a woman had been sitting at a desk working on the computer.

It was Micah Shaw she was telling that someone strange had been snooping around in the administrative area. Staying low, Demi walked along the outside of the cubicles, the walls concealing her.

She heard Finn's voice now, and then Carson and Elle.

"What's going on?" Elle asked.

"A woman sneaked in here and was going through Miller's computer," Micah said.

Demi made it to the front of the administrative area and walked down the hall toward the back where Lucas had said he'd take Queenie. Outside she walked along the fenced enclosure, seeing the equipment shed in the distance, one of the two doors cracked open. She heard Queenie growling and the sound of a fight. Something crashed inside the shed and then Lucas's body came flying outside, banging the doors against the shed.

A gun had fallen to the shed floor and Devlin appeared in the opening, bending to pick it up. Lucas corrected his balance and kicked Devlin, sending the man falling backward, away from the gun. But Devlin picked up a pry bar and threw it at Lucas, who held up his arm to protect himself.

Devlin used the distraction to crawl toward the gun. Lucas punched him, preventing him. Devlin picked up a metal bucket next, hurling that at Lucas. Then he rammed into Lucas, sending them both falling outside the shed.

Getting to his feet, Devlin scrambled for the gun.

"Stop or I'll shoot!" Demi shouted, pulling her pistol from the back of her jeans. She was a pretty good shot.

But Devlin picked up the gun and aimed it at Lucas, who had just gotten to his feet.

"Drop your gun or I'll kill him," Devlin growled. "I will."

He was going to shoot Lucas!

"This is all your fault!" Devlin hissed.

"Don't do this, Devlin. Enough people have died." She aimed for his hand that held the pistol. "Put down the gun. It's all over." He'd killed too many and had almost succeeded in killing her. She tasted victory. At last Devlin would pay, pay for all those victims and pay for framing her.

"It's not over until you're *dead*!"

"You'll be dead if you don't drop that gun."

"If you want your precious boyfriend to live, you better be the one who drops their gun."

Demi wavered, afraid if she shot first if he'd get a shot of his own off and kill Lucas. If she hesitated Devlin might get the upper hand. She could not allow him to escape again.

Seeing Lucas inch his hand closer to his own gun, Demi took a chance and fired her well-aimed pistol. She hit Devlin's hand. His gun dropped as Lucas drew his.

Devlin bent over with a wail, holding his bleeding hand.

"There she is!" Hayley cried out as several Red Ridge police officers rushed forth and saw the scene that had just played out. A few K-9 cops poured out from the building—Shane and Brayden, Hayley and Carson, and a few others.

Lucas pointed his gun at Devlin's head and kicked the fallen pistol away. "Give me a reason to pull this trigger."

"Drop your weapon!" Seeing Carson made the demand of her, Demi dropped her gun and lifted her hands, showing everyone she would surrender, never more frightened in her life.

Would she ever see Wolf again? The concept terrified her and soured her core with dread.

She glanced back to see Lucas shoving Devlin against the shed wall and cuffing him, reading him his rights.

What would happen to her now? She hated not knowing. She'd worked so hard to stay free, to prove her innocence. All of that was uncertain now.

She faced the crowd of officers.

Finn approached her with a displeased frown. Lucas pushed Devlin toward Shane, who took control of the madman, holding his cuffed wrists while Hunter appeared and held a gun on him.

"I've waited a long time for this day," Hunter said to Devlin.

"You have the wrong person," Devlin shot back.

"Oh, really? Is that why you almost killed Lucas Gage?"

Devlin grumbled something unintelligible, the ramblings of an insane man. Then he yelled, "You can't do this!"

Stopping before Demi, Finn reached for her hair and pulled off her wig. He studied her a moment.

"Hello, *Demi*."

Apprehension reared up higher. Her heart slammed and she debated whether to run or not.

"That's Demi!" Devlin yelled some more. "She's the one who's the killer! She's right there. You have her! Why aren't you arresting her?"

"Quiet." Shane gave Devlin a jab with his gun.

Lucas went to Demi and pulled her behind him, facing Finn. "You're not arresting her." Queenie sat beside him, panting.

Finn's brow turned stormy. "You had her all this time and didn't tell me? I knew something was going on."

"Nobody is arresting her," Lucas repeated.

Finn said nothing.

Lucas told Queenie to stay and guard, and she went to stand beside Demi. His protectiveness warmed her and eased her tension.

Standing beside Finn, Lucas said, "I need to show you something."

Demi perked up. Had Queenie found something?

Lucas led Finn into the shed. Demi moved closer so

she could see, Queenie staying right by her side. Lucas pried a board from the floor of the shed, tossing it on top of the others he'd removed.

Excitement chased through her. Brayden and Shane came to stand to her left, the other K-9 cops, including Hayley, also stepped closer. Queenie turned and growled, baring her teeth in warning.

"We won't come any closer," Hayley said.

Lifting a duffel bag, Lucas put it on the shed floor and parted the opening enough for all to see. Demi saw two guns inside.

"Queenie tracked Devlin to this shed and to these guns," Lucas said.

Finn looked up from the guns to Lucas. "How did she track him?"

Lucas would have to explain how Queenie had gotten Devlin's scent. Finn wanted to know if he'd followed legal channels, and of course he hadn't.

"I obtained an article of clothing."

"From?"

"His house."

"Without a warrant?" Finn wore a disapproving frown. "You know—"

"If his prints are on these guns, it won't matter," Lucas cut him off.

Finn had to know that. He was just angry Lucas had kept him in the dark.

Demi took out the printout and handed it to Finn. "I found this on Miller and William's work computes."

Finn reached up, took them and read. Then he lifted his head. "I'm not even going to ask how you got these." "You aren't arresting Demi," Lucas said again. "She's staying with me."

Finn stood and Lucas stood with him. "Ordinarily I'd remind you I'm the chief."

Demi waited, glancing behind her to see the other cops waiting for Finn's order. She'd be arrested any second. She glanced up at Brayden, who held his hand out and moved it up and down as though telling her to simmer down.

"But I'm going to allow her to stay in your custody until we get these guns through forensics."

Demi nearly sagged in relief. She put her hand on Brayden's forearm and he put his arm around her in support.

"Queenie, come." Queenie moved to Lucas's side.

"Get a crime scene team in here," Finn demanded.

"I'll go." Brayden left Demi's side and went inside the building.

Finn stopped before Demi. "Don't try to get away."

"I didn't kill anyone."

"I know. I need you to stay put until we can prove that. Do I have your word?"

She glanced at Lucas, whose eyes were full of heat and triumph over succeeding in protecting her.

"Yes. You have my word. I won't leave Lucas's sight."

"The whole town is going to be abuzz over this one," Hayley said.

"Everybody, back to work," Finn said. "Get Mr. Harrington in a jail cell over at the police department."

"Gladly." Shane handed a complaining Devlin over to a RRPD officer, and he and two other officers took him into the training center. They'd take him to the RRPD and throw him in jail, something that was long overdue.

Finn turned to Lucas and Demi. "I won't be forgiving if you go against your word and try to run again."

"I won't run."

He looked at Lucas. "I'll let you know as soon as forensics is finished."

"Where is your baby?" Hayley asked. "Didn't you have one?"

Demi didn't answer. She took Lucas's offered hand and walked with him along the outside of the building toward the front and his car.

"Trust me now?" Lucas asked.

She stopped by the car and faced him. "I do."

He sort of faltered over the way she said that, as though she were uttering a vow.

Chapter 16

Demi's trust had a strange effect. Lucas had half teased her the other day, but the other half was what had him in a conundrum. He liked her trust. When she had said *I do,* she'd addressed her confidence that he'd ensure no one arrested her, but he felt her meaning reach deeper. Did she trust him as a man? The surge of satisfaction with the prospect alarmed him.

Right now they were in Edson's home, sitting in his office. Layla had contacted him this morning, asking him to help her work something out with his father to help her bail out her father's company and fund the K-9 center. She had likely come to some decision on Edson's terms.

Able to move freely now as long as she was with Lucas, Demi dressed as herself and the previous night she had changed her hair back to its natural color. She'd said she couldn't wait for it to grow long again. In gray slacks and a long-sleeved white blouse, her butt looked great and he liked her natural breasts. Her green eyes needed no enhancement.

Layla entered the office, her beautiful blue eyes sharp with intent. She stopped before Lucas and Demi. "Thank you for coming." She hugged Demi. "I'm so glad you're back." Demi had thought them being there would help Layla's cause, Lucas being Edson's son and Demi being one of Layla's cousins and so close to being eliminated from the Groom Killer suspect list. Demi and Lucas made a powerful alliance. It was time for unity.

"Edson," she greeted Lucas's father, going over to shake his hand.

His face was unreadable he returned the shake.

"I've given it a lot of thought and I agree to your terms," Layla said.

Edson considered her and then walked around his desk to come closer. "What about your father? Surely he won't agree as you have. Doesn't he have the final say?"

"Let me worry about that. The future of his company will be what sways him. He won't allow it to crumble."

Edson's proposal was not an unfair one. If he hadn't been a Gage, Fenwick would've jumped at the opportunity. Any savvy businessman would. With his father's old money, Edson could afford to make this conditional proposal.

"It must be difficult for him to fall from such wealth to having to beg for help." Edson didn't sound offensive using the word *beg*. Fenwick and Layla would have to act soon to avoid potentially irreversible damage to their livelihood.

"He's not the one doing the begging."

Layla wasn't exactly begging, either. She was making a business move, one that her father would never have made on his own.

"I hope you know that this proposal is intended as a peace offering and not revenge or any kind of payback for a century-old poker loss."

"I hope that in time my father will see that."

"He'll agree to the sale of land at the price I proposed?"

It was below the actual value of the land, but Edson stood to make money and Fenwick would have his K-9 center funded. Both would benefit over the long term.

"In exchange for a bailout and K-9 center funding for five years, yes, after some persuading."

More like a *lot* of persuading.

"And if he doesn't agree?"

Layla's head lowered and then lifted. She did have her doubts.

"There has to be a way to convince him," Demi said. "Everything has changed over the last year."

"She's right," Lucas said. "Everyone worked together on the Groom Killer case and in bringing the Larson twins to justice, and Fenwick backed off on Layla's marriage to Hamlin. I've never seen the Coltons and the Gages closer than they are now." He kept to himself that he, himself, had grown closer to a Colton.

"Then we must make Fenwick see that and get past the old feud."

Lucas had never been prouder of his father. He had obviously forgiven the Coltons, and this amicable deal he had on the table would satisfy both the Gages, who still felt slighted, and Coltons, who still felt they owed the Gages nothing. After all, the Coltons would gain something in return. They'd gain five years of stability and prosperity.

A commotion erupted at the entrance of Edson's estate, which was sizable, making the sounds far away but growing closer. The housekeeper must have opened the door because now it sounded as if someone was forcing their way toward them.

"Oh, no," Layla said, spinning to face the doorway.

Her father, Fenwick, appeared, an angry scowl distorting his face, a much different face than the one that had repented almost allowing his own daughter to marry in order to save his company and his wife's pet project, the K-9 center.

"How could you?" Fenwick entered the office with the housekeeper chasing him, yelling, "Stop!"

Edson walked to the doorway as Fenwick approached his daughter.

To the poor, sweet-looking housekeeper, Edson held up his hand and said in a soothing, grandfatherly way, "It's all right." When she smiled with an exhale and turned, he closed the office door.

"I told you I will not make a deal with a Gage!" Fenwick shot a look at Lucas. "What is he doing here?" Then he glanced at Demi—a Colton and part of the family. Not that Fenwick cared much for their kind of Colton.

"Father, stop and think. Put your animosity aside for just a—"

"You're crossing a dangerous line!"

Dangerous seemed a bit extreme. Was the line between Coltons and Gages? Fenwick wanted to stay firmly on the Colton side and keep any Gage far from it.

Lucas stayed out of the argument, content to see where this would lead. He could intervene if necessary.

"Do you want to make another mistake like you made arranging a marriage between me and Hamlin?" Layla asked. "I thought we made a good connection after you stopped pursuing that. You *cried* in front of everyone!"

Fenwick breathed heavily a few times. Then he implored his daughter with what appeared to be heartfelt eyes. "That was different. I do deeply regret trying to set you up with Hamlin, Layla. That was wrong. You're my daughter. Nothing is more important to me. But…"

"But you can't let go of that meaningless feud."

Fenwick stretched his arm out toward Edson. "Neither can he if he passes an ultimatum to settle a hundred-year-old score."

"My father is trying to mend that old fence," Lucas said. "It's not an unfair deal."

"It's time for everyone to get along," Demi said.

Edson approached Fenwick. "I'm not only thinking of myself or my relatives from long ago with this proposal," Edson said. "I'm thinking of the good of everyone. It's no secret there've been Coltons and Gages intermixing this last year. How many weddings do you suppose there'll be after Devlin is proven to be the Groom Killer?"

"What did you just say?" Fenwick was clearly incensed. "Weddings?" He shot a glance toward Layla.

She wasn't marrying a Gage and neither were any of his other children, but many other Coltons were.

"You wait and see," Edson said. "As soon as the Groom Killer is charged, there will be an explosion of weddings in this town, not only between Gages and Coltons."

"It's time to accept it, Fenwick," Lucas added. "Christmas is a week away. Agree to this deal and help bring us all together."

"I'll allow you to choose the property or properties that equal the value you need for both your company and the K-9 center," Edson said. "It is a good business move, for both of us. Your daughter has already agreed to a fair proposal. Honor it. Honor *her*."

Fenwick took time mulling that over.

"If it was offered by anyone other than a Gage, would you take this deal?" Layla asked.

Her father met her eyes, indecision swarming.

"You would," she said. "Forget that it's Edson Gage. Think about the *business deal*."

"Edmund would turn over in his grave."

Layla put her hand on her hip, looking every bit the corporate leader she was. "Then he's long overdue for that turn. It's time to put the feud behind us, Dad, and I agree this deal is a good way to do that. Who cares what happened a hundred years ago? We need our company back on track."

Her angle on the company seemed to have an effect on Fenwick. He loved his company as much as Layla.

"And don't forget Mom," Layla said.

Fenwick blinked once, twice, eyes softening.

Just then Lucas's cell phone rang and he saw it was

Finn. That could only mean one thing—the results of the forensics testing had come back.

"Excuse me. This is important." He answered.

"Lucas. We managed to get a rush on the fingerprint testing. We got a match."

Whose prints? The brief amount of time that passed seemed an eternity.

"There were prints on the guns, good prints. They belong to Devlin. He's being formally charged right now with the murder of Bo Gage and other victims in the Groom Killer case, and of course, Officers Williams and Miller."

Lucas shut his eyes in relief and nodded at Demi, who tipped her head back with a huge smile and let out a, "Woo-hoo! Yes!"

"Devlin's fingerprints were on two guns we found," Lucas said to Layla and the two other men.

After Lucas ended the call, Demi threw her arms around him. He chuckled and held her, and then they kissed. A few seconds later, he looked down into her happy eyes and realized two things. One, Wolf had gotten his happy disposition from her and might have to overcome a similar passionate temper as he grew older, and two, they'd just kissed in front of his father, Fenwick and Layla.

Demi seemed to realize the latter just after him. Her radiant smile died and she withdrew, looking from Edson, to Fenwick, to Layla.

"There you have it," Layla said brightly, as though breaking ice. "You're seeing it with your own eyes, Dad. Love blossoming between a Colton and a Gage."

Fenwick closed his slightly open mouth. "I…"

"Just say yes, Dad. Agree to Edson's proposal." Her strong tone left no opening for argument.

Fenwick looked at Edson, who waited patiently. At last Fenwick gave a single nod.

With a shriek of joy, Layla hugged him and planted a kiss on his cheek. "Thank you! You won't regret this."

"I trust your business sense, Layla, and I love you."

"I love you, too." She withdrew and let her father go to Edson, and the two shook hands.

"I'll have the necessary papers drawn up and have them sent to you for your review."

Fenwick gave a single nod again.

Layla went to Demi, "We knew you were innocent." She hugged her. "I'm so glad things are working out for you." Her eyes rolled toward Lucas. "In more ways than one."

Demi just smiled and didn't respond, likely as uncomfortable as Lucas was.

"Just think, after you're married, the Gages and the Coltons will be family."

Lucas almost said, "Hey, wait a minute." He and Demi weren't getting married.

But for the first time in his life, the idea of marriage didn't make his skin crawl.

The next day, Lucas found that observing a suspect before interviewing them sometimes proved advantageous. He gained insight into their disposition. How patient were they? Did they fidget or appear nervous? The patient and calm ones usually proved to be guilty. Devlin, however, seemed to fall outside the bell curve.

After just ten minutes in the small interrogation room, he was fidgeting and pacing. He also talked to himself.

"I don't belong here." He reached one side of the room and turned to head for the other. "I should be home with Hayley and Demi should be in jail." He reached the other side of the room. "This is all wrong, all wrong."

Devlin stopped at the one-way glass and stabbed his forefinger through the air. "I'll get you for this."

Demi flinched and Lucas rubbed her back. Then he turned to Finn and Hunter. "Okay, it's time. He's stewed enough. He'll talk."

Hamlin had also joined them after he'd been notified that his son had been arrested for multiple murders. He stood watching Devlin ranting with bleak eyes.

Leaving the observation room, Lucas entered the interview room.

"It's about time." Devlin stopped pacing and zeroed in on Lucas. "What do I have to do to get out of here?"

He actually thought he had a chance to be released? Lucas decided to play along, hoping to get him talking sooner rather than later. "I need your statement."

"Statement of what?"

Lucas went to the table and sat. "Have a seat."

Devlin took the chair across from him.

"Let's start with Bo Gage's murder."

"I didn't have anything to do with that. Demi Colton killed him."

"We have evidence that links you to certain Groom Killer murders. Prints on the murder weapon. Your prints."

Devlin pondered that a moment. "Someone put them there, then. Demi."

"You wrote her name in blood at Bo Gage's murder

scene. You left her necklace there for police to find. We also know you paid a man to lie about seeing her there."

Again, Devlin took time to mull over some kind of response. "I'm not the Groom Killer."

"You are the Groom Killer, Devlin. That's what I'm trying to tell you. We *know* you are. We have irrefutable evidence."

After several seconds of simply staring at Lucas, Devlin's head lowered. He was beginning to crack.

"Tell me what happened the night Bo was killed."

For endless moments, Devlin just sat there with his head down. Judging by what Lucas could see of his changing expression, he seemed to be going over events that had led up to his motive to kill.

"I asked her out and she said no," Devlin said in a quiet voice.

"Who?"

"Hayley. I asked her twice and she said no both times. I don't understand why she's playing with me, why she refuses when I know she wants me."

"Hayley was engaged to Bo. She wasn't interested in you." *That ought to spark some reaction.*

Sure enough, Devlin's head sprang up and his brow V'd. "She didn't love Bo. She loves me. She just won't admit it."

"She doesn't love you. I think you know that, Devlin. You can't stand that she rejected you."

Devlin pounded his fist on the table. "No one can have her! I couldn't allow Bo to have her. Don't you see?"

"Yes, I do. Tell me what happened the night you killed Bo."

Once Devlin calmed a little, he said, "After I found

out he was engaged to my Hayley, I followed him to The Pour House. I shot him after he got out of his vehicle. He didn't see me coming."

It was difficult for Lucas to hear this, the details of his brother's last moments.

"I put the necklace by the tire of the parked car near where his body fell and wrote Demi's name in his blood."

"Why Demi?"

"She had a reason to kill him. Bo betrayed her by asking my Hayley to marry him. I had to kill him. Hayley was meant for *me*, not him."

"What about the others? Why did you keep killing?"

"Hayley wouldn't have me. It's not fair that anyone should be able to get married to the one they love when I can't. I had my love taken from me by her fiancé. They all *deserved* to die. If I can't have my bride, no one else can!" He broke down into tears.

After a while, Devlin calmed and stared off into space. Then he looked up at Lucas. "Do you think Hayley will visit me in prison?"

"Doubtful. We're finished here." Lucas left the interview room and went into the observation room, where Demi, Hunter, Finn and Hamlin had witnessed the entire thing.

Devlin had also confessed to killing Miller and Williams, not only to escape, but to keep them quiet about the payoff. He hadn't wanted anyone to discover he had paid crooked cops to arrest Demi.

Hamlin stood with his head in his hand and appeared to be tearing up. "I can't believe he killed all those people. My own son. My own flesh and blood. How did this happen?"

"It isn't your fault." Demi went to him and put her hand on his arm.

He turned his head toward her. "You're awfully forgiving toward the father of the man who framed you for his crimes."

"I'm not forgiving of him. You, on the other hand, did nothing wrong."

Hamlin rubbed his forehead and then dropped his hand. "I feel like I owe the community, like I should do something to make up for what my son did."

"You don't owe anyone anything," Demi said.

Hamlin seemed to search for something, some kind of solution to attempt to rectify this terrible wrong. "Fenwick said he had the K-9 unit and the training center covered for five years."

What did that have to do with his son turning out to be a serial killer? Lucas waited for him to explain further.

"What if I pledge to provide support after that? I could support the center if Colton Energy can't. I will always be there for you." He looked at Finn as he spoke.

"We would be ever grateful for the support," Finn said.

"I know it won't bring back lives lost, but at least I can do something good for the community."

It was an honorable gesture. True, Hamlin could not reverse the horrible things his son had done, but he could make amends in a small way, and in a way that everyone in Red Ridge would appreciate.

Confusion plagued Demi well into the evening. She'd put Wolf down for the night and came back out into the living room, where Lucas was absorbed with his computer. Demi suspected he needed some space. He'd been quiet ever since they'd left the RRPD, as though what had been said at his father's house bothered him.

She needed her own space and felt the same as he did, weighed with sobering thoughts. Somewhere along the line their relationship had progressed into something serious. Demi, surprising herself, was more open to exploring what they had together. He wasn't. That brought her to her next thought. Why was she still here if there was no hope for the two of them? She could go home now, go back to her life.

One thing she knew she couldn't do was stay in this relationship if he wasn't willing to try. If he stuck to his old conviction about love, then she had to get out now, before he hurt her even more than she hurt now.

Demi went to him and sat on the couch beside him. He closed the web browser, but not before Demi saw it was just the news. He shut down his computer and leaned back, looking at her.

She couldn't tell what he was thinking. Her heart began to pound with apprehension. She'd never been any good at these serious talks. Normally she just waited to see how things went. If they worked out between her and a man or not. But normally she didn't have much investment in men. It was easy to walk away. This was different.

"Is something wrong?" Lucas tipped his head as though trying to see her face better.

She moved so she sat at an angle, tucking one leg beneath her, and met his eyes. "Can I ask you something?"

"Sure." He seemed to grow wary.

"Where do you see this going? Me and you?"

He didn't say anything for a long time. Seconds seemed like minutes.

"I don't know. I haven't really thought about it."

"Have you thought about what Layla said about how, after we're married, the Gages and the Coltons will be family?" That was difficult for her to say. Layla had shocked her when she'd said that.

"I had mixed feelings."

He had? Did that mean he'd considered marriage? Maybe the idea didn't repulse him as much as he expected. Maybe that's why he'd been so quiet.

"Where *do* you see us going, Lucas? I need to know and I need to know now."

"I honestly don't know, Demi." He raked his fingers though his hair with a sigh. "I've been thinking about us all day."

"Do you want to date for a while and then split up?"

"I like you. I want to keep seeing you."

"Do you think there's more to this than to keep seeing each other and then break it off? No talk of marriage?"

"It's too soon to talk about that. Marriage?"

He was taking a copout. "We've known each other for years."

"Can you commit to a long-term relationship?" Demi wasn't sure she could agree to that, not with the uncertainty of Lucas's stance on marriage.

"We're good together," he said.

He was beginning to sound as though he'd ticked

off all the positives about them together. He liked her. Check. They were good in bed. Check.

"And I love Wolf."

Whoa. He liked her but he *loved* Wolf? Demi stood abruptly, stinging sharply from the obvious difference in his feelings for her and his feelings for Wolf.

She lifted her hands, palms facing him. "I can't do this. In the morning, I'm taking Wolf home and you and I can go back to competing over bounties." She started to turn.

"Wait, Demi." He stood and came to her. "What did I say?"

She cocked her head incredulously. He didn't know?

"What did I say that offended you?"

"You like me? Hello?"

He let out another sigh and this time pinched the bridge of his nose, eyes closing briefly. At last he dropped his hand and looked at her.

"It's more than like."

She waited. She needed more than that to be convinced.

"That's what's been bothering me ever since Layla said that thing about marriage and family. It didn't grate me like it usually does when people make assumptions about me getting married. The way I feel about you..." He looked off over her shoulder and shook his head. "I don't know what it is, okay? I just know it's more than like."

So, he couldn't face his feelings for her, so he tagged the word *like* to it. That wasn't much better.

"I can't stay with a man who isn't sure about his feelings. That isn't fair to me. I deserve more from a man. Wolf deserves more. Tell you what. Wolf and I will go home tomorrow and leave you alone. If and when you come to any conclusions about us and your place in this relationship, then let me know. If not, we move on."

Demi hated the thought of moving on without him. Her mind had to overrule her heart this time. What's more, she realized she wasn't doing it out of defense, to protect her heart. Well, she was, but not from an insecure standpoint. She would be unhappy for a while without Lucas, without kissing him, without making love with him, but she had to do what was right for her. Staying in a relationship with a man who would never commit was not right for her, not even for a little while longer to satisfy her cravings. And she did crave him. She craved him like mad, his affection and, most of all, his love.

In that very instant she realized she loved him. She'd begun to fall in love with him a long time ago, long before she'd gone on the run. She'd buried it until now.

"I don't want you to leave," he said.

"I don't want to leave, either, but I can't stay if you can't commit to me. This has grown into more than something casual for me. I have strong feelings for you, Lucas, stronger than I think you realize." He didn't even realize his own feelings. How could he estimate hers?

"Are you saying you won't stay with me unless I ask you to marry me?"

Yes, she wanted to say. That was the only way she'd be absolutely sure he was committed.

"I won't stay because you can't even envision the possibility of us getting married."

He sort of turned white. "Envisioning that shocks me."

Shock? She didn't understand.

"Terrifies me."

Ah, terrifies.

"You were right about me in that regard. I am afraid of marriage."

Because of what he'd seen his father go through. Because he'd lost his mother. And probably because his father had taught him it was best to live alone than trust in marriage lasting a lifetime. For the first time ever, she saw a man who might be able to overcome his past.

She smiled a little and put her hand on his chest, moving closer. "Well, then I think you're just going to have to man up."

They engaged in a stare down of wills.

"Layla invited us to a Christmas party at the training center tomorrow night," Lucas said. "Do you want to go?"

He was denying again, running. Demi almost refused outright then. Was he trying to get her to stay with him for as long as he needed her? Some attempt to have her until the time came when he would run?

"Is this…?"

"Just go with me to the party, Demi."

Taking in his muscular arms and the darkly handsome face that sent messages of resignation even if temporary, she couldn't stop her response.

"I'd love to." One last night, and then she'd leave.

Chapter 17

The administrative staff at the Red Ridge K-9 Training Center had pulled out all the stops decorating the white party tent. Lucas checked their coats at the door.

"All the dogs have to wear a red bow," the coat checker said, handing one to him.

Lucas crouched to attach the bow to Queenie's collar, then walked with Demi farther inside the tent. Carrying Wolf with one arm, she hooked her other arm with Lucas's, her slender fingers resting on the material of his suit jacket.

He had all but eaten her up when he'd first seen her come out of her room. In a knee-length black cocktail dress and zircon-bejeweled black stilettos, every inch of her body called to his male instincts. She wore dangly zircon earrings and a matching necklace and bracelet. No rings.

She'd dressed Wolf in a little man suit with a red bow tie. He looked so adorable and now looked up at Lucas, fascinated as always.

Familiar faces and dogs with red bows sat or stood around tables topped with white linen cloths that filled the events tent, each adorned with burning candles surrounded by evergreen branches with pine cones. A dance floor made to resemble an ice rink had been set up at the far end. Beyond that, a long table had an ice sculpture on each side, a champagne fountain in the middle and a variety of hors d oeuvres. Fairy lights hung from the top of the white tent, intermixed with snowflakes. To the side of the dance floor, a tall, colorful Christmas tree glittered, wrapped boxes and stuffed polar bears underneath. At the opposite side of the dance floor, a DJ played "Have a Holly Jolly Christmas." Heat lamps had been set up throughout the tent, keeping the temperature cozy warm.

"Wow," Demi said, echoing his impression.

He put his hand on her lower back and walked with her to a table where Brayden and Shane sat with Esmée and Lucas's sister Danica. Esmée's nearly three-year-old son, Rhys, sat beside his mother, the top of Echo's head peeking up over the top of the table where he sat beside Rhys's chair. Echo was a big yellow Lab. Both Brayden and Shane wore black suits. Esmée wore a gray V-neck, horizontally banded dress that turned black down the sides as she moved and light hit it at different angles. Danica had on a gold mesh dress with sparkling beads and sequins that overlapped in petal shapes.

Elle appeared with Anders Colton, the strapping ranch foreman, and their bulldog, Merlin.

"Hey, Lucas." Elle leaned in for a quick hug, giving him a subtle whiff of nice-smelling perfume. "Thanks to you, Anders and I can finally get married."

Lucas glanced around at all the other couples. All the K-9 team was here, as well as anyone else who'd helped track down the Groom Killer. His older brother, Carson, stood beside Serena Colton at the hors d'oeuvres table; he was piling a plate full and Serena was picking, sampling this and that while holding her nearly one-year-old daughter, Cora. Justice, Carson's German shepherd, must have been standing next to him although Lucas couldn't see with the white tablecloth shielding his view of the other side of the table.

Micah Shaw and Bea Colton also stood at the food table, holding plates and smiling at each other. West Brand and Quinn Colton had gone to the DJ booth with Quinn's black Lab.

Everywhere he looked he saw couples who'd hidden their romances. "Looks like there'll be a lot more of those around here."

Elle came to Demi. "Can I hold him?"

"Sure." Demi handed over Wolf.

"It was so hard to give back the baby girl that was left on Anders's doorstep. We thought she was yours. We thought you left her there to keep her safe."

Lucas saw Demi smile softly as she witnessed Elle adore her baby.

Elle bounced Wolf gently, and he rewarded her with a delighted squeal. "You might not get him back tonight." As though she'd make good on the threat, she wandered over to Brayden and Shane as though she planned to take Wolf around and show him off.

"Danica and I are going to get married, too," Shane said aloud.

"Congratulations," Elle said. "What about you?" she asked Brayden.

"We're engaged."

Esmée held up her left hand to reveal a beautiful diamond engagement ring, her smile full and pretty.

Lucas still had his hand on Demi's back. "Something to drink?" he asked her.

With a glance at Wolf, she nodded. "Some ginger ale."

He left her and walked to one of two bars that had been set up next to the food table and near the entrance. He got himself a beer.

"Nice job nabbing Devlin."

Holding the drinks, he turned to see Hunter Black, Layla beside him. At their feet was Goose, Hunter's basset hound, the very one who'd sniffed out some drives that proved Devlin had hacked into Layla's computer.

"Thanks. It wouldn't have been possible without you." Hunter had tipped the balance and found someone other than Demi to label a suspect.

"We can all sleep easier knowing that menace is behind bars."

"And plan some weddings." Layla smiled at Hunter.

Lucas looked for Edson Gage and Fenwick, Rusty and Judson Colton. They didn't seem to be in attendance tonight, although Finn had made certain every one of them had been invited.

"They won't show," Hunter said, as though reading his thoughts. "It will take weddings to knock them off their feuding behinds."

The suggestion got Lucas's mind churning. Layla's father was Fenwick. Demi's father was Rusty. Valeria's father was Judson Colton, and Vincent's father, of course, was Edson Gage. Valeria and Vincent planned to marry on Christmas Eve. If they made it a three-way…

Lucas could not believe the idea had struck him. What was the matter with him? He was actually contemplating *marrying?*

Demi. He would be marrying Demi.

Lucas looked across the room and found her sitting at the table where he'd left her. Valeria and Vincent and Quinn and West had joined them. Another survey of the room showed him all the other Coltons were sticking to their kind—sort of. Elle had taken Wolf and Anders over to a group of Gages standing near the Christmas tree. Carson had his arm around Serena and Finn held Darby Gage's hand. Gages and Coltons mixing.

Except for Layla, Fenwick's offspring occupied two tables, eating and drinking champagne while their red-bow-wearing K-9s sniffed each other and played with dog toys that had been left on the floor. Blake Colton leaned toward Juliette Walsh in an intimate conversation. They'd obviously overcome discovering Pandora was his daughter after returning to Red Ridge from a long absence. Their daughter played in a front corner of the tent with some other kids on a fort with a slide surrounded by bales of hay.

Bea Colton received a kiss from Micah Shaw. Fenwick had split them up years ago, but apparently they'd gotten back together. Did Fenwick know?

Patience Colton engaged in a lively talk with her man, Nash Maddox. She looked five or six months pregnant. Would they get married now that the Groom Killer had been caught? What did her father think of her being pregnant?

Gemma Colton laughed at something her newfound love, Dante Mancuso said. None of the Fenwick Colton kids had happened to fall for a Gage, which worked against Fenwick softening his stance on the feud. He may have agreed to Edson's deal, but that was just business. What would he do if one of his kids married a Gage?

While attending Layla's wedding wouldn't make Fenwick family with the Gages, a three-way wedding with everyone there might open the path to closer ties. The business deal was a step in the right direction, but something like a wedding was personal and romantic. Love could melt any remaining animosity. It would certainly sweeten the deal Layla had worked with Edson, making it less painful for Fenwick and even heping him realize friendly relations *were* possible.

"You drifted off."

Lucas returned his attention to Hunter, but wondered if his wandering thoughts were more of an excuse to marry Demi. He must be internally convincing himself there was a good reason to do so—bringing the families together. But his heart told him something entirely different. He had fallen in love with Demi.

Maybe he'd loved her for years and had kept the feelings from developing into anything real.

"I have an idea."

Demi watched some kids playing in a corner near the entrance of the tent, where the K-9 center staff had set up the bales of hay and a fort with a slide. She also kept a close eye on Wolf. Elle had confiscated him for the evening, apparently. Wolf loved the attention. His big smile never faltered with each new face he encountered. Right now Elle had wandered over to where her close friend Juliette Walsh sat. Juliette stood and smiled into Wolf's face.

"We're going to make our announcement tonight," Valeria said.

Shane and Brayden were involved in a conversation about Esmée's upcoming documentary on the Groom Killer. She could conclude it now that Devlin had been arrested.

In a navy skater dress with a festive white pattern on the bodice, Valeria looked radiant. Vincent held her hand on the tabletop, looking like a proud and satisfied young groom-to-be.

"What announcement?" Demi asked.

"We're getting married on Christmas Eve. We've made arrangements and plan on inviting everyone."

"Have you told your father?"

Valeria's face drained of some of her joy. "Yes, and he isn't happy at all. He doesn't know Anders and Serena are both engaged to Gages. I'm not sure Finn counts, since Darby is only a Gage because she married and divorced Bo. But I doubt he'll be happy when he finds out they're going to be married, too."

"He'll get over it. He doesn't have a choice."

"We're hoping our wedding brings the families together," Vincent said.

What a lovely gesture. Vincent had such a warm heart, and Valeria was so cute and attractive, these two young lovebirds had nothing but goodwill for all.

"We were thinking about having poker tables at the reception, but instead of money, we want to use individually wrapped chocolates."

Demi laughed. How fun that would be, and a tease on the century-old feud that should be laughed at by now.

"The chocolates would be different brands, each representing a dollar amount. Tens, hundreds and so on," Vincent added.

"That's brilliant!"

Lucas appeared back at their table, setting down Demi's ginger ale. "Vincent, I need to talk to you."

Vincent looked up, perplexed.

"Come with me."

With a glance at Valeria and a quick kiss, Vincent stood and followed Lucas to the DJ booth, joining Hunter there.

Layla had gone to sit at the table with her siblings and their romantic partners, but she watched Hunter.

"What are they up to?" Valeria asked.

"Heck if I know. Something, though. Look at the way they're talking."

Shane and Brayden stopped talking when Esmée

and Danica twisted on their chairs to look where Demi and Valeria's attention had gone.

Vincent began to smile and nodded his head, then he shook both Hunter's and Lucas's hands.

Lucas spoke with the DJ, who ended the music and handed him a microphone. Hunter took the mic.

"Ladies and gentlemen, may we have your attention." Hunter's voice boomed.

The crowd quieted and all eyes went to the trio.

"Lucas has something to say."

Hunter handed the microphone to Lucas.

"Merry Christmas, everyone." His deep voice penetrated the tent.

"Merry Christmas," most of the crowd responded, some lifting champagne glasses.

"It's been a tense year. We at the Red Ridge Police Department have accomplished a lot."

"Hear, hear," someone shouted out.

"We've apprehended dangerous criminals. We worked as a team. Gages and Coltons working side by side for the greater good. As many of you now know, with Layla's help, we saved the K-9 center. We hope this will be the ice breaker in a feud that doesn't belong to this generation of families." Lucas put his hand on his youngest brother's shoulder. "It's a start, but it's not enough. So with no further ado, I have an announcement to make. My little brother, Vincent, is getting married on Christmas Eve. He's going to marry Valeria Colton."

Murmurs spread through the tent, most of them without shock. Many had already assumed as much but there were some who hadn't.

"He and Valeria hope their union will end the feud once and for all by making the Gages and Coltons family. When I discovered this, it made me realize our fathers aren't here tonight and they should be."

Lucas handed the microphone back to Hunter.

"That's why I'm making another announcement. Darby Gage and I are also engaged to be married, and Vincent has agreed to allow us to join him and his fiancée at the altar on Christmas Eve. That means my father, Vincent's father and Valeria's father will all be there."

Cheers erupted in the tent.

Demi turned to Valeria, whose mouth had dropped open. "Are you okay with that?" She'd have to share her wedding day with another couple.

"I think it's a great idea!" She smiled and laughed. "Our wedding is getting bigger by the second! And Vincent and I want our families to stop fighting. He knew I'd support this."

"This show isn't over yet, folks." Hunter handed the microphone to Lucas.

"I have an announcement of my own, but before I can make it, there's something I need to do."

Lucas looked right at Demi and her heart climbed up into her throat. What was he thinking?

"Demi?" Valeria queried. "Oh, my gosh."

Lucas walked toward her and stopped before the table. "I've spent many years avoiding relationships."

Demi clutched the napkin on the table in front of her, entranced by Lucas's confident dark eyes. His certainty sent a tingle through her.

"I believed love wasn't for me, but after being with

Demi these last few weeks, I've realized how wrong I was."

A more excited, thrilled murmur passed through the crowd.

"I've known this beautiful woman for several years. Nobody would have called us friends."

Some laughed at that one—he and Demi had been enemies, or seemed like it.

"But no one saw what was really going on. I was attracted to her the moment I set eyes on her and I'm convinced she felt the same about me. But past relationships and heartbreak prevented us from acting on that attraction. We both weren't ready. But now we are. I am." He stopped talking and Demi wondered what he'd say next. So did everyone else in the tent, given how quiet they were.

"I need to find a way to convince you of my love, Demi," he said.

He'd said the L word. Lucas Gage had actually said the word *love*.

"Ohhh," Valeria cooed from beside her.

"And I found a way." Lucas stepped closer.

Demi moved on her chair so she faced him more, astonished when he went down on one knee. She planted her hand over her gaping mouth as he fished inside his jacket pocket and people said, "Whoa," or "Oh," or other exclamations.

Lucas removed two or three green pine needles he must have taken from one of the table decorations and fashioned into a makeshift ring, complete with a tiny bow. He fumbled with the microphone and Danica took it from him, holding it near his mouth and freeing both his hands.

"Demi Colton, will you marry me?" Lucas took her hand from her mouth—her left hand—and poised the pine-needle ring over the tip of her ring finger.

"I want to spend the rest of my life with you," Lucas said. "I know that now. I love you, Demi."

Tears sprang to her eyes. "What about Wolf?"

As though responding to his name, Wolf gave a shriek of glee, making everyone burst out laughing. Demi saw Elle happily watching, still holding Wolf, whose arms bounced as he stared up at her.

"I love him, too, but it's you I want to marry," Lucas said. "Will you?"

Gladness and love escaped her hold and she said, "Yes!" as she threw her arms around him.

Everyone clapped and cheered.

Demi backed away to see Lucas's eyes smiling into hers. He kissed her and she kissed him back, curbing the desire for more.

"I'm not finished yet," Lucas said.

"What…?"

He took the microphone from a beaming Danica and addressed the crowd. "With Vincent and Valeria's blessing, I'd like to propose Demi and I also marry on Christmas Eve. We'll invite Rusty Colton, which will bring all of our families together on a very special day."

Christmas Eve? That was less than a week away! Was he out of his bleeping mind?

Other couples began to come forward and, one by one, the men announced their own engagements. Anders joked that he and Elle wouldn't crowd the altar on

Christmas Eve any more than it already was. Brayden and Shane took turns declaring their engagements to Esmée and Danica. Carson came forward to say he and Serena Colton would have a spring wedding.

It was a liberating celebration at this K-9 Christmas party. No one had to fear being killed for admitting their love and marriage plans.

Nash Maddox said he'd do the honorable thing and marry his pregnant fiancée, Dr. Patience Colton. Dante Mancuso was next.

"I'm the lucky groom-to-be for Gemma Colton. I love you, Gemma."

Micah joined in on the fun and revealed he and Bea Colton were to be married in the summer. Blake Colton and West Brand took the microphone next, Blake introducing his fiancée, Juliette Walsh, and West telling all he was a lucky man to have won over Quinn Colton.

Finn took the microphone last, looking at Darby Gage and saying, "I'm going to marry the love of my life. Thank you for finding your way into my life, Darby."

She mouthed the words, *I love you.*

The atmosphere was electric and alive with love and happiness. The crowd grew loud with talk and the music started up again. A jazzy "Jingle Bells" drew couples out onto the dance floor. Demi forgot how charming this town could be without murder and mayhem.

Lucas offered his hand and she took it.

"Let's dance."

She felt light as a feather, as though she could dance her way through the rest of her life, with Lucas and her son. Her family.

Chapter 18

Demi had to scramble to get ready for her wedding day. Her wedding day! She stared at herself in the mirror as she finished getting ready. Layla and Valeria were talking excitedly behind her in the church room. She couldn't believe she was getting married. Furthermore, she couldn't believe she was getting married to Lucas.

Had she been too rash, saying yes when he'd proposed so unexpectedly? Everything he'd said rang true in her heart. She believed he had come to his senses, accepting that his thinking on marriage had been biased and based on his father's experiences and not his own.

Anything could happen in life. In twenty years she could be divorced like so many other couples, except she didn't feel she and Lucas would end up that way.

When he'd proposed she had felt his certainty. His confidence had brought hers forth, setting her free to love without fear. She trusted him. She could dive into this wedding without second thoughts.

Swept up into a whirlwind of preparation, she'd raced against the clock every day. Luckily Valeria had been planning for months. She had the church and the reception already arranged. Demi extended invites to friends and family—her father included. Lucas had done the same. She, Valeria and Layla had all decided not to have maids of honor or bridesmaids. The altar would be crowded enough. They each had something in common, in that all that really mattered was getting married and unifying the Coltons and the Gages.

Valeria already had her wedding dress, so Demi and Layla went to Bea Colton's bridal shop and picked out their own. Bea had been thrilled to be back in business after a year of struggling. The Groom Killer had scared off couples from having weddings. Now she couldn't keep up with the demand.

Layla chose an eye-catching, figure-hugging gown that flared from above the knees and flowed into a short lacy train. Off-shoulder sleeves drooped from spaghetti straps. Scrolling lace overlaid stretch chiffon, sheer to give the illusion of a thigh-high slit on the left side. Very elegant and Layla's style.

Demi preferred a more earthy look, maybe more traditional but not quite Cinderella. The strapless vintage lace bodice had a sweetheart neckline and a corset back. A crystal sash circled the waist and soft tiers of lace adorned the A-line skirt, gently flowing into a court train.

Valeria had chosen a gown worthy of a princess. The strapless bodice had sweetheart beading and a lace-up back. Sequins sparked on the tulle ball-gown skirt, overlaying satin.

Demi turned from the mirror. Layla and Valeria looked at her and all three of them smiled.

"I wonder if our fathers have gone at each other's throats yet," Layla said.

"When I invited mine, he didn't seem very excited," Demi said. "I think he'll be the least of our concerns today."

"Mine went ballistic," Valeria said.

"Mine didn't approve of Coltons marrying Gages, but he supports my wedding to Hunter," Layla said.

Bea poked her head in the door with a big smile. "It's time, ladies." She had been a big help coordinating this event.

Demi's stomach fluttered. Valeria let out a little giggle. Layla must have been feeling similar to Demi—excited and nervous.

Picking up their bouquets of red roses—appropriate for Christmas Eve—Demi followed Valeria and Layla out of the room. Her father waited with Valeria's and Layla's. Before they abruptly stopped talking in what sounded like an argument she heard Fenwick saying to Rusty "...doesn't mean we're going to get all chummy."

Judson turned from them and his frown didn't improve much when he saw Valeria. But he did what he was supposed to and offered his arm. They walked down the hall. Layla took her father's arm, both of them smiling, and followed.

"You look beautiful. So much like your mother."

If her dive-bar-owning father could have said anything great today, that was it. She loved that he'd brought up her mother on this special day. She didn't have the best relationship with him, but today was a day of putting differences aside and bringing people together.

She looped her arm with his, smiling genuinely at him in return. They followed the others down a hallway toward the sanctuary.

Demi heard voices and a harp playing. She lined up behind Layla and Valeria, and could see the pews. Everyone had turned their heads to see them. The church was packed, a good sign that many supported the union of Coltons and Gages. Garlands with red flowers decorated the pews.

At the altar, Hunter, Vincent and Lucas stood in black tuxes with red cummerbunds and bow ties. She had eyes only for Lucas. He looked at her and from here she could feel his intensity. Any doubts she had fled. This felt too right to be a mistake, rushed or not.

When the traditional wedding song began to play, Valeria began her walk down the aisle.

When she was halfway to the altar, Layla started her walk. Demi stood on the threshold of the sanctuary, seeing Lucas had not taken his eyes off her. She heard a few of the attendees whispering about how beautiful Layla's gown was. They must have commented on Valeria's, as well. Rusty began walking with her down the aisle and she heard more comments on her own gown. Demi never felt more beautiful in her life.

Valeria's father handed her off to Vincent and found his seat in the first row. Layla's father kissed her on her cheek and handed her off to Hunter. Then it was Demi's turn. She reached the altar and could see Lucas's eyes clearly now. They smoldered as they gobbled up the sight of her.

Rusty kissed her cheek and said in a low tone, "Love you." He handed her over to Lucas.

She hooked her arm with his and they all faced the officiant. A fifty-something man with cropped white hair, he wore a suit and tie and held sheets of paper. They'd kept the ceremony simple, with a few short readings and no prayers.

"Today is a special day," the officiant began, "and not only because three couples will be married. Today is special because this ceremony represents the joining of families."

Valeria had wanted the officiant to talk about this.

"Families share close bonds and new bonds are formed through marriage. These three couples bring three families together. Families give a place to call home and celebrations of life accomplishments and milestones. We as humans aren't meant to go through life without families. Disagreements come and disagreements go, but they should never last generations."

The officiant passed his gaze over the crowd and then each couple. "Whatever negativity existed before this day, let these marriages and the love between these men and women, bring us all peace and a long future of togetherness."

The officiant addressed each couple. "Valeria and Vincent, Layla and Hunter, Demetria and Lucas, you all come before me today to pledge your love for each other. With that pledge comes the duty to be faithful, to trust, and to support each other in all matters of life. Whether sickness befalls you, whether financial troubles descend upon you, your pledge obligates you to share each of these experiences together and to work your way through them *together.*"

Moving to Valeria and Vincent, the officiant told them to now read their vows. They had written their own.

"Vincent, I knew the day I met you I wanted to spend the rest of my life with you. You are kind and funny and my best friend. I promise to be there for you in the ups and downs as our lives go forward from this day. I will never betray you and will always have faith in you. I take you as my partner, my best friend and my husband from this day on for all the days of my life."

Demi had to swallow the burn of happy emotional tears as Vincent read the same vow to Valeria.

The officiant moved on to Layla and Hunter, who had opted for traditional vows. Once they finished, it was Demi and Lucas's turn.

He faced her and held her hands between them. They had opted for a variation of their own vows that was nondenominational.

"I, Demetria Colton, take you, Lucas Gage, as the man I know up to this day and the man you may grow into as we age. I take you with your flaws and your strengths. I take you as my husband and promise to love you and trust you. I will respect your integrity and have faith in your love for me in return, through all our years together and through anything life may bring."

Lucas's eyes never left hers. "I, Lucas Gage, take you, Demetria Colton, as the woman I know up to this day and the woman you may grow into as we age. I take you with your flaws and your strengths. I take you as my wife and promise to love you and trust you. I will respect your integrity and have faith in your love for me in return, through all our years together and through anything life may bring."

"The rings, please."

The officiant began with Valeria and Vincent, then moved on to Layla and Hunter.

Demi and Lucas had gone together to pick their rings. She had always loved sapphires and so her center stone was a small rectangular sapphire and round diamonds surrounded that. His was a white gold band with *love and trust* engraved on the inside.

When the officiant reached them, Lucas began. "With this ring, I thee wed." Lucas slipped the ring on her finger.

"With this ring, I thee wed." She performed the same task on his finger.

"Grooms, you may kiss your brides," the officiant said.

Her surroundings faded to the background as Lucas pulled her close and pressed his lips to her. She slid her hand up his chest to his neck, her thumb on his chin, falling into the warmth of his soft touch, so full of meaning and heating her up.

Appreciative cheers rose and fell from the crowd as they parted.

"I now pronounce you husband and wife."

The cheers and applause grew louder as the three couples faced them. The harpist played a vibrant closing tune as Demi and Lucas led the way down the aisle. People threw red rose petals at them as they passed.

Demi laughed her glee and heard Lucas's deep chuckle. Outside, they climbed into their limo, the third in a line of three. Sitting flush against Lucas, Demi couldn't stop smiling. Lucas smiled, too, and took her hand, holding it all the way to the reception.

Lucas saw Finn approach with Darby at his side. Valeria had planned the reception at the new house she and Vincent had bought, a four bedroom in one of the nicer middle-class neighborhoods in Red Ridge. Lucas said his father had put up a sizable down payment as a wedding gift. Guests filled the great room, kitchen and adjacent den.

"Lucas, Demi." Finn gave a nod to Demi. Finn wasn't known for liking the Rusty Colton clan but he seemed to have changed his mind. Hooking up with Darby and finding out Demi wasn't guilty of murder might have had something to do with that. Maybe also all the Colton–Gage weddings on the horizon.

"It was a beautiful ceremony," Darby said. "I think Finn and I will get married at that church, as well."

Rusty came to stand beside Demi as Darby finished talking. "You could have your reception at my bar."

"We have plenty of room at the ranch," Finn said. "But thanks for the offer."

"I'd like to personally thank you for catching Bo's killer," Rusty said to Finn and Lucas. "I never believed my daughter killed anyone, and having a murder take place outside my bar is bad for business."

"We're all glad the killer was caught." Lucas put his arm around Demi.

After talking a bit longer, Finn and Darby turned to

Judson. Edson walked over to Lucas and Demi. Nearby, Fenwick stood with Layla and Hunter. Lucas didn't think the four fathers had ever stood so close together.

Fenwick seemed to notice the same, pausing in conversation to look from Rusty to Edson to Judson.

"Not so bad, huh, Dad?" Layla asked with a smile.

Edson and Judson turned to look at her and then noticed where their attention had gone, seeing Rusty and Fenwick and then exchanging a glance between themselves.

"At least Fenwick's kids aren't marrying up all the Gages," Judson grumbled.

His petite, blond-haired, blue-eyed wife stood beside him and said, "Get over it, Judson. Look how happy Valeria is."

He did look and his face smoothed. "That's why I didn't fight it too hard. Still wish she would have fallen for someone who wasn't a Gage, though."

"We Gages aren't so bad," Lucas said. "My dad made a deal with Fenwick. Why not just be part of the family?"

"I think we all make a fine family," Demi said, Bouncing Wolf, who smiled up at her and made a high-pitched sound.

Judson saw that and smiled.

Demi handed him over. "He's got Colton blood in him."

Judson took the baby and laughed a little as Wolf pumped his little arms up and down, toothlessly smiling at Judson and staring into his face.

"Patience told me she and Nash are getting married next weekend," Demi said. "We'll all be together again."

Edson glanced up at Demi and then returned his pleasant attention to Wolf. "You're right. It was a stupid poker game. I should have stopped listening to my father a long time ago." He let Wolf play with his little finger. "Besides, this feels a whole lot better."

"It's time for our first dance." Lucas took Demi's hand, seeing Hunter and Layla already on the dance floor with Valeria and Vincent.

He swung her around and held her close as they began to move. Just looking at her face warmed him. Her hands—one on his chest and one in his hand— were right where they belonged. He'd savor every day, each new moment cherished.

And this. He scanned the crowd of happy faces— Coltons and Gages everywhere. Yes, this. Family.

* * * * *

COMING SOON!

We really hope you enjoyed reading this book. If you're looking for more romance, be sure to head to the shops when new books are available on

Thursday 13th December

LET'S TALK
Romance

For exclusive extracts, competitions
and special offers, find us online:

- ![f] facebook.com/millsandboon
- ![twitter] @MillsandBoon
- ![instagram] @MillsandBoonUK

Get in touch on 01413 063232

For all the latest titles coming soon, visit
millsandboon.co.uk/nextmonth

Want even more
ROMANCE?

Join our bookclub today!

'Mills & Boon books, the perfect way to escape for an hour or so.'

Miss W. Dyer

'Excellent service, promptly delivered and very good subscription choices.'

Miss A. Pearson

'You get fantastic special offers and the chance to get books before they hit the shops'

Mrs V. Hall

**Visit millsandbook.co.uk/Bookclub
and save on brand new books.**

MILLS & BOON